CAMBRIA Sky

LINDA SEED

CAMBRIA *Sky*

This is a work of fiction. Any characters, organizations, places, or events portrayed in this novel are either products of the author's imagination or are used fictitiously.

CAMBRIA SKY
Originally published as LIKE THAT ENDLESS CAMBRIA SKY
Copyright © 2016 by Linda Seed.

The author is available for book signings, book club discussions, conferences, and other appearances.

Linda Seed may be contacted via e-mail at lindaseed24@gmail.com or on Facebook at www.facebook.com/LindaSeedAuthor.

ISBN: 9781693238666

First Trade Paperback Printing: February 2016

Cover design by Kari March

For Chloe, Evan, and Condee
With all my love

Chapter One

Genevieve Porter had a hangover.

This was not an ordinary hangover, the kind that could be brought under control with copious amounts of water and a couple of Extra Strength Tylenol. No, this was the kind that made one pray for sweet, sweet death. Or at least an extended period of unconsciousness.

Gen hadn't had a hangover of this proportion since college, a good ten years before, when keg parties and tequila shots had made them a semiregular occurrence. These days, she usually didn't drink more than a couple of glasses of wine, maybe a good craft beer.

Last night had been different.

Her best friend, Kate, had thrown a party to celebrate the fact that her boyfriend of six months had moved in with her. It had been a housewarming of sorts for Jackson, a celebration for Kate, and a reason to get together with good friends for everyone else.

Usually at a party, Gen would have a few drinks, eat some of the chips and salsa, and call it a night well before she was drunk enough to worry about how she'd feel in the morning. But last night she'd lost control of the situation—of herself—for reasons she hadn't yet talked about to anyone.

How could they understand?

How could Kate understand that while Gen was happy for her—honestly, genuinely happy—she was also jealous as hell? Kate had found love, a love that by all appearances was destined to make it for the long haul, and that was great. That was fine. But here was Gen, at thirty-one (actually thirty-three, but so used to lying about it that who remembered anymore), no closer to finding anyone to share her life with.

That was bad enough, but now she didn't even have Kate anymore.

Well, she did, but it wasn't the same.

Gen lived in an apartment that occupied the bottom floor of Kate's house. Before Jackson had come into Kate's life, Gen had treated Kate's place as her own, coming and going as she pleased, enjoying morning coffee upstairs with her best friend, rehashing work problems and guy problems at the end of the day, ordering food, watching Netflix, and just generally living inseparably, like sisters.

Now that Jackson had moved in, Gen could hardly pop in at seven a.m. in her pajamas. She was jealous because the easy closeness she and Kate had shared couldn't stay the same now that a third party had been added to the mix. And she felt like shit about the jealousy, because what kind of person couldn't be happy when someone she loved had found her soul mate?

And that was only part of it. The other part, the other thing that had driven her to behave irresponsibly the night before, was the news that her former boss had died.

She had so many feelings about that. None of them was grief, and none of them was simple.

Davis MacIntyre had owned the most influential art gallery in New York before his untimely demise at age forty-eight due to an accidental drug overdose. Gen had begun working for him as an intern right out of college, with her shiny new art history degree and her ambitions to be a player in the art world.

She'd known right away that Davis MacIntyre was a sleaze. She'd known about the drug use, about the sex in his office with bimbos who never showed their faces more than once. She'd known about the shady deals.

As she'd risen from intern to full-time gallery employee, she'd put up with the sexual harassment—the occasional hand on her ass, the double entendres, the suggestions that perhaps she should try being "friendly" to a top collector—because she knew that an association with Davis MacIntyre was like gold in the New York art world.

But when she'd learned that Davis was selling forgeries—paintings with doctored signatures and fraudulent provenance—she couldn't keep her mouth shut any longer. Knowing what she knew, she could have gone to jail right along with Davis if she hadn't done anything and he got caught. So she spoke up. She told him that she knew what he was doing, and that he had to stop.

The result had been swift and merciless. She'd been fired, and Davis had made it known not only in New York but nationwide that anyone who hired her would never find favor with MacIntyre again.

Broke and unemployed, she'd done the only thing she knew to do.

She'd blackmailed him.

She told Davis that she would go to the police about the forgeries—and she would sue him for sexual harassment and for the damage he had done to her reputation—unless he gave her enough money to get set up somewhere far away, where he wouldn't have to see her or hear from her again.

He'd taken Option B.

The money he'd given her wasn't extravagant, but it was enough for her to come to Cambria, California, buy a small art gallery on Main Street, and have enough left over for a healthy savings account.

Now the son of a bitch was dead, and that meant so many things. It meant she could come out from under the rock where she'd been hiding. She could go back to New York if she wanted. She was fairly certain that she could find work there again. Davis's reputation was such that it was likely everyone knew she'd done nothing wrong—she'd simply gotten on Davis's bad side. It hadn't mattered whether anyone believed the things he'd said about her. They probably hadn't. It only mattered that an important door would have been closed to them if they'd worked with her.

Now that door no longer existed.

The disappearance of the only major obstacle that had been standing in her way should have filled her with joy. But she didn't know how to feel. Now that she was no longer boxed into a corner, the possibilities before her seemed terrifying.

So, last night, she drank.

She'd stood around upstairs in a crowd as big as they could fit into Kate's tiny house, drinking margaritas and watching the gorgeous Ryan Delaney drool over Lacy Jordan, who, along with Kate, was one of her three closest friends.

And why wouldn't he drool? Lacy was a tall, leggy blonde with pale blue, hypnotic eyes and skin like fresh cream. The fact that she was entirely unaware of her striking beauty made it even worse, somehow. It was impossible to hate her—impossible, in fact, not to love her.

Gen herself had none of Lacy's graceful height. At five-foot-two, she felt positively stunted by comparison. Her wild, curly, red hair was completely unmanageable, and her fair complexion freckled at the very mention of sunlight. She wished she had Lacy's effortless elegance—wished, in fact, that she had been the one to catch Ryan Delaney's attention—but instead, she had to work hard not to feel like a garden gnome.

And right now, she felt like a gnome with a thundering headache.

She groaned and her stomach roiled as she rolled over in bed and looked at the digital clock on the nightstand. It was past nine a.m.

Shit.

She had to get up. The gallery was supposed to open at ten o'clock.

It wasn't like she was going to get in trouble if she was late; she owned the damned place, after all. And the foot traffic in January tended to be slow, unlike in the summer months, when the tourists kept things busy.

The more she thought about it, the more appealing it was to just lie there and wallow in her misery.

But the misery was too intense to make wallowing pleasurable, so she dragged herself out of bed.

She opened the sliding glass door and stepped out onto the patio. The house where Gen rented her tiny apartment was perched on the side of a hill with one of the best views in Cambria. Normally, she'd have a 180-degree view of breaking waves from the patio, but this morning a layer of fog obscured the view and shrouded the world in gauze. Not uncommon for January. It was cold outside, and the chill cut through the haze of her hangover and made her feel a little bit better. Thank God it wasn't sunny. She wasn't sure she'd be able to cope with sun.

When she started to shiver, she went back inside, closed the door, and turned on the big gas fireplace in the corner of the apartment's single room. She pulled a blanket around herself and went into her miniscule kitchenette to make coffee.

She could hear the sound of footsteps moving around overhead—Kate's, or maybe Jackson's. Before Jackson had moved in, Gen would have taken the sound of the footsteps as an open invitation to go upstairs in her pajamas, help herself to the coffee in Kate's kitchen, and flop onto Kate's sofa for a little morning camaraderie. But she couldn't exactly do that when the two of them were likely floating around on a cloud of post-coital afterglow.

Gen sighed, and her head throbbed.

She rooted around in the medicine cabinet for some kind of pain killer, found some acetaminophen, and took two with some water from the bathroom faucet. By that time, thankfully, the coffeemaker was hissing and the smell of French roast was wafting through the room.

As she was pouring, she heard a gentle knock at her door. Still wrapped in her blanket, she went to the door and opened it. Kate was standing there with a steaming mug in her hand, wearing a big hooded sweatshirt that said UCLA. She had a suspiciously big smile on her face.

"Hey," Gen said, backing up to let Kate come in.

"Hey. I heard you moving around. Thought I'd come down and see how you're doing this morning."

"Eeaarrrgh," Gen said.

Kate nodded. "I suspected as much."

Gen went back into the kitchenette and put sugar and milk into her coffee. Normally she skipped the sugar and milk—she usually drank it black—but this morning she needed whatever energy the extra calories could provide to her.

She took a long drink of the coffee and groaned.

Kate and Gen went over to the sofa bed, which was, at the moment, a bed, and plopped onto it with their mugs, sitting cross-legged, enjoying the warmth from the fireplace.

"You look ridiculously happy this morning," Gen said.

"I love morning sex," Kate replied.

"Shut up," Gen said. "You and your morning sex smugness. Why don't you go back upstairs and have more of your damned morning sex, if it's so great?"

Kate considered. "Well, I could, but Jackson's gone to work, so it would be awkward." Kate, five-foot-six with short, tousled, dark hair, had never looked happier, or more beautiful. Life with Jackson, the head chef at one of the local restaurants, was obviously agreeing with her. "You're testy this morning," she observed.

"God. I'm sorry. It's this hangover. The relentless drumming in my head won't allow for warmth and graciousness." She drank some more coffee.

"You want me to go?" Kate looked at her, eyebrows raised.

"No, no. Stay. I want you to stay."

They sat for a while, propped on pillows, letting the caffeine seep into them. After a while, the Tylenol started to kick in and Gen began to feel marginally better.

"Kind of an adjustment for you," Kate ventured. "Having Jackson move in."

"Yeah," Gen said miserably.

Kate reached out and rubbed Gen's upper arm with her hand. "I'm sorry if it's hard."

Gen shrugged. "It's not your fault. What were you supposed to do, stay lonely and unhappy for my sake? It's ridiculous. I'm being ridiculous. And I love Jackson. I do. And I'm happy for you. It's just … "

"I know," Kate reassured her.

"Listen, sweetie," Kate said after a while. "I've got to go and get dressed for work. You going to be okay today? Seems like you really drank a lot last night. You've gotta be … "

At that moment, Gen turned faintly green, put down her mug, dashed into the bathroom, and hurled into the toilet.

"Um, okay, then," Kate said. "I'll just … I'm gonna go now."

Why did she drink so much? Why hadn't she just stuck with a glass of wine or two? *Stupid, stupid, stupid.* She wasn't a twenty-one-year-old having a kegger in the dorms, for God's sake. That part of her life was over. And good riddance.

She berated herself as she pushed through the fog in her head to unlock the gallery and go inside. The Porter Gallery, just down Main Street from Kate's bookstore, was bigger than many of the storefronts in this part of town—thought that wasn't to say it was big. The main part of the gallery consisted of two fair-sized rooms, and she had a small office and storage space in the back. When she'd originally acquired the space, it had been a clothing boutique. She'd stripped it down to its bones until now it was all sleek white walls and gleaming honey-colored wood floors.

Flipping on the lights, she surveyed her business with a sigh. Some of the artwork on display was quite good—she had some abstract expressionist paintings from a young artist she thought had a promising future, and she had a beautiful display of art glass by Jackson's friend, Daniel Reed—but she also had a large number of the watercolor seascapes she considered to be more souvenir than fine art.

The watercolors were the kind of thing that would prevent her from being taken seriously in cities like New York or Los Angeles. Breaking waves at sunset wouldn't get you a reputation as a savvy dealer. But this was Cambria, and the seascapes sold. She could advocate for serious art all day long, but in the end, she had to pay the rent.

The rent had been the motivating factor that had persuaded her to stock a display of ceramics and handmade jewelry, as well. The pieces were lovely, and they sold well, but they were crafts, not fine art. She'd adapted to the realities of the art world in a tourist town, but not without some reluctance.

Because of the hangover—and the fact that she'd overslept—she was opening the gallery a little late today. It was 10:25 by the time she flipped the sign on her door to OPEN. Sure, one of the benefits of having her own place was that she could open whenever she wanted. But arriving late was just a bad business practice.

She was dressed in a close-fitting, sleeveless black sheath dress and black pumps with three-inch heels, her curly red hair pulled up into a chignon with a few stray curls dangling beside her face. The look was standard New York. Here in Cambria, the shop owners were more likely to wear a flowing, hand-woven shawl or a maxi dress with a painted silk scarf, but Gen had never quite been ready to go native. She'd been a New York girl once, and she planned to be one again. It was best to act like it, so the transition would be easier when it was finally time to go home.

Home.

With Davis MacIntyre gone, and with him all of the obstacles he'd placed in her path, the idea of returning was a possibility once more. But she couldn't simply show up on 57th Street and announce she was back. While Davis MacIntyre would no longer be spreading hurtful rumors about her, that also meant that everyone had probably forgotten who she was.

She needed a plan.

She was thinking about that when Daniel Reed came in the front door toting a carton the size of a mini refrigerator.

Daniel was tall, dark, and gorgeous, all rugged masculinity with his faded jeans and his close-fitting T-shirt—just the kind of man she was usually attracted to. Too bad she wasn't the least bit attracted to him. There was no accounting for it. On paper, they'd have made the perfect couple. She was a gallery owner, he was an artist. She was single, he was single. She was delighted by his company, and he by hers. But there simply was no chemistry. After more than a year of working with him, he seemed more like a brother. Life could be unfair sometimes.

"Hey, Gen," he said jovially.

"Ugh," she answered.

He put down his carton, put his hands on his hips, and looked at her with his head cocked. "You don't look so good."

"That's funny, because I feel ... like hell."

"Last night around the time you took your third tequila shot, I said to myself, 'Daniel, that girl's going to have a rough day tomorrow.' And look how right I was."

"But at least you aren't smug at all, so that's something," Gen said.

"Something bothering you last night?" His tone was casual, but the invitation was there for a heart-to-heart, something she might have welcomed on another occasion, but that she just couldn't deal with right now.

"What's in the carton?" Gen said.

"You're changing the subject," Daniel observed.

"Imagine that. What's in the carton?"

He looked at her for a moment, probably waiting to see whether she'd crack under the pressure of his gaze and pour out her problems. Fat chance. She waited, arms crossed and eyebrows raised, until he relented and opened the carton.

He pulled out a heavily Bubble-Wrapped item, freed it from its protective layers, and held it out to show Gen. He held a large, shallow bowl in shades of orange, streaked with graceful, dark lines that suggested the branches of a late-fall tree that had been stripped of its foliage.

Gen cooed appreciatively. "That's nice," she said. "Really nice. Mrs. Freeman is going to love it. She's been asking me when you were going to bring in some new pieces." Adele Freeman, a wealthy older woman with a summer home in Cambria, was Daniel's most reliable collector.

Daniel nodded. "I made it with her in mind. She was telling me last month how much she misses the seasons since she moved here from the East Coast. Said she loves fall. So, I thought of this. But this kind of evokes the stark, harsh, it's-almost-winter fall. Maybe I should have gone with foliage."

"No. Don't second-guess yourself. I love this. If Mrs. Freeman doesn't take it, someone else will." Daniel's work was always a top seller in her gallery. She'd tried to convince him to show his stuff in Los Angeles or San Francisco—she felt certain he could do well in a bigger art market—but he'd balked every time. Once or twice she'd raised the subject of what the self-help gurus would call Daniel's "success blocks," but he'd shut her down, much the way she'd shut him down on the subject of what had made her drink so much the night before.

Maybe they both had issues they weren't ready to explore.

After Daniel left, Gen went into the back room and made a pot of coffee to clear the remaining dust bunnies the hangover had left in her head. She hadn't had her morning run, and that had put her in a bad mood. She hated to miss her morning run, and whenever she did, it made her feel sluggish and out of sorts for the rest of the day. Maybe she'd get to the gym after work. If she could get the nagging ache in her head to go away.

When she had a mug of hot, black coffee in her hand, she sat at her desk in the rear of the main room of the gallery and sighed. The place was pretty much deserted, but that was no surprise on a late morning in January. Here in Cambria, foot traffic peaked during the summer tourist season, with another good bump in December when visitors came for the holidays. Sometimes people with families came during spring break. Other than that, Cambria was a sleepy town with little activity on Main Street.

Gen couldn't keep a business like this running with foot traffic. The tourists weren't the ones who brought in the real money, anyway. They bought the seascapes, the ceramic mugs, the hand-made moonstone jewelry. That was a good and essential part of Gen's business, but they were lower-ticket items. Her real income came from the things she did behind the scenes, the matchmaking between artists and collectors. The best artworks that came through her hands never made it to the gallery walls—or, at least, not with a price tag on them. The best stuff was promised to deep-pocket buyers before the public ever saw it.

So much of what she did was schmoozing and socializing. Today she had a lunch with a wealthy couple who kept a weekend place down in the exclusive Sea Clift Estates neighborhood. He'd made a fortune in the pharmaceuticals business, and she had old family money. Their "weekend place" was more like a palace, with a back yard perched on a bluff overlooking the ocean. Justin and Colleen McCabe collected art not because they loved art, but because they believed it was what cultured people did. Knowing that they, themselves, didn't have a feel for quality—or for what might increase in value over time—they relied on Gen's tastes to guide them. She'd placed a number of excellent abstracts with them over the years, sales for which she took a hefty forty percent commission. That was how the doors of the Porter Gallery stayed open—the deals she made with the McCabes and others like them.

She'd prepared for today's lunch by speaking with a number of artists whose work she thought would be suitable for the McCabes, to see what they were working on and what might be available. But even that wasn't straightforward. The artists who believed their work was hot—and Gen wouldn't be talking to them about the McCabes if it wasn't—usually hemmed and hawed about how they worked with a New York dealer and not with a nobody from Cambria, or about how the McCabes weren't the kinds of collectors who would build the artist's reputation, or about how they'd promised their best work for a solo show in Los Angeles.

You'd think that, in the end, it would come down to price. That's what the McCabes believed, and they didn't see why it was sometimes an effort for Gen to acquire a desired work of art for them. But, in truth, it was about so much more than money. It was ego-stroking and reassurance and strategizing; it was promises made for future deals with people Gen hadn't even met yet.

It was exhausting.

She loved it.

She looked at the clock on her laptop and saw that she still had an hour before she had to leave to meet the McCabes. She looked over the images of the artworks she'd selected for them, e-mailed to her by the artists. For the McCabes, name recognition was key. They wanted to collect artists who were being talked about, whose work appeared in *Art in America*, who were profiled in *The New Yorker.* That was good for Gen, because it meant big-ticket sales that would keep the lease on the gallery space paid for months to come. But as profitable as such deals were, she saw them as short-sighted.

She pulled up an image of an abstract work by a young artist from Chicago. The canvas was all reds and blacks and brilliant blues, with slashing brushwork that suggested a raging storm. This artist wasn't being talked about—not yet—but looking at the painting, she had a nagging feeling that he was on the verge of something. Some kind of artistic breakthrough, some revelation that would transform his work from promising to brilliant. She sighed. She would show this to the McCabes, tell them her thoughts about this artist's bright future. And, of course, she'd push hard her belief that buying his work now, before he became the darling of the premier galleries, would be an outstanding financial investment. But the McCabes would never go for it. They wanted to collect artists who were impressive now, not those who might be impressive ten years from now.

She snapped the laptop shut.

That was one of the frustrating things about her job: having the vision to spot true talent before others did, but being unable to persuade anyone to act on it.

The lunch went the way Gen had expected. The McCabes had cooed over the artists she'd known they would. She had instructions from them to pursue a particular work that she may or may not be able to get for them; it likely would involve promises to also take lesser works that the artist hadn't been able to move any other way. If she could swing it, the commission would provide her with a nice financial cushion.

But the deal with the McCabes was just one thing to think about.

She also had to think about how to get back to New York.

Cambria was nice—you'd have to be blind not to love it—but it was a small town tucked away in the middle of nowhere. Her ambition to become a player in the art world wouldn't happen here, no matter how many rich couples like the McCabes she cultivated, no matter how many artists she cooed to and pleaded with over the phone or on her occasional trips elsewhere.

She had to go back to New York, but it wasn't as simple as selling the gallery and packing her stuff. She had to develop a reputation first. She had to get some buzz, some gravitas, or she'd get eaten alive in New York.

Chapter Two

Ryan Delaney was up early the morning after the party. He was up early every morning, before sunrise, regardless of what he'd done the night before. Running a cattle ranch didn't allow for sleeping in.

By five thirty, he was downstairs and in the kitchen, pouring himself a cup of black coffee from the pot. His mother was already there, busy at the stove, frying eggs and bacon for his father and his uncle.

Coffee mug in hand, he kissed his mom's cheek.

"I've got some oatmeal going for you," she said, giving him the usual morning side-eye. "Though my life would be a lot easier if you'd just eat the eggs and bacon like everybody else."

"You don't have to cook for me, Mom," he said. Like the side-eye, it was also part of their routine. "I've been a grown man for a while now. I can make my own oatmeal. You don't need to trouble yourself."

She grunted. "I can't very well cook for your father and your uncle and just ignore you, now can I?"

Ryan had been a vegetarian for six years, and his family had yet to adjust to it. Having raised beef cattle for generations, the Delaney family could not make sense of the idea of foregoing steaks and burgers in favor of salads and brown rice. His mother viewed his dietary choices with suspicion, and his father and uncle simply scoffed at him as though not eating meat were comparable to announcing that he'd be wearing only blue from now on, or hopping from place to place on one foot. To them, it seemed frivolous and arbitrary. But to Ryan, it was the natural result of getting up close and personal with the eventual providers of the steaks and burgers.

He couldn't eat them when he'd raised them and sometimes even bottle-fed them. It surprised him that the rest of his family could.

Sandra Delaney, a woman in her midfifties with dark brown hair now starting to gray, fussed around at the stove, deftly managing the eggs, the bacon, and the oatmeal at the same time, an apron wrapped around her middle, fuzzy slippers on her feet. She wore Levi's and a San Francisco 49ers T-shirt, her hair pulled back into a ponytail. Sandra was trim and small but strong and wiry, the result of a lifetime of hard work outdoors.

"Well, don't just stand there. Grab a bowl," she said.

Ryan grinned as he opened a cupboard over the counter and took out a bowl. His mother's perpetual ill humor amused and comforted him for reasons he couldn't begin to understand. Sandra was Sandra, and if she ever stopped being Sandra—if, say, she ever became warm and nurturing, with a kind word and an easy smile—he'd take it as a sign of the impending apocalypse. She was a deeply loving woman, but that deep love was buried beneath a layer of porcupine quills. Her constancy, her predictability, was north on the compass of his life.

He poured oatmeal into his bowl from the saucepan on the stove, bustled around adding butter, milk (he had no philosophical problem with butter or milk), and brown sugar, then carried the steaming bowl to the kitchen table. The world beyond the windows was still black, with sunrise more than an hour away.

Ryan's brain was a little foggy after staying late at Jackson and Kate's party the night before. He didn't drink much, knowing he had an early morning and a long workday ahead, but he did stay into the early hours, and he'd had to hit his snooze alarm three or four times this morning before he'd been able to drag himself out of bed.

He would never mention such a thing to Sandra, who wouldn't tolerate nonsense like sleeping in. Parties were fine, staying out late was fine, hell, even getting drunk off your ass was fine on occasion. But that ass had better be up and seated at the breakfast table no later than six a.m.—five thirty was better—unless you were sick or dead.

Ryan was on his second cup of coffee, halfway into his breakfast, when his father came into the kitchen, dressed and ready for his day. Orin Delaney was an ox of a man even into his early sixties, tall and broad, with hair that was once dark brown, near black, but was now thinning to such an extent that the main color to reach one's eye was the pink of his scalp. Now, the older man pulled a mug from the cupboard over the coffee pot and poured himself a cup, which he drank black. He took a seat at the table next to Ryan and peered into Ryan's bowl.

"Why the hell would you want to eat horse food?" Orin asked, looking pained.

Sandra came to the table and set a plate of eggs, bacon, and toast in front of Orin.

"Why the hell would you want to eat dead pigs?" Ryan retorted.

Ryan's uncle Redmond came in just as Sandra was placing his plate on the table. Similar in appearance to Orin—tall and broad, with a powerful build—Redmond had shrunk some with age. A good ten years older than Orin, Redmond had retired from actively working the ranch about five years before, but a lifetime of rising before the sun had made him incapable of sleeping in, even in what were supposed to be his leisure years.

"Morning, Uncle Redmond," Ryan said as he got up from the table to take his empty bowl to the sink.

"Morning," Redmond replied.

"How's your back doing this morning?" Sandra inquired.

Redmond grunted as he lowered himself into his chair. "Been better." As always, Redmond was a master of brevity.

The Delaney Ranch had been in operation for seven generations, since one of Ryan's ancestors—an immigrant from Ireland—had received the acreage as part of a Mexican land grant in 1846. The original buildings weren't standing anymore, except for the ruins of an old cabin on the eastern edge of the ranch. The modern buildings—main house, old barn, stables, guest house, and bunkhouse—were built in the 1950s, except for the new barn, which was built ten years ago. Most of the structures showed significant wear, but the house was in good shape, and it was big enough for Orin and Sandra, Redmond, Ryan, Ryan's sister, Breanna, and Breanna's two boys, ages five and seven. Breanna had moved back to the ranch a few years ago after her husband, a Marine, had been killed in the Middle East. It wasn't an ideal situation for her, but she'd been grateful to have the family home to return to. At least here, she didn't have to raise her boys alone.

Ryan had two brothers—Liam, who ran a ranch in Montana, and Colin, who was a lawyer in San Diego. With Redmond retired and Orin getting older, they were all looking to Ryan to take over the operation of the ranch. That was fine with him; it had always been his intention to manage the ranch when his father and uncle were no longer willing or able to do so. He'd gotten his degree in farm and ranch management from Iowa State with just such a goal in mind.

He had a different idea of how to do it than they did, but that was okay; he'd ease them along, and eventually they'd accept the changes he was planning to make.

When Ryan had announced his intention of taking the ranch organic—for the good of the land, for the benefit of the cattle, and for the increased prices organic beef brought over conventional—his family had looked at him the same way they had when he'd sworn off eating meat. True, raising cattle organically was more cumbersome and more costly, but he believed the benefits would outweigh the trouble and the expense.

Orin had been reluctant to accept the idea, but bit by bit, he was coming around.

Ryan had been less successful at persuading his father to invest money in upgrading the various buildings on the ranch. The money wasn't the issue; Orin's lifelong resistance to change was the problem. If something was still working, why fix it? If the house was still keeping the rain off their heads, why renovate it? Here it was ten years later, and Orin was still grousing about how they hadn't really needed to build the new barn. But Ryan had plans for the ranch, plans to put his mark on things and make the place his own.

His parents and his uncle would just have to learn to roll with it.

By sunrise, Ryan had finished with his morning barn chores and was on his way out to check the fences in the northeast pasture. He'd be moving the herd there in the coming week, and he had to make sure they would be secure. Checking fences was a job that never seemed to end, especially on a ranch as large as this one. One broken fence and you'd be busting your ass to retrieve your herd from a neighbor's land,

and that was a dicey operation at best, especially this time of year, when the amount of hired help was minimal.

For many jobs, Ryan preferred his four-wheel-drive truck over the four-hooved variety of transportation. But for checking fences, it was horseback or nothing. He rode Annie, a five-year-old mare, through the heavy early morning fog as daylight began to brighten the gauzy world around him.

He loved this time of day, loved this time of year, when the air was cool and the world was softened by the mist at first light. Being out here by himself—just him and the powerful animal moving beneath him—gave him time to think, to reflect, to plan and prioritize.

He thought about the work he had ahead of him today, about his long-term plans for the ranch, about friends and women and his place in the world.

He thought about Lacy Jordan.

Ah, Lacy. He had long been an admirer of her beauty, her gentleness, her effortless grace. He'd found himself unable to approach her, and he was beginning to understand why. It was because, on some level, he knew that she did not return his interest. If he were to ask her out, she would be too kind to shut him down the way another woman might. Her efforts not to hurt his feelings would likely result in false encouragement, which would draw out his eventual failure with her to uncomfortable lengths. Ryan, with his good instincts for people, somehow knew that, and that was what had prevented him from making a move.

It should have worked between them, though. It should have been right. Lacy was gorgeous—no question about that—but she was also perfect for him. She'd lived in Cambria her whole life, like he had. She valued family relationships, like he did. She wanted a solid home life, a house full of noise and kids, just like he did. At least, that was what he'd heard from friends—both his and hers—in his inquiries about her. He hadn't been bold enough to ask her himself.

But in the times he'd approached her for a tentative conversation, something had been missing. Some undefinable element, some spark that would be needed if they were to eventually ignite a flame. He stubbornly continued to believe he could get that spark going, though. He just hadn't rubbed enough rocks together yet.

As he thought about exactly which rocks he might rub together, and how, his thoughts drifted to Gen Porter. He'd spent some time talking to her at the party last night, mostly hoping to get some insight into Lacy. Gen had seemed sad, irritated, keyed up. She'd been drinking a lot. He'd known her, casually, for a while now, and he'd never known her to be a drinker, at least not to any noticeable extent.

He wondered what was wrong, and while he was thinking about that, he also wondered what kind of person she was, what undefinable mechanism made her tick. It might be interesting to find out.

The fog began to thin slightly as the day brightened. Annie huffed a heavy breath that steamed in the cool morning as she picked her way through the grass. Ryan adjusted his baseball cap. He wore it in lieu of a cowboy hat because he didn't want to be a cliché.

Just as he began to crest a gentle, rolling hill covered in knee-high, green grass, he saw a place where a post on one of the older stretches of fence had sagged to the ground, leaving a gaping opening that might as well have been labeled COW EXIT. He sighed. He climbed down from the horse and gave the animal a pat on her side.

Well, there was his morning.

Chapter Three

"I know," Gen was telling Rose Watkins one evening a few days after the party as the two of them climbed side-by-side staircases to nowhere at Hard Bodies, the gym where they worked out far too seldom, in Gen's opinion, and far too often in Rose's. "I don't drink like that normally. I'm not planning to do it again anytime soon. You don't have to be a mother hen."

Rose's hair was blue this month, a bright, bold blue one might see in a box of Crayolas, and it had grown out a bit from the chin-length bob she'd sported for most of the summer. Now, it was just long enough that she was able to pull it into a tiny, perky ponytail at the back of her head for the sake of workout comfort. Rose's exercise ensemble consisted of a pair of black spandex capris and a T-shirt that sagged off her left shoulder, exposing a bit of a rose tattoo just beneath the strap of her exercise bra. Rose's left eyebrow, pierced with a silver barbell, quirked up.

"I'm not being a mother hen. I'm just, you know, wondering. You didn't seem like yourself. As your friend, I'm allowed to wonder."

"I guess," Gen said sullenly. She kicked the stair-climber up to a higher setting and wiped the sweat from her face. The exercise felt good. Exhaustion always helped to clear her anxiety, calm her thoughts.

"So?" Rose prompted.

"So, what?"

"So, what was bothering you? Jeez, it's like pulling teeth. Just come out with it already." Rose took a long slug from her water bottle and then fixed her gaze on Gen.

"It's Kate," Gen said finally. "Or, actually, Jackson. Kate and Jackson."

"I thought you liked Jackson," Rose said.

"I do!" Gen threw her hands into the air for emphasis, then had to grab the rails on the stair-climber to regain her balance. "I do. I love Jackson. And I'm so happy for Kate. I am. But ..."

"But?" Rose prompted.

"But now she's *busy* all the time! With him! Probably having lots and lots of really great sex, and I can't just ... just *barge in* to her place anymore like I used to, because she's happy and all coupled up and she's moved on, and I'm left all by myself downstairs with no one to talk to, thinking about the fact that I'm *not* having great sex."

"That's a lot."

"I know!"

Rose considered for a moment. "Okay, let's take those points one at a time. One: How busy can she really be? Jackson's a chef. He works crazy hours, including nights five days a week, sometimes six. I'm thinking it's not actually, technically, impossible to spend time with Kate."

"Well ..." Gen grumbled.

"Two: She has not moved on. Moving on suggests that she's done with you, me, and all of her friends, and she'll be doing nothing except having great sex exclusively from now on. When, in fact, I think she'll need to emerge from time to time, if only for hydration."

Gen shrugged. "Hydration is important."

"And three," Rose continued. "You could have great sex. There are plenty of men out there you could have great sex with."

Gen took a slug from her water bottle, breathing hard, sweat making her face gleam. "Name one."

"Well … I saw you talking to Ryan Delaney for quite a while at the party. A solid nine on the hotness scale. The dark hair, the deep brown eyes, that firm, muscular cowboy body." She wiggled her eyebrows. "Not to mention the manliness factor of the whole ranching thing."

Gen tsked. "He's not a nine."

"Why not?"

Gen glared at Rose. "I don't know what your criteria are, but if that man doesn't score a ten, I don't know who would."

Encouraged, Rose sped up her pace slightly and waved an arm at Gen. "Well, there you go!"

"No. There's no 'there you go.' You know what Mr. Ten On The Scale and I were talking about all that time?"

"Uh oh. What?"

"Lacy."

"Ah."

There was no need to explain. In the years that Gen, Rose, and Kate had been close friends with Lacy, each of them had, at least once, experienced chatting up an attractive man only to have him inquire about Lacy.

"The man makes my palms sweat. My palms were actually sweating." Gen shook her head to emphasize her own pathetic state. "There I was with my sweaty palms and that dry mouth thing—because apparently my body can't even function when I'm around him—and he's asking me what Lacy's interests are, and if she's seeing anyone, and what's the best way to talk to her. Gah!"

"Aw, honey. So what did you tell him?"

"I said that I talk to her about shoe sales and *The Bachelor,* but I didn't think that was going to work for him."

Rose laughed. "Good one."

They climbed side by side in silence, panting and sweating companionably.

"She's not interested, you know," Rose said finally.

"I know!" Gen shook her head. "God, what a waste."

Rose slowed her machine, came to a stop, and climbed down. She looked up at Gen, who was still pumping away. "You know what you need, you need a hot artist to come to Cambria and sweep you off your feet."

Gen sighed. "You know, I really do."

Rose's comment about the hot artist didn't solve the issue of Gen's nonexistent love life, but it did spark an idea.

Gen needed to rebuild a reputation in the art world if she were ever going to return to New York and become a player there. She needed to generate some buzz, gain some credibility. That was hard to do in an out-of-the-way town like Cambria, because the kinds of artists who had major influence didn't live here. She could call them on the phone, e-mail them, deal with them via Skype, but it wasn't the same as being able to schmooze with them over lunch or cocktails.

You need a hot artist to come to Cambria, Rose had said.

That was just what she needed—a hot artist. But not sexy hot. She needed an artist who was my-career-is-about-to-take-off hot.

An artist whose career had already gotten traction would not bother with Gen and Cambria. But one who was likely to emerge soon—but hadn't yet—just might. If she could some-how spot an artist like that and bring him here, maybe create an artist-in-residence program through her gallery, she could have her name associated with his—or hers—when they even-tually did get showered with fame and recognition.

It was a gamble, of course. If she bet on the wrong horse, she'd have invested time and money for little return. But if it worked, she could make a name for herself nationwide before she ever left town.

Gen thought about it as she drove home from the gym, still sweaty and hot from her workout. She thought about it some more in the shower, as the hot water soothed her aching muscles. Afterward, warm and comfy in her bathrobe with her hair wrapped in a towel, she opened her laptop and Googled artist-in-residence programs to learn what she could about what would be involved.

She was still researching when Kate knocked on her door half an hour later.

"Come in!" Gen called, not looking up from the computer screen.

"Hey." Kate leaned in the doorway. "You want to come up? Jackson's working. It's lonely up there."

"Mm, sure," Gen said.

When she had moved to Cambria about a year and a half earlier, Gen had considered herself lucky to be able to rent Kate's downstairs space for such a reasonable price. True, the apartment was tiny, with a galley kitchen that allowed for only miniature appliances, and a single living space that had to double as bedroom and living room. But that presented no problem, as Gen was used to apartment living in Manhattan. Compared to her place there, this was positively cavernous.

Gen had considered herself fortunate even before getting to know Kate. Afterward, she considered herself positively blessed. She and Kate had become close immediately.

Kate, who owned Swept Away, a bookstore on Main Street, was in her after-work relaxed mode. She was wearing Levi's torn at the knees and an oversized T-shirt that said Book

Nerd, with a pair of glasses as the two Os. Her feet were bare, and her short, spiky, dark hair was askew.

"You eat yet?" Gen asked her. "I just came from the gym. I'm starved. All those burned calories."

"I did," Kate said, still leaning in from the door frame, "but we have some great leftovers. Jackson cooked last night."

"Ooh. I'm in." There were definite benefits to having a chef living upstairs.

Tonight's leftovers consisted of herb-crusted leg of lamb and zucchini soup with crème fraiche and cilantro.

"Jeez," Gen said as she settled in at Kate's dining room table and dug in. "This is what he cooks at *home?*"

"I wish. No, not usually. He wanted to try some things out before doing them at the restaurant. What do you think?"

"I'd order it."

Kate didn't cook, and before Jackson's arrival, the offerings upstairs had consisted mostly of Pop-Tarts and frozen pizzas. When Kate had offered Gen the so-called foods that made up Kate's own diet, it usually resulted in a lecture on health and nutrition. Gen had to admit, this was better.

"So, what were you working on so intently when I popped in?" Kate sat across from Gen at the dining table, sipping a glass of white wine.

"An idea." Gen took a drink from her own wineglass, then had another bite of the lamb. "Yum."

"An idea for the gallery?"

"Could be." She told Kate about her idea for an artist-in-residence program, but she didn't tell her that she was considering it as a way to get back to New York. She rarely held anything back from Kate—they were like sisters—but this, she sensed, would cause some difficult feelings. How could she tell

Kate that she wanted to leave? How could she explain that if all went well, the two of them might be separated not only by thousands of miles, but also by the giant cultural chasm that separated Cambria from Manhattan?

"Huh," Kate said, thinking about Gen's plan. "How would that work? Where would this artist live? How would you pay for it?"

Kate echoed the questions that were crowding around in Gen's head. "I don't know."

"It's an interesting idea, though," Kate said.

"Yeah. It could be. It really could be."

"You could solve all of those problems. I mean, it's doable," Kate said. "There are a million rental houses around here, and if you could get one of your wealthy collectors to sponsor the program, you'd be all set. The rest would be … details."

"I think I even know the artist I want." Gen munched on another bite of lamb and thought. "But the place. That's the first step. I have to find a place."

Chapter Four

It was time for Ryan to stop thinking about the run-down buildings on the ranch property, and time for him to start doing something about them. The main house wasn't bad; no one would claim it was an architectural gem, with its 1950s exterior that was long past needing a new coat of paint, but structurally, it was in good repair, solid and warm and sheltering for the family within. The new barn had been built recently enough that it was in very good condition, but the older barn—the one built back in the fifties—needed some refurbishing. Or they needed to just tear it down.

The guest house, though—that was the worst. The little one-bedroom cottage had plumbing problems, wiring problems, roof problems. Nobody had stayed in it for as long as Ryan could remember. Shame, too. The location was prime, with shade trees, rolling, grassy hills, and a creek close enough that you could just hear the rushing water—during the seasons when the water was high enough, anyway.

There was no excuse for letting it go. The Delaney family had simply had other priorities over the years.

But Ryan had ideas.

Ryan's ideas had gone mostly unspoken up to this point, because his father and his uncle were set in their ways, much like a mountain was set in the earth. They were about as immovable as the mountain on any given thing when it came to the running of the ranch.

But now that Redmond was retired and Orin was slowing down, Ryan saw his opportunity to change a few things. Do a little tweaking. Put the Ryan Delaney touch on the place, as he'd been longing to do.

Late in the afternoon, with the hazy sun slanting in through windows that were filmed with dirt, Ryan surveyed the inside of the guest cottage. He saw the dirt, the broken moldings, the disrepair.

But he also saw possibilities.

He adjusted the baseball cap on his head and poked around in the bedroom, the tiny bathroom, the closet. His shoes scuffed against the wood floor as he went from room to room.

Wood floors. Yeah, they were beat to hell, but he could get someone in here to refinish them. He walked to the front window in the main room, wiped a clean spot with his sleeve, and peered out. Fantastic view. Oak trees and tall grass and, off in the distance, a strip of blue ocean.

The best way, he figured, was to just get some workers going on it, and then tell his parents after the fact, when they started asking about the trucks and the hammering and the invoices. The dishonesty of that—the sneakiness—might have bothered him for a minute or two, but he knew they'd be pleased when the work was done.

That's how his family was. They had to be dragged toward progress, usually by the ankles.

He wasn't sure what they would do with the cottage once it was done. Breanna and her boys could use some privacy, no doubt, but the place was too small for them. Ryan himself sometimes longed to break away from the whole living-with-the-family thing, God knew. But he also knew he'd miss the busy bustle of the main house.

If he could spin it to his dad as income property—get some tenants in the place, maybe even put it out there as a vacation rental—then the family would have a hard time arguing that there was no point to having the work done.

Vacation on the coast, at a working cattle ranch. That had some potential.

He pulled out his cell phone, scrolled through his contacts, and called Will Bachman, a friend who worked as caretaker at a big estate up the highway. He'd know some construction guys, some plumbing guys. Hell, better get some interior decorator guys—or girls, he guessed—on the job too, while he was at it.

The crew Will had recommended to him had been on the job for two days before Orin noticed. That wasn't anything unusual; the guest cottage wasn't visible from the main house, and the crews had taken an access road to get to the site. Eventually, though, the noise and dust became obvious.

"What in the hell you got going on over there?" Orin asked Ryan one day as the two of them were just coming in from the workday, Ryan dirty and sweaty, Orin considerably less so, since he'd cut back on his ranch duties.

Breanna's boys—Lucas, age five, and Michael, age seven—mobbed Ryan as he came in the door, as was their habit. Ryan lifted Michael high into the air and set the boy on his shoulders, and he picked up Lucas and held him under one arm like a log of firewood. The boys giggled with glee.

"Just fixing the place up," Ryan said, continuing the conversation as though he didn't have a hundred pounds of squirming boy all over his body.

"What the hell for?" Orin demanded. The look on his face suggested that he was troubled by some irritating condition like poison oak or heat rash.

"You seen it lately? Place is practically falling apart. It's about time it got some maintenance," Ryan said. He carried the boys over to the big leather sofa that stood in front of the stone fireplace. He dumped Lucas onto the sofa with a *whump,* then lifted Michael off his shoulders and deposited him beside his brother. Then he proceeded to tickle both of the boys until they were in helpless hysterics.

Orin scratched at one ear. "Well, what are you havin' 'em do out there?"

Ryan shrugged. "Fix the plumbing. Do a little roofing. Maybe some paint." He left out a few details—like the new electrical system—that he thought would send his father into more discomfort than either one of them could handle.

"Aw, hell," Orin said.

Ryan went through the usual coming-home routine with the boys, in which he tickled them until they screamed and begged him to stop, and then he stopped, and then they begged him to do it all over again.

When the screams of "Uncle Ryyyaaannnn!" got to be too much, he patted them on the butt and sent them off to find their mom or their grandma.

"I wish you'd told me you were going to do all that before you started," Orin said, sounding irritable but not angry, as was his way. Orin never got truly angry, but he had a way of scrunching up his face and looking as though he'd just dis- covered his hat was full of bees.

"If I'd told you, you'd have said no," Ryan said as he plucked Michael's jacket off the floor and hung it on a peg near the front door. "Tell me I'm wrong."

"Well, you're not wrong," Orin admitted. "I guess I don't see the point, is all, since nobody ever uses the place. I don't see why that old guest house would be a priority."

Ryan continued moving around the living room, straight- ening things up. He put away some Legos the boys had left out on the coffee table, scooping some off the floor and into their plastic bucket.

"That's just it," he said. "It's never been a priority. That's why it's just about falling down. Aren't you the one who taught me how important maintenance is? Well, I'm doing maintenance."

Orin scratched at the back of his head. "Well, I guess when I said that, I meant maintenance on the stuff we actually use."

"If we fix up the guest house, we'll use it," Ryan said.

Orin scrunched up his face in a mask of skepticism. "How you figure? Who's going to use it?"

Ryan stopped what he was doing and started ticking off points on his fingers. "Colin or Liam might use it when they're here for visits," he said, referring to his brothers. "Or some of the cousins, during the holidays. Or we could rent it out, bring in some income. Or ..." He'd saved this option, his favorite, for last. "Or we could rent it as a vacation place."

Orin looked puzzled. "Well, who'd want to take a vacation here?"

"Jeez, I don't know, Dad. What with the ocean and the grass and the trees and the fresh air, this place isn't much better than a Turkish prison." He looked at his father with scorn.

"All right, all right," Orin said. "You can just quit with the sarcasm."

"Well."

"And who's going to deal with all these vacationers, when we get them?" Orin was arguing with renewed vigor, now that he'd seized on a new argument.

"I will."

"You."

"Yes, me. Why not me?"

Orin squirmed with discomfort. "Well, what about all the work you do around here? How are you gonna have the time?"

"I'll figure it out." Ryan slapped his dad on the back in a way that was supposed to be both friendly and reassuring. "Trust me."

Gen was still pulling together her idea when, one day while she was hanging out at Kate's bookstore, she heard Jackson mention that the guest house on the Delaney Ranch had been remodeled, and that Ryan was trying to figure out whether to rent it to a regular tenant or make it into a vacation place.

The thought of a guest house on the ranch property clicked perfectly with her artist-in-residence idea. Sure, she could put her artist—whoever it turned out to be—up someplace in town, but that lacked the charm and serenity of the ranch. She could just imagine her chosen artist working on plein air paintings under the canopy of a hundred-year-old oak tree, with an ocean breeze ruffling his (or her) hair.

Would Ryan Delaney be open to hosting her artist? She'd never been to the ranch, and she reflected that it might not be nearly as scenic as it was in her imagination, what with the cows and all of the dirt and smells that went with them.

Being on a cattle ranch could be a draw, depending on the artist's personality. She'd have to find someone who was into nature, someone not too hung up on the whole animal rights issue of beef production. PETA members need not apply.

Leaning against the counter in Swept Away, listening to Kate and Jackson chat, Gen considered the options. She asked Jackson what he thought, and he said he'd talk to Ryan. Within a couple of days, she had an appointment to go out and see the place. The thought excited her in more ways than one.

❖

Ryan Delaney made Gen's knees weak. It probably had something to do with his big, expressive, deep brown eyes, framed by dark lashes so thick any woman would envy them. Those eyes made Gen want to envelop him in her arms and make everything all better—even though she had no reason to believe he had a problem that needed solving, or a hurt that needed soothing.

She did, though.

She had the big, empty space in her middle that reminded her she hadn't had sex in a really long time. Now, there was one hurt that Ryan could make all better.

"So? What do you think?" Ryan was standing in the kitchen of the tiny guest house, his butt leaning against the counter, his arms crossed, waiting for Gen's appraisal.

Gen tried to tear her thoughts away from Ryan's tall, lean physique and focus on the house—the reason she was here. The cottage really was beautiful. It was tiny—a sitting room, a bedroom, a galley kitchen, and not much else. But the kitchen had been updated with miniature stainless steel appliances and butcher block countertops, the walls were a buttery yellow, and the hardwood floors gleamed in a warm shade of caramel. One side of the sitting room was dominated by a stone fireplace. She crossed through the little bedroom and into the bathroom, and found new fixtures, spotless and inviting.

"This place looks brand new," she said, emerging back out into the main room.

Ryan chuckled and rubbed at his chin, which sported a day's worth of stubble. Gen wanted him to rub that stubble all over her naked body, but suggesting such a thing would have made for an abrupt change of topic.

"Not exactly," he said. "This place has been sitting here more than sixty years. Just had it redone, floor to ceiling."

"Well, it looks amazing."

"Shoulda seen it before. Lucky it was still standing."

The guest cottage would be perfect for her program for several reasons. One, the setting was quiet and peaceful, just what an artist might need for maximum creative output. Two, the beauty of the surroundings would be inspiring. Three, the fact that it was on a cattle ranch was just unique enough to draw attention. And four, there was the landlord.

On second thought, that might be a drawback rather than an item in the plus column, considering how difficult it was for Gen to form a coherent thought with Ryan standing there, looking at her with those liquid eyes. Plus, there was his attraction to Lacy.

"The program would run for five months," she told him. "Jackson said you were planning to rent the place by the week, as a vacation house. I'm hoping that as a monthly rental …"

"I could knock the price down some," he said, anticipating her question.

"I'd appreciate that."

"Then there's the question of studio space."

He quirked an eyebrow. "What exactly did you have in mind?"

When Gen had said "studio space," she hadn't been thinking of a barn. And yet, here it was. The barn was cavernous, with a hay loft, stalls for livestock, and enough space that you could probably land a plane in there.

Gen took in the square footage, the natural, hazy light that wafted in through the open doors, and the pure, tangible ambiance you could only get from an abandoned barn.

"So, is this the original barn?" she asked as Ryan led her into the place with its dirt floors and weathered walls.

"No, not even close," he said, looking amused. "The original barn was built around 1850, I'd say. It either fell down or got torn down, probably a hundred years ago. This one dates back to about 1956. Or so my dad tells me. We don't use it anymore, obviously. Built a new one about ten years ago when we outgrew this one."

"You outgrew *this* barn?" she asked, taking in the sheer size of it.

"Well, it wasn't just the size that needed upgrading. The new one's got all the technology."

"Huh," Gen said.

"This one's got electricity, water. Ventilation. Size works out, if your guy does big canvases."

"Yeah, I don't think size will be a problem," Gen said.

Until now, the idea—the whole artist-in-residence thing— had seemed like a fuzzy fantasy that hadn't really taken shape. But the barn—the vision of someone setting up in here, throwing paint around, being inspired by the smell of hay and dirt and sea air—that's what did it for her. That's what made it real.

She turned to Ryan. "I want it. But I don't have the details on the dates yet. Or, actually, how I'm going to pay for it. Give me a couple of weeks. Don't rent it out before then." Her voice was excited, adamant.

His eyebrows rose. "I don't know if I can promise that."

"A deposit, then. I'll give you a deposit now, and tell you the dates when I've got them."

He rubbed at his chin. "That works."

They went back to the main house to work out the details as Gen mentally reviewed the contents of her business account, and winced.

Chapter Five

"You should see the place. It's so great. Holy cow. No pun intended." Gen was lying on Kate's sofa and munching from a bowl of popcorn. Lacy was sitting on the other end of the couch, with Gen's legs across her lap. Kate and Rose were both sprawled on the floor with blankets and pillows around them, as though they were thirteen-year-olds having a slumber party. They all were dressed in either sweatpants and T-shirts—Lacy and Rose—or pajamas—Kate and Gen. An episode of *Gilmore Girls* was playing on the wide-screen TV, but they were only paying attention to the show sporadically. There was no need, as they'd all seen it many times before.

"Sounds like a pretty cool project," Rose said. She sipped from a glass of chardonnay. "Artist on a cattle ranch, painting in a big barn. Sweet."

"The visuals of this place, I'm telling you, it's going to get me featured in all the art magazines."

"And then there are the visuals of Ryan Delaney," Kate remarked.

"Ah, God. Don't remind me. I could barely focus on the real estate," Gen said.

Emily Gilmore said something rude to Lorelai, and Lacy threw a piece of popcorn at the screen. "Shut your trap, Emily. Some kind of mother you are. Jeez."

"Speaking of Ryan Delaney," Gen said, nudging Lacy with her toe. "You were all he could talk about at Kate's party."

Lacy's forehead scrunched up in sympathy. "Aw. That's sweet. But it makes me feel bad."

"No chance there, huh?" Gen said. She tried to sound like she was idly curious, tried not to betray the fact that her heart was hammering as she waited for the answer.

Lacy shook her head regretfully. "No. I mean, he's great. I like him. But ..."

"But what?" Gen probed. "He's really sexy."

"Yeah. He is. I can see that, objectively. But he doesn't ring my bell."

"Ah, the Lacy Jordan Hotness Detector Bell," Rose said knowingly.

"The bell is never wrong," Lacy said.

"I think it's wrong this time," Gen admitted. "I think that bell of yours should be ringing right off its damn holder thingie. Whatever you call the thing that holds up a bell."

"Really." Lacy looked at Gen with interest. The messy bun atop Lacy's head was askew, and strands of her long, blond hair were falling into her face. She had no makeup on, and she was wearing an old pair of grey sweats, but even so, she was so beautiful—so radiant—that Gen could hardly blame Ryan for being taken with her.

Gen sighed. "I just think it's unfair, is all. Here he is, all smoking hot, all doe-eyed and tall and ... and ... and so *Ryan,* and all he can think about is you, and your bell won't even ring!"

Lacy put a hand on Gen's shin. "If I could make the bell ring, I would."

"I know."

Kate propped herself on one elbow and faced Gen. "Maybe this project of yours will give you a chance to get to know him better. Maybe get his mind off of Lacy and onto a certain curvy, red-haired art goddess." Her eyebrows wiggled.

"Ah, I don't know," Gen said.

They all watched the screen in silence for a few minutes. Lorelai was making jokes at the dinner table in a futile effort to cut the tension.

"There's no point anyway. It wouldn't make sense to start anything," Gen said. Her heartbeat sped as she prepared to say what she'd been keeping from them for weeks. She swallowed hard. "I really need to go back to New York anyway."

Rose looked up from her place on the floor. "Ooh, a trip to New York. We should all go. Hit some clubs, see some shows. Do some shopping. That would be fabulous."

"I'm in," Lacy said.

Gen sat up and cleared her throat. "I mean … What I'm saying is, I really need to move back to New York. You know … permanently."

Kate sat up straight from her position on the floor. "What?"

Rose, who had been lounging on the floor beside Kate, popped up and put her hands out in front of her in a classic traffic-cop gesture. "Stop. Wait. What are you talking about?"

"Gen?" Lacy prompted. She sounded hurt. Lacy reached for the TV remote and turned off the set.

"It's just … I don't want to leave you guys. I love you guys. You know that." Gen could feel herself starting to get teary-eyed. "But New York is where everything happens in the art world. I can't make a career here in Cambria. Not really."

"I thought the gallery was doing okay," Rose said. "If you need money …"

"It is," Gen said. "It is doing okay. But … that's all it'll ever be. It'll never do better than okay."

Kate got up abruptly. "I just … I need to …" She went into her bedroom and closed the door.

"Kate?" Gen called after her. "Kate, come on."

Lacy put her hand on Gen's arm. "She'll be all right. She just needs a minute."

"I thought you were hiding out," Rose said. "I thought that big-deal New York guy was intimidating you, and ..."

"He died," Gen said.

Lacy's eyebrows shot up. "He died?"

"Yeah. A couple of months ago. And now there's nothing keeping me here."

"Oh, really? Nothing? That's nice," Rose said. "Yeah, maybe you better go, then. Good luck with that." She got up, hunted for her shoes, and slipped them on her feet. Then she grabbed her purse.

"Aw, Rose. Don't go," Lacy said.

"Well, you know, there's nothing keeping me here." Rose shot Gen a look that was one part hurt, one part anger. "I gotta go. Bye, Lacy. Tell Kate I'll see her tomorrow." She went out the door with a slam.

"Shit," Gen said, wiping at the tears that were now starting to fall. "That went well."

Lacy rubbed Gen's upper arm. "They'll be okay. They're just sad. And maybe a little hurt. "We thought ..."

"Thought what?" Gen prompted her.

"Well ... We thought we were like a little family. The four of us."

"We are." Gen pulled her feet up onto the sofa and hugged her knees. "We really are. But families are supposed to support each other in doing new things ... in ... in reaching their goals!" Gen threw her arms up. "Where's the support? I have goals!"

"What about this new artists' thing you're planning? Is that off, then?" Lacy asked.

"No! That's why I'm doing it. If I can just have some success with an emerging artist, that'll set me up to go back to New York, open a gallery there, have some real influence. It's all part of the plan." She sighed, feeling miserable. "Hurting people's feelings and getting everybody pissed at me wasn't part of the plan."

"No, I guess not," Lacy said.

Gen peered sideways at Lacy. "Why aren't you mad?"

"Me? I don't know. I guess because I get it."

"You do?" Gen made a snuffling noise and blew her nose with a tissue she'd grabbed from a box on the side table.

"Oh, hell yes. I'd love to get out of here."

Gen raised her eyebrows. "Really? I had no idea. I mean, you've been here your whole life, your family's here …"

"Exactly. I've been here my whole life." Her expression took on a mixture of frustration and grit. "I mean, Cambria's great. And I love my family. But … there's more out there. I want to try other things, see other places. And I don't want to be a barista for the rest of my life."

"Huh," Gen said. "I didn't know."

"Yeah, well, I don't think anybody does. It's not like I can talk about it with my family. You can imagine how they'd react."

Gen gave Lacy a half grin. "Kind of like Kate and Rose?"

"Exactly. But with plate-throwing. There'd probably be plate-throwing."

After Lacy went home, Gen waited a while for Kate to come out. When she didn't, Gen went downstairs to her apartment and slept restlessly. She felt unsettled—things weren't right in her world if her friends were unhappy with her—but she also felt a renewed sense of determination. She couldn't let her friends' feelings get in the way of the things she needed to do for herself and her career.

Kate and Rose would come around. And if they didn't ... Well. They would if they cared about her, and that was all there was to it.

Chapter Six

It didn't take long. The next morning, Gen was just dragging herself out of bed when she heard a gentle knock at her door and found Kate standing there holding two mugs of coffee.

"I brought you caffeine," Kate said, looking sheepish. "Can I come in?" It was still early, and a heavy fog on the ground made everything look soft and gauzy. The morning was chilly, and Kate was wearing flannel pajama pants and an over-sized UCLA hoodie.

"Sure." Gen stepped back to let her inside. "Jackson go to work already?"

"No, he's still asleep. He had a late night at the restaurant."

They went into Gen's bedroom/living room, and Gen turned up the gas fireplace to ward off the morning chill. She sat cross-legged on her bed, wrapped a blanket around her shoulders, and reached out for the coffee mug. Kate handed it to her, and Gen took a satisfying sip. "Thanks."

"Gen, look, I'm sorry about how I reacted last night." Kate looked miserable. "I am. I know you have to think about your career, and I know Cambria isn't exactly the center of the universe. It's just … If you go, I'm really going to miss you." She sat on the bed next to Gen, and Gen squeezed her knee.

"I know. I'll miss you too. And Rose and Lacy. God, I don't know what I'll do without you guys. But …" She gathered her thoughts. "I kind of came here in the first place to run away from my problems. You know? And now …"

"Now it's time to face them."

"Yeah."

"I get that," Kate said, nodding. "I hate it like hell, but I get it."

"And anyway … you don't really need me anymore. Now that you have Jackson." She'd been thinking it for months, and she'd hinted at it the morning after Kate's party, but it had taken her this long to come out and say the words to Kate. She braced herself for Kate's reaction.

"What?" Kate looked at her as though Gen had lost her mind. And maybe she had. "What makes you think that just because I'm in a relationship, I don't need my *best friend* any-more?"

Tears came to Kate's eyes, and Gen immediately felt guilty for having said it. She knew she was being ridiculous.

Gen put a hand on Kate's knee. "I'm sorry. It's just … I'm happy for you. Really. But you've got this … this *life* now. And I want a life, too."

"Okay." Kate nodded. "Okay. But I do still need you. I'll always need you."

They sat in front of the fire and drank their coffee.

"There are phones. There are planes," Gen offered.

"Right." Kate nodded again. "There are."

"And Skype. There's definitely Skype."

They sat there, and Gen thought some more about how that would be, how she would cope without Kate and Rose and Lacy in the giant, relentless world of New York.

In the gallery that day, Gen thought some more about her artist-in-residence program. Now that she had the detail of lodging worked out, there were the two simple matters of who would be the artist, and how she was going to pay for it.

She had the answer to the first question—or, at least she hoped she did. The abstract artist from Chicago whose work she'd tried to sell to the McCabes would be perfect. Gordon Kendrick's work was raw, emotional, expressive. And he hadn't been discovered yet, not really. He was getting a little bit of attention—Gen had heard of him, after all—but not enough. Gen had good intuition regarding this sort of thing, and her intuition told her Kendrick was a caterpillar inside his cocoon, and when he came out, shook out his wings and started to fly, his work was going to be amazing—and potentially very expensive. If she could ally herself with him now, get her name and his linked, she could capitalize on his eventual success.

But she'd have to get him to say yes to her proposal. And to do that, she'd have to make that proposal attractive. Which meant she'd have to pay for all or part of his stay. While many artist-in-residence programs asked for the artist to contribute to or even fully pay the cost of lodging, Gen didn't want to do that. She wanted to woo him.

Sitting behind her desk in the main room, she looked over her income and expenses, her expected sources of revenue, and the quote Ryan had given her for rental of the cottage and barn space. He'd said he could come down on the rent if she booked the place for a full five-month term. But he hadn't said how much he could bring down the price. She decided to reduce the rate he'd given her by ten percent, and work with that figure. That seemed safe.

The last deal she'd done for the McCabes had been lucrative, and had given her a good cushion in her business accounts. She could use some of that money for Kendrick. But that wouldn't get her all the way there.

Inspired, she thought again of the McCabes. They had more money than they knew what to do with. If she could find a way to appeal to their narcissism, maybe she could persuade them to sponsor the program. She had the skills to do it. Appealing to people's narcissism was ninety percent of what she'd done at McIntyre's gallery in New York.

She got on the phone and made an appointment to meet the McCabes for another lunch, and began writing up a plan.

❖

"You're gonna do *what?*" Orin asked, peering at Ryan through eyes squinting with skepticism.

"I'm gonna rent the guest house. We talked about this, Dad. When I fixed the place up, we talked about how it would make a good rental, bring in some extra income."

"Yeah, but I thought you were gonna rent it to a regular tenant or a vacationer or some damn thing. Now you tell me you're gonna rent it to an *artist.*" He said the word *artist* the same way he might have said *prostitute* or *meth dealer.* In Orin's mind, the latter two were probably more useful.

"Genevieve Porter's gallery is going to rent it for a visiting artist. I don't see what the difference is if it's that or some vacationer."

The two of them were in the barn—the new barn—checking out a heifer that had been showing decreased appetite and poor coordination. They'd culled her from the herd until they could figure out what was going on. The barn was still chilly with the crisp morning air, but the sunlight slanting through the windows was quickly warming it up. The place smelled like hay and cow shit—two smells as familiar to Ryan as the scent of his own skin.

Ryan talked gently to the heifer and put a hand on her back to soothe her as he examined her. He noticed a little bloating on her left side. That was worrisome.

"The difference is," Orin went on, "a vacationer would just be … I don't know … going to the beach or up to Hearst Castle, or doing whatever the hell they do. An *artist …*"

"He's likely going to be painting," Ryan went on impassively as he went to the front of the animal and checked her for nasal discharge. "I don't see what's so bad about painting."

Orin shifted uncomfortably from one foot to another, scratching at the back of his neck. "Well, he's going to have his stuff all over the place, using the barn ..."

"The old barn," Ryan added.

"Old barn, new barn, what's the difference?" Orin said.

"The difference is, we don't even use the old barn, except for storage. What do you care if the guy's got some paint and canvases and, hell, I don't know. Turpentine. He might have some turpentine, I guess. And easels."

"Well," Orin said. That was what he always said when he didn't want to give up an argument but he didn't have a good case to make. Just, "Well."

"Look." Ryan put a hand on his father's shoulder too soothe him, much as he soothed the cattle when necessary. "It's only five months. I'll take care of whatever this guy needs, so you won't have to do it. It's gonna be fine, Dad."

Orin grunted. "Well."

Chapter Seven

Gordon Kendrick was hopelessly self-centered. Nothing about that surprised Gen. She was used to self-centered people in the art world. The artists, the dealers, the collectors—all of them tended to be wrapped up in themselves to a degree that would be alarming in any other line of work, except maybe acting. And this was acting, when you thought about it. Dealers had to act powerful and knowledgeable. Collectors had to act like they were influential enough that their interest in an artist could elevate his career. And artists had to act brilliant and eccentric.

Gordon Kendrick didn't have the brilliant part down just yet. But damned if he didn't seem eccentric.

Once Gen had convinced Kendrick to consider her offer—which wasn't hard, considering she would be footing the bill for his lodging in a stunningly beautiful locale for five months—they'd gotten down to the nitty-gritty of their arrangement.

She wanted exclusive rights to sell the art works that he produced during his stay. He wanted a limo to bring him from the airport in San Luis Obispo. She wanted him to make a personal appearance at the show she would hold for him at the end of the residency. He wanted her to provide a specific list of items at the cottage, ranging from particular art supplies—reasonable—to a foreign brand of yogurt that was not sold in most U.S. stores—less reasonable. She wanted him to meet at least once with the McCabes, who had agreed to sponsor the program in exchange for a painting and a mention of their names whenever the program was publicized. He stubbornly argued that the McCabes were bush-league collectors and unworthy of his time, let alone his art.

By the time the negotiations had been completed, she was nearly ready to tell him to screw it, she'd find another artist, one who would eat Yoplait like a normal person and who would shut his goddamned trap about what he *needed* for *maximum artistic expression*. But then she reminded herself how talented he really was, and how deeply she believed that he would eventually have breakout success. This was a guy whose paintings would one day be reproduced on coffee mugs and museum gallery gift shop T-shirts; she could feel it. And when they were, people, or at least people who knew about such things, would think of Genevieve Porter as the person who had discovered him. And even if they didn't, she had negotiated to keep one of his art works for herself. If his career went where she thought it would, the eventual resale of the painting she selected would more than compensate her for the trouble he was putting her through.

He arrived at San Luis Obispo's tiny commuter airport on a Tuesday in May. She felt ridiculous riding in the back of a big, black stretch limousine to pick him up. Who the hell demanded a limousine? Who would even want one? They were unwieldy in traffic, and you couldn't even park the damned thing. The back was stocked with Perrier, with an ice bucket and crystal glasses, and she poured herself some fizzy water on the way down the coast.

"I'll bet you meet a lot of assholes in this business," Gen mused to the driver, a guy in his forties with close-cropped greying hair and wire-rimmed glasses, as they zoomed down Highway 1.

"You have no idea," he said. "Half of them get so drunk I have to carry them out of the car or clean puke off the carpet, and the other half put up the divider and have sex back there, think I don't know it. Then another half won't even talk to me, act like I'm not even there."

"That's more than two halves," Gen pointed out.

Considering the limo, the special yogurt, the Egyptian cotton bed linens Kendrick had demanded, Gen should not have been surprised when he made her carry his luggage. Somehow, though, she was. He'd brought a full-size suitcase, two carry-ons, and what Gen could only describe as a man purse, and Gen had it all piled onto her little five-foot-two body as they made their way back to the car. Kendrick was yammering on about a solo show he'd done back in Chicago, and how oppressed he felt because no one appreciated his style, when Gen caught the eye of the limo driver with her own desperate gaze.

Startled by the sight of her laboring under the weight of all that luggage, the driver jerked up from where he'd been leaning against the car in the passenger pick-up zone and hurried over to Gen.

"Thanks," she murmured as the driver took the bags from her shoulders and hauled them to the car. Kendrick was going on about the unreasonable demands at the Museum of Contemporary Art in Chicago.

"Do you have any physical disabilities I can help you with?" the driver asked Kendrick in a solicitous tone.

"What? No. Why?" Kendrick said.

"Oh." The driver's eyebrows rose in apparent puzzlement. "I just thought you must have a disability, since you had the lady carrying all of your luggage."

"Oh, ha, ha," Kendrick said, laughing as though the driver had shown a sparkling wit. "It's all part of the service. Right, Genevieve?"

"Sure," Gen said. When Kendrick was climbing into the back of the car, the driver holding the door for him, Gen arched an eyebrow at the driver and gestured toward Kendrick. "Which half is he?"

"The back half," the guy said before Gen climbed in, and he shut the door.

Kendrick was in his midthirties, medium height, with a receding hairline and a sharp, angular face that put Gen in mind of a fox, or maybe a weasel. In what Gen considered to be a self-conscious display of hipness, he was wearing Birkenstock sandals and a man bun. The open top button of his loose white linen shirt showed a dark blue bead on a cord around his neck.

"Pleasant flight?" Gen inquired inside the limo as she poured him a glass of Perrier and handed it over.

"Ugh. We were all shoved in there like sheep in a pen. And they don't even provide a meal anymore—as though anything they might feed people would be edible in the first place. I should have insisted on first class, or at least business class. Why I let you talk me into flying economy, I will never know."

"Ah. Well. I'm sorry it wasn't more comfortable."

Kendrick was an ass, but he was the ass who was going to get her back to New York. She looked out the window at the strip of blue ocean to the left side of the car, and reflected that this was going to be a long five months.

Thank God Rose hadn't stayed mad at her, because Gen really needed a drink after she got Kendrick situated in the cottage. She sat at the bar in De-Vine, the wine tasting shop where Rose worked, and sipped a glass of pinot grigio as Rose leaned on the counter, listening to her moan about her day.

"And it wasn't even the right damned yogurt!" Gen exclaimed, throwing up her hands. "I had to search for days to find a specialty grocery store that would order it, then I had to drive to goddamned Paso Robles to pick it up, and apparently, he wanted Icelandic style, with added goddamned probiotics. Did you even know Icelandic style yogurt was a thing?"

"No, I did not," Rose said.

"Well, it is! And I didn't get it! And now all he can do is bitch about the yogurt and how his goddamned digestive tract is going to be all atwitter without it. Good. I hope he's backed up for days!"

Rose looked at Gen, her pierced eyebrow raised in question. "Did that rant make you feel better?"

"Not yet."

"Would another glass of wine help?"

"Wouldn't hurt to try."

Rose refilled her glass and went back to doing whatever it was she did behind the counter. She arranged bottles, washed a couple of glasses, opened a new case of merlot.

"How did Ryan react to your digestively challenged artist?" she asked while she worked.

"With bemusement. Yes. That's the word. He was bemused." Gen took another drink of her wine. "As anyone would be who was a normal, sensible person and not a self-centered pain in the ass."

Rose pointed one finger at Gen. "You're the one who invited the self-centered pain in the ass to Cambria. You didn't just invite him. You 'wooed' him. I think that's what you said at the time."

"True." Gen nodded. "I wooed."

"And now he's here."

"Yes. And now he's here."

A couple had come in and sat down at the bar, and Rose explained the wine tasting menu to them.

When Rose returned, Gen had calmed somewhat, the wine relaxing her, making her feel loose and slightly tingly. "You know, that's a nice place he's got over there. Ryan. The guest house is gorgeous. And the barn. The old barn, he specifies, not the new one. It's an artist's paradise. God. I hope Kendrick appreciates it."

"He won't," Rose said.

"Probably not," Gen said with a sigh.

Chapter Eight

Ryan found himself wanting to call Gen, but he wasn't even sure why. He just knew that he'd enjoyed talking to her—simply having her around—when she'd been to the ranch to get that Kendrick guy settled into the guest cottage. And he knew that he wanted to have her around again. His thoughts didn't go any further than that. He didn't try to make sense of the urge to see her—didn't wonder what it meant. Why did it have to mean anything?

He was still pondering whether to call her when his mother pointed her fork at him that evening at dinner, scowling her usual scowl. "You should take that gallery owner around, show her the ranch. She's only seen the guest house. You oughta give her the tour, show her some of the places where that artist might want to go set up his easel."

Orin looked uncomfortable—as he nearly always did—and shifted in his seat as he stabbed at his steak with his fork. "Aw, now, Sandra, I don't know that I want that artist poking around everywhere. Bad enough that he's in the guest house in the first place."

Sandra let out a burst of air that communicated her disagreement as clearly as any words would have. "He's here, isn't he? Why else did he come, if it's not to have a beautiful place to paint? Might as well make it worth his while."

"There's that place by the creek where we had that picnic that one time," Redmond said helpfully.

"Gen Porter's a pretty girl," Breanna said. "Don't you think, Ryan?" She was seated on one side of the table with her boys on either side of her. She had to sit between them so they wouldn't fight at the dinner table.

"I guess," Ryan said.

Sandra let out the scoffing sound again.

"Show her around," she said, as though the matter were settled. "Be a good host, for God's sake."

"Well, now, I'm pretty busy around here most days," he said. He knew even as he said it that he sounded exactly like his father.

"You'll find time," Sandra said.

"Well."

He felt the need, for some reason, to scowl as though he were being pushed into something unpleasant. In fact, he was satisfied with the way his family had neatly solved his problem of whether to call Gen, and why. Family could be useful sometimes.

She showed up at the main house early on a Wednesday. Now that the weather was warming up and the tourists were starting to show up in town again, the gallery was open every day. But it didn't open until ten a.m. on weekdays, and that gave her time to take a tour of the Delaney Ranch with Ryan.

She'd been surprised when he'd called her to suggest it. She'd first talked to him about renting the guest cottage, what, three months ago? He hadn't said a thing about showing her around then. She'd wondered if maybe the larger expanse of the ranch was off-limits to her and her artist, and she hadn't really questioned it. Now, the thought of seeing the place—and seeing it with Ryan—pleased her and maybe even excited her. Until she learned she'd be doing it on a horse.

"Wait. A horse? I don't know how to ride," Gen told Ryan as the morning activities of the house went on around her.

"You'll do fine," Breanna called to her from the kitchen, where she was getting her kids ready for school—giving them breakfast, getting their backpacks ready. Gen had met Breanna and the boys numerous times around town. The boys were cute, with their noisy, happy temperaments and their thick shocks of dark hair, and Breanna had always struck Gen as being a solid sort of person—friendly and decent.

"Couldn't we just … you know … walk?" Gen said.

Ryan scoffed. "This is a ranch. You don't walk on a ranch when you could ride. Breanna's right. You'll do fine."

In the kitchen, Lucas, the little one, was refusing to eat his pancake because it had arrived on his plate with a bump on one side, where an extra drop of batter had fallen into the pan. Michael, who suffered no such apprehension about bumpy pancakes, asked for a second helping as Breanna slid his sack lunch into his backpack. Done with that, she calmly cut the bump off of Lucas's pancake and instructed him to eat.

"Ah, jeez," Gen said miserably.

Ryan's mother, Sandra, bustled into the room, looking harried but efficient, shooed the boys out of the kitchen with friendly spanks on their butts, and started cleaning up the breakfast dishes.

"I'll clean this up when I get back, Mom. You don't have to do it," Breanna told Sandra, planting a kiss on the older woman's cheek.

"Oh, now, you just get those boys off to school before they're late," Sandra grumped at her.

"Good morning, Mrs. Delaney," Gen said.

"Is it? Seems just like every other morning to me," Sandra said, stacking plates into the dishwasher.

Gen smiled. She didn't know Ryan's mother well, but she knew her well enough to know the grumbling was just a part of the Sandra Delaney gestalt.

"Can I help you clean up?" Gen offered.

"What?" Sandra demanded. "Well, I think I can clean up my own kitchen! You just get on with what you came here for. Ryan, show her around the place like you should have done months ago. I swear, you've got no manners despite my best efforts."

"I would, but she's afraid to get on a horse," he said, some amusement in his voice.

Gen sensed that she'd been set up—Ryan had lobbed an easy ball right toward Sandra, who was about to smash it over the net.

"Afraid of a horse! Oh, holy … Girl, are you kidding me?" She assessed Gen, hands on her hips. "What kind of upbringing did you have, anyway, if you're afraid of a perfectly noble, people-friendly animal like a horse?"

"I … uh … well, I'm from Manhattan, so …"

"That's no excuse!" Sandra declared. "Ryan, you go and get this girl into a saddle, for God's sake." She inspected Gen. "Well, I guess you're dressed all right for it. The shoes aren't the best, but they'll do."

Gen looked down at the Nikes on her feet, feeling defensive. She'd thought they would be walking. She hadn't known special footwear would be required.

"You heard her," Ryan said to Gen, grinning. "We better get going, before she grounds me."

"Don't think I won't!" Sandra said.

The horse Ryan had chosen for Gen was named Bailey. She was a chestnut mare with a white blaze on her forehead, and she stood there with longsuffering tolerance as Ryan saddled her for Gen.

"Are we really sure about this?" Gen said, sizing up the mare.

"Don't worry. Bailey's gentle as a kitten. She's the one we let Lucas ride."

"Well ... that's reassuring, I guess."

He sized up Gen with his eyes, then adjusted the stirrup height.

"I think you're gonna need a mounting block," he said.

"I don't know what that is."

"Don't worry about it," he said again.

Fifteen minutes later, Gen was atop Bailey, following Ryan along a trail that led up a hill and toward God knew where. Gen had never considered how ridiculously wide a horse was. How in God's name had five-year-old Lucas ridden this thing? It had a smell, too. While Gen had to admit that the earthy, horsey scent that wafted up toward her wasn't entirely bad, it was, nonetheless, an aroma she was not accustomed to smelling.

The horse seemed to tolerate her in its own world-weary way. It plodded along, jostling Gen around, seeming to barely notice her as it fixed its gaze on the rear end of Ryan's horse and got along with the business of walking the trail. Gen was holding the reins, but she wasn't sure what she was supposed to be doing with them. Nothing, she supposed. The horse seemed to know what to do without any guidance from her.

The morning was cool and clear, with bright sunlight streaming through the leaves of the trees that lined the trail. She could hear insects buzzing in the grass and birds communicating with one another in their unfathomable language. Ahead of her, Ryan sat atop his horse with comfort and authority. San Francisco Giants T-shirt, Levi's, a ball cap. The T-shirt displayed his broad shoulders and tanned, muscled arms. The jeans—well, they displayed other things that were equally good. Ryan was wearing some sort of boots with a short heel that, she'd been told, fit into the stirrups in some sort of way that was supposed to be helpful. That explained Sandra's disparaging remark about Gen's footwear. Nikes didn't usually come with a stirrup-friendly heel.

"How you doing back there?" Ryan called to her in a friendly voice.

"Okay, I guess. I ... whoa!" Bailey suddenly veered to the side of the trail, lowered her head, and started munching some kind of greenery from the ground.

Ryan raised his eyebrows at her. "You can't let her do that."

"How am I letting her? How is this my choice?" Gen said. She tugged ineffectually at the reins. Bailey didn't seem to notice.

Ryan shifted in the saddle with a creak of leather and looked at her as though she were a student who hadn't studied for a quiz that should have been an easy ten points. "Pull up on the reins."

"I am."

"Harder than that. Don't jerk them, but pull up firmly. Let her know you're in charge."

"Are we really sure I'm in charge?" Gen said. Bailey continued to snack on something tender and green.

He maneuvered his horse close to Bailey, took the reins from Gen's hand, and made some sort of noise to the horse that Gen didn't understand, but that Bailey apparently did.

Gen's horse raised her head, looked at Ryan, and then climbed back onto the trail. He handed the reins back to Gen.

The ease with which he handled the big animals was ridiculously hot. Gen wondered how easily he could handle her, given the chance.

"So ... um ... where are we going?" she called ahead to him as they continued on the trail.

"Oh, I've got an agenda. My uncle wanted you to see the creek, which is running pretty nicely right now, by the way. My mom wanted you to see the view from on top of that ridge over there." He pointed. "Breanna wanted you to see her herb garden. And the boys just wanted to make sure I showed you the cattle."

"That's a lot," Gen said, amused. "What about your dad? Didn't he have anything to add to your list?"

He looked over his shoulder at her. "My dad? He pretty much wanted me to show you the road back to town."

"Oh," Gen said, a little bit hurt.

Ryan chuckled. "It's not you. It's the whole idea. Having an artist here on the ranch. He thinks the guy's going to be poking around, getting in the way. Plus, my dad thinks art's about as useful as male nipples."

Gen guffawed. "Well, it's not about *usefulness* exactly. It's about expression."

Ryan shrugged. "I get that. But you try explaining it to him."

"Maybe I will."

"I'd really like to hear that," Ryan said with a grin. He made that *move along* noise to the horses again, and they picked up their pace slightly as they rose up the trail and crested a grassy hill.

The creek ran through the middle of a woodsy area to the northeast of the main house. Before she could see it, Gen could hear it—the musical sound of water rushing over rocks, making its way toward the ocean.

Ryan dispensed with the tour-guide duties with business-like efficiency, but it was clear to Gen that he was proud of the land and its grandeur. "The creek will be kind of low in another month if the drought keeps up," he told her as they emerged on the trail into a shady, rocky area bisected by the creek. "Right now, it's running pretty good, though."

Bailey let out a gentle snort as Gen took in the scene. Dappled sunlight breaking through the leaves to scatter on the ground. The sound of birds twittering to each other, the humming of unnamed insects under the leaves and in the grass. And always, the gentle murmur of the water, in a white froth as it tumbled over rocks, then clear and clean as it rushed its way west.

"Oh," Gen said.

"Want to get down for a bit, take a rest?" Ryan offered.

Gen did, but she wasn't sure she'd be able to get back onto Bailey again without the benefit of a mounting block.

Ryan saw her hesitation and read it correctly. "Don't worry, we'll get you back up there."

"Uh ... okay." She considered the prospect of climbing down from the mammoth animal and found it daunting. In a moment, Ryan was on the ground at Bailey's side, coaching Gen.

"Okay, now, throw your right leg over to this side," he told her. "That's right. Now take your left foot out of the stirrup and just slide on down. I got you."

It seemed like a long way down, but Ryan was there, and he put his hands around her waist and lowered her gently to the ground. This unexpected contact, this feeling of his hands on her, made her pale skin blush. She could feel the heat in her cheeks. She turned to him, and he was just inches away as she tipped her face up to look at him.

God, he was tall and broad, and the way he looked at her, with a kind of gentle indulgence, made her wish he were looking at her with the same kind of animal hunger she felt, but struggled not to show.

"Thanks," she said.

"No problem." He stepped back, giving her room.

"Uh … Are you going to tie the horses to a tree or something?"

He chuckled. "Nah. These two are pretty well trained. They know not to run off." He pulled Bailey's lead to the front and let it drop to the ground, as he'd done with his own horse. "See how I've got the lead hanging straight down in front of her? When you do that, they know to stay put."

"That's amazing," Gen said.

Ryan shrugged. "They know their manners."

Gen's butt was sore, and her thighs were burning. Who'd have thought that just sitting on top of a horse would make your thighs sore? Bailey was the one who'd done all the work. Gen felt like she was walking funny as she stepped over toward the creek.

If she was, Ryan didn't comment on it.

Chapter Nine

Ryan should have felt annoyed. He should have felt irritated. This little trail ride was taking time away from all of the things he had to do. They were heading into calving season, and he needed to check the pregnant cows to see which ones might deliver soon, make sure the calving pens were clean and ready to go. He had to check his equipment, do some work with the newer hands he'd hired for the season to make sure they'd know what to do. He didn't have time to give tours.

But as much as he knew he should be rebelling against this thing his family had pressured him into doing, he found himself feeling relaxed and happy. It was a pretty day. He liked being out here, away from his day-to-day tasks, enjoying the sights and sounds of nature. He liked taking the time to just breathe.

And he liked being here with Gen.

Something about seeing her outside of her native environment—out of the little black dresses and the high heels and onto the back of a horse—made him feel good. Nature agreed with her. He liked her nervousness about riding, liked the way she gamely pressed forward despite her fear and awkwardness.

Truth was, she wasn't bad at riding for a first-timer. He'd seen much worse. He could tell from the way she sat the horse, the way she carried herself, that she had a natural aptitude. Shame that it had never been nurtured.

They walked together toward the creek, and Gen appraised her surroundings, looking around her and above her, before turning to Ryan. "This spot would be great for plein air painting. Look at the light." She nodded her head in appreciation.

"Is that the kind of painting this guy does? Landscapes, that sort of thing?"

Gen laughed. It was a nice sound. "God, no. He does abstracts. Bold colors. Big, slashing brushstrokes. Some of them look like the paint's been shot out of a cannon. He'd scoff at landscapes."

Ryan took off his hat and scratched at his head. "Why'd you bring him to Cambria, then? Seems like he could do that kind of thing anywhere."

"He could." She turned to him, her hands tucked into the back pockets of her jeans. "But environment influences an artist's work—even abstract work—in ways you can't predict. Everything he experiences—sights, sounds, the argument he had with his ex-wife—it all goes into this big blender and comes out as the artwork. You want to change the artwork ..."

"You change what you put into the blender," Ryan finished for her.

She nodded and smiled. "Right."

He walked over to the creek and sat down on a big boulder. "So, are you setting out to change this guy's artwork?"

"Sort of." She sat beside him. "He's good. He's very good. But he hasn't had a breakthrough yet. I think he's going to. He just needs to shake things up a bit. Put some different stuff in the blender, see what comes out."

Ryan considered her. He rubbed at the stubble on his chin. "That's gonna be good for you, he has his big breakthrough while he's here."

"That's the idea."

They sat side by side on the boulder for a while, listening to the birds and the rushing water. A gentle breeze rustled the leaves overhead. Nearby, a dragonfly circled lazily over a still pool of water and then lowered itself to the surface.

Gen's hair was twisted into a bun at the back of her neck, but a few tendrils of red hair had come loose, and they curled around her face. Ryan wanted to pull her hair out of the bun and set it free.

"So, have you talked to Lacy?" Gen asked.

Lacy. He hadn't been thinking about Lacy, not at all.

"Not lately. Why do you ask?"

"Oh." She shrugged and avoided his gaze. "I just wondered. That time at Kate and Jackson's party, it seemed like you really wanted to go out with her. I wondered if you'd asked her yet."

"Nah." He shook his head, feeling uncomfortable.

"Why not?"

"I don't think she'd be amenable."

"Really." The *really* came out as a statement of fact rather than a question.

"I get a certain vibe from her that's … I don't know what it is." He shook his head.

"A vibe?"

"Yeah. It's kind of, *Oh, look how cute Ryan is, I'll try to let him down easy.* That kind of vibe."

"Ah."

He peered at her. "I take it I'm not wrong."

She looked at him tentatively, probably trying to gauge whether her response would hurt his feelings. "No. You're not wrong."

He nodded. "That's what I thought."

Gen was silent for a few minutes, and Ryan wondered what unfathomable thoughts were going on in her head.

"I don't want to talk about Lacy right now," he said.

❖

He gave her the full tour—all of the sights his family had recommended, and then a few he added in himself—and had her back to the main house by late morning. She was late to open the gallery—she'd wanted to be there by ten, and it was well after that already—but she didn't seem concerned about it. In the spring and summer, when the tourist traffic started to pick up, Gen had an assistant working with her at the gallery. When the tour hadn't wrapped up by nine thirty, she'd called him—a guy named Alex who Ryan knew a little bit—and asked him to open for her. Ryan had offered to cut off the ride and get her back, but she'd said that Alex would be fine and that she was enjoying herself too much to quit.

And she did seem to be enjoying herself. By the time they got back to the house, her face was pink with sun and exertion, and her hair was askew in a way that he found pleasantly distracting. She was smiling, looking healthy and vibrant and pleased with the events of her day.

The house was unusually quiet, with the boys off at school and Breanna running errands in town.

At first Ryan had thought he would be able to avoid putting Gen through a grilling from his mother, as it looked as though no one was home. But a few minutes after they came in the door, he heard Sandra scuffing down the stairs in the fuzzy slippers she always wore inside the house, calling to him.

"Ryan? That you?" She sounded less irritated than usual, a happy state of affairs.

"Yeah, Mom. I've got Gen Porter with me. Just finished showing her around."

"Well, what did you think?" Sandra came to the foot of the stairs and planted her hands on her hips, addressing Gen as though in challenge.

"Your property is gorgeous," Gen said, her face and her voice full of enthusiasm. "I wasn't sure about the whole idea of riding a horse—I'd never done it, and they're really big. But Ryan taught me a few things, and I think it went okay." Gen looked exhilarated, actually, all pretty and pink-cheeked.

Sandra squinted at Gen in that way she had, as though she were using laser vision to X-ray someone and inspect for internal injuries. Then her face broke into a grin. "He take you on Bailey?"

"Yes, ma'am," Ryan confirmed.

"Good. That's about as gentle a horse as you're likely to find. If you can't ride Bailey, you can't ride, period." She nodded. "You think your artist is going to like the place?" Sandra asked.

"I don't see how he couldn't. Or, wait. Yes I do. Because he's kind of ... well. Kind of socially challenged." She looked embarrassed to have said it. "But this place, it's lovely. It's inspiring. It's the perfect place to bring an artist. Even him."

"Is 'socially challenged' code for asshole?" Sandra inquired.

Gen hesitated. "In this case, yes, ma'am, it is."

Sandra let out a belly laugh that made Ryan blink. Laughing was not something that came naturally to Sandra Delaney, nor was smiling, for that matter. And here he'd seen her smile and laugh, both, within the space of a few minutes. It was puzzling, but not entirely unwelcome.

Sandra waved Gen toward the kitchen. "Come on in here and we'll have coffee."

"Oh, you don't have to do that," Gen said. "I know Ryan must be busy. I've already taken up too much of his time."

"Ryan's busy, all right. That's why I'm inviting you, and not him." Sandra made a shooing motion toward Ryan.

Was that how a mother was supposed to treat her son? "Well, now, I'm not that busy ... and I like coffee," he said.

"You better go check on your father, give him a hand in the barn," Sandra told him. "You know he's not as young as he used to be."

Ryan left the house reluctantly, bothered by the nagging sense that something had been plotted without his knowledge, something clear and obvious to the women but inaccessible to him. He had the sense that his mother had taken something important out of his hands, something fragile, like a newly hatched bird stretching its tiny wings, its eyes closed tight against the sun.

"Can I help?" Gen asked as Sandra led her into the kitchen and started getting out coffee filters and beans.

"I think I know how to make coffee by myself," Sandra groused at her. "Been doing it for a good forty years. It's good that you offered, though." She nodded. "Shows manners. I've got no patience for people who don't have manners."

"Yes, ma'am," Gen said, feeling like a Catholic school girl who'd narrowly escaped getting her knuckles rapped by the Mother Superior. "Have you lived on the ranch long?"

Sandra chuckled—a low and rough *heh-heh* sound. "Well, let's see. I married Orin Delaney thirty-five years ago, and I moved to the ranch the day of the ceremony. So, I guess you could say I've been here a while."

Gen sat at the kitchen table—a long, rectangular, solid-wood affair that was exactly what you'd expect to see in a farmhouse—and leaned forward on her elbows as Sandra turned on the coffee pot and started gathering cups, spoons, sugar, and milk.

"You don't see a lot of cattle ranches in Manhattan," Gen said.

"I guess not," Sandra said. "You miss it?"

Gen thought about it. "I do. Everything is just so ... *busy* in New York. There's a sense of energy, a sense of importance. This feeling that you're at the center of the world. But when I go back, I think I'll miss this, too."

Sandra turned to Gen and raised her eyebrows in question. "You're going back to New York, are you?"

"Not right away. I'm not sure when. I need to work out some things first."

Sandra carried a mug of hot coffee to the table and put it in front of Gen with a plate of big, puffy muffins. She sat across from Gen. "Now, me, you couldn't pay me to live in a city. That's just not how I'm built. Stick me in a tiny apartment in a twenty-story building, people all stacked up like books on a shelf?" She shook her head. "I couldn't do it."

Gen sipped at her truly excellent coffee and considered that. "I can understand feeling that way, if you're used to this." She gestured to include the house, the ranch, the land beyond. "There's a kind of magic to being around all this nature."

Sandra nodded approvingly. "A lot of people don't get that."

"I wouldn't have before I moved here," Gen said. "Cambria is special."

"It is at that. Here, have one of these muffins. Breanna made them."

"Mmm." Banana walnut. Gen's favorite.

Chapter Ten

"My ass is sore," Gen complained to Lacy later that day, after she'd closed the gallery. She was sitting uncomfortably on one of the barstools at Jitters, drinking her third and last coffee of the day. Any more than that, and she'd be wide awake at one a.m. watching cat GIFs on Facebook. "I'd never been on a horse before in my life. How do people do it for more than a half-hour at a time?"

"Ass calluses?" Lacy suggested. She was bustling around behind the counter, an apron around her waist, making espresso and steaming milk. She managed to keep up her end of the conversation effortlessly while turning out hot beverages for the modest crowd in the coffee shop.

"Ryan's ass must be like steel by now," Gen said. "Oh, God."

"'Oh God' what?"

"Just thinking about Ryan's ass."

Lacy grinned at her. "It is a nice one."

Gen plucked a napkin from a nearby dispenser and started tearing it into tiny pieces. A little furrow formed between her eyebrows. "He makes me all gooey and stupid. Which is ridiculous, because he's not interested in me."

"What if he were?"

"What do you mean?"

"Gen." Lacy reached over the counter and put a hand on Gen's, stilling them. "Put down that poor napkin and focus."

Gen did.

"What if he felt the same way about you that you do about him, and sparks were flying everywhere, and you two were crazy in love, with animated birds and kittens and unicorns and all of that crap?"

"I could go for that," Gen offered.

"Yeah. You could go for it right up until you leave for New York. Which is what you've said you plan to do. Ryan's not going anywhere. His family has been on that land for 170 years. What are you going to do, have a long-distance relationship while you're three thousand miles apart?"

It surprised Gen that she hadn't thought of it that way. *Why* hadn't she? She knew she was planning to leave, and she knew Ryan never would.

"No. I guess I haven't considered the realities, because it *isn't* real. There's nothing there. It's just a fantasy. And that's all it's ever going to be."

"Well … I wouldn't count on that."

Gen's head snapped up and she looked at Lacy.

"What do you mean?"

She shrugged. "You never know, that's all. You just never know."

When Gordon Kendrick wasn't grousing about the yogurt, he was bitching about something else. Less than a week after he'd moved into the guest cottage on the Delaney Ranch, he was on the phone with Gen, complaining that the bed linens weren't organic, and that had caused an unsightly rash on the tender flesh of his thighs. Gen didn't want to think about Gordon Kendrick's thighs.

"I have sensitivities to environmental toxins," Kendrick was going on. Gen had him on speakerphone in the gallery, and she was bustling about, doing her usual tasks, while he groused.

"Well, I'm sorry to hear that," Gen said as she sorted bills and perused her e-mail.

"Yes, well. It's difficult to be productive, from an artistic standpoint, when my system is out of sorts."

"Because of the inorganic sheets," Gen continued.

"Among other things."

She wondered about the *other things*. What was he going to ask for next? A personal acupuncturist? An aromatherapy consultant?

"Well, you're unlikely to find organic sheets in Cambria, since we lack a major department store," she said, keeping her voice even. "But maybe if you drive into San Luis Obispo …"

"I don't have a car at my disposal."

Gen sighed and rolled her eyes. "I'm sure I can arrange for a rental car for you. Or, if you prefer, you can order the sheets online."

Kate came through the front door of the gallery at that moment, and Gen gestured with her fist behind her head, throwing her head to the side and sticking her tongue out, in a mime of hanging herself.

"I had really hoped that you would attend to such things for me," Kendrick went on over the speaker. "The whole point of a retreat such as this is that I should be able to focus on my work exclusively."

"Mr. Kendrick …"

"Distractions like this … procuring bed linens and rental cars and the like … I don't know how I'm supposed to work at my full potential." His voice sounded whiny and petulant.

"Oh, miss? Miss?" Kate broke in. "How much is this painting? Miss?"

Gen smirked at her. "I'm sorry, Mr. Kendrick, but I have a guest in the gallery. Can we finish this conversation later?"

"Well, I ..." Kendrick began.

"Miss! I want to buy several very expensive paintings but I'm in a terrible hurry!" Kate said.

"I'll be right with you!" Gen said. "Mr. Kendrick, I have to hang up now. I'll talk to you soon! You take care! Good-bye!" She punched the button to disconnect the phone and slumped against her desk in exaggerated exhaustion.

"God," Gen said.

"That guy sounds like a real asshole," Kate observed.

"You have no idea."

Kate was carrying a small paper sack and two to-go cups of coffee. "I went to the donut place," she said.

"Donuts?" Gen's eyebrows rose. She didn't usually eat junk food like donuts, but she'd skipped breakfast and her stomach was growling.

"Don't worry. Donuts for me, an egg white wrap for you."

"Oh, bless you. You're a doll. I'm starving."

Kate spread the food out on Gen's desk and took a seat in her visitor's chair while Gen settled in behind the desk. It was still early—before ten a.m.—and the gallery was empty.

"So, how's married life?" Gen asked, taking the cover off of her coffee and taking a sip.

Kate snorted. "I'm hardly married."

"You might as well be. I mean, you've got to pick up his dirty underwear. That's like marriage. There's dirty underwear, right? I'm assuming."

"He mostly deals with his own dirty underwear."

"Well, thank God for that."

Kate broke off a piece of chocolate donut and popped it into her mouth. "It's good. Really good. I'd thought it would be hard—the adjustment—but it just feels ... right."

"Oh, honey. That's great."

"Jackson is just … he's everything Marcus wasn't. He lets me be me. He …" She'd started tearing up, and she wiped at her eyes. "Oh, jeez. Look at me." She let out a breathy laugh.

"That's wonderful, Kate. I mean it." And she did. While Gen had dealt with a lot of feelings when Jackson had moved into the house, she had to admit that her friend was practically glowing with happiness these days. She loved Kate, and so she loved Jackson, too, for making Kate feel this way.

If there was still a nagging feeling eating at her—a feeling that she wanted what Kate had but was worried that it might never happen—well, that was her own issue to deal with and it wasn't something she should put on Kate.

"So, the artist is a real pain in the ass, huh?"

Gen was glad for the change in topic. "Oh, yeah. He needs special yogurt and special sheets, and he can't be bothered to go online and order the crap he wants because he wants me to be his goddamned personal assistant." Gen shook her head and bit into her egg white wrap. The eggs were steaming and fluffy.

"Can you just tell him no?"

Gen considered. "Yeah. I mean, there's nothing in his contract that says I have to run errands and buy sheets for him. The deal was for transportation to and from Cambria and lodging while he's here. But if he's not happy …"

"Then he's not going to take you along for the ride on his art success gravy train. When it happens," Kate finished for her.

"Well … yeah. But it sounds bad when you say it like that."

"Oh, it's not," Kate assured her. "Thinking strategically is just business. So what are you going to do?"

Gen shrugged. "I guess I'm going to buy some goddamned organic sheets and drive them out there."

"Ooh. Maybe you'll get to see Ryan again." Kate waggled her eyebrows.

Gen had to admit, privately, that the thought had occurred to her. "Hmm? Ryan?" she said, as though she had no idea about whom Kate was speaking.

"Oh, drop the act. You're not fooling anybody," Kate said.

Gen's shoulders slumped. "He'll probably be out … oh, jeez, I don't know … birthing calves or something. Or … or … checking the back forty. In movies, ranchers are always checking the back forty. I'm going to bring sheets to the asshole artist and I'm not even going to get eye candy."

"Hmm," Kate said.

"What?"

"Maybe there's a reason you'll have to run into him." She sipped her coffee. "Let me think about it."

Chapter Eleven

Kate did think about it, and the idea she came up with was for Gen to bring Kendrick the sheets and then deliver the old sheets, washed and neatly folded, to the main house to give to Ryan.

"But couldn't I just put them in a closet at the guest house?" Gen had asked, not unreasonably.

"You could, but then you wouldn't get eye candy," Kate said.

Gen calculated that her best bet for finding Ryan at home would be to go after dark. Did ranchers work after dark? Could they even see the cows? If it was calving season, she supposed he might be busy in the barn. She imagined him having to shove his arm up inside some poor cow to turn a calf around, and inwardly winced. Sure, it was possible she still might miss him. But an evening visit would be her best bet.

She sent Alex, her assistant, to the Pottery Barn in San Luis Obispo to buy organic sheets. She thought of having him take the sheets to Kendrick and bring back the others so she could wash them at home, but she didn't know if Alex—a guy who wasn't known for his diplomacy—had the necessary people skills to smooth over whatever the hell it was Kendrick would be upset about this time. So she left him in charge of the gallery and went out there herself.

When she knocked on the door of the little guest cottage just after six p.m., nobody answered at first. She was just about to conclude that Kendrick was in the old barn painting—a happy thought—when she heard feet shuffling just on the other side of the door.

He opened the door looking bleary-eyed. His hair was askew, sticking up in various directions from his scalp. He was unshaven, with a shadow of stubble covering his chin. He was wearing nothing but a drawstringed pair of pajama pants, his bare feet looking somehow sad and vulnerable.

"Mr. Kendrick?" she said tentatively. His pale chest looked somehow shrunken without the fortifying cover of a shirt.

"Oh. Genevieve. Hello." He scratched absently at one elbow.

"I brought the organic sheets you requested," she said, holding up the neatly folded pile of linens. "Is this a good time?"

"A good time?" He said it as though he were working out the translation from Sanskrit.

"Yes. A good time to bring the sheets. I thought I'd just put these on your bed and collect the old ones. Is this a good time?"

"Oh. I guess so." He stepped back to let her in.

"You might want to …" She gestured vaguely toward his chest. "Just put on … you know. A shirt."

He looked down at himself as though he hadn't noticed he was missing one. "Oh. Of course. Just a second."

Kendrick went into the bedroom and closed the door. It gave Gen a moment to survey the condition of the guest house.

The little dining table was covered with empty food containers and crumpled pieces of sketch paper. The kitchen counters held drinking glasses, forks and spoons, an empty granola box. A half-empty bottle of Jack Daniels stood next to the sink. The floor was littered with discarded clothing.

A moment later, Kendrick emerged from the bedroom wearing a white T-shirt and a rumpled pair of khakis. His pale, innocent feet were still uncovered, the toes sprouting a meager crop of hair.

"Okay. You can do the sheets now."

Gen ventured tentatively into the bedroom and found more chaos. Clothing, more crumpled sketch paper, empty cups with a dark residue of coffee shadowing the bottoms.

She changed the sheets, made the bed neatly, and came out into the main room, holding the used sheets in her arms. They smelled faintly of whiskey. Gen wondered whether he'd spilled some of the Jack Daniels on the sheets, or whether it had simply emitted from his pores.

She felt a low rumble of panic in her belly. This wasn't good—wasn't good at all.

"Mr. Kendrick?"

"Oh, just call me Gordon." He waved an arm dismissively.

"Okay. Gordon. Um … Why don't we have a seat on the sofa and chat for a little bit?"

She looked over at the sofa and saw that it was buried under dirty clothes, used towels, and other detritus. She set the sheets down on the coffee table and cleared off the sofa.

When they were sitting, him slumped and foggy, her perched primly on the edge of the cushion, she proceeded carefully.

"How are things going out here, Mr. Kendrick? Gordon," she corrected herself.

"Oh, fine," he said. He seemed to have barely heard her.

"Really? Because … Well. It looks as though maybe you're having some difficulty."

He looked around the little house and blinked.

"How is your work coming?" Gen ventured.

His gaze fell upon a pile of crumpled sketch paper on the coffee table. He rubbed at his forehead with one hand.

"My work is ..." He trailed off and shook his head.

She reached out and picked up one of the crumpled pieces of paper between two fingers. "May I?"

He waved a hand to gesture his assent.

Carefully, she opened the piece of paper and smoothed it on her lap.

The paper was a jumble of pencil marks, slashes, swirls, hints of geometric shapes.

"Is this an idea for a new abstract?" she guessed.

"No. No, Genevieve." He took the paper from her. "This ... is dog excrement." He crumpled it again and threw it back onto the pile on the table.

Uh-oh. That was just what she needed. To bring an artist out here and have him suffer a complete collapse of confidence. She sighed.

"Have you been working?" she said. "I mean ... beyond the sketches?"

He looked at her wearily. "It's not as easy as just throwing paint on a canvas, you know."

"I do know that. Yes," she reassured him.

Gen took a mental inventory of what she was dealing with. She'd spent thousands of dollars of her own money and the McCabes' money to bring an artist to Cambria who appeared to be a drunk in the middle of an epic personal crisis. Unless he was always like this, which she supposed was possible.

"My muse ..." he began, then trailed off, looking vaguely into the distance.

Gen resisted the urge to roll her eyes. She had a tendency to immediately dismiss any creative person who uttered the word *muse*, but that wouldn't do this time. She'd hitched her wagon to this guy, and there would be no unhitching it now. If he didn't produce while he was here—or if he did produce, and what he came up with was crap—then her investment would be for nothing. As much as she hated the idea of babysitting an egotistical, puffed-up, maladjusted whiner with a drinking problem, she didn't see where she had much choice.

"Gordon, is there anything I can do? Anything that might help you to ..." She inwardly winced. "... to awaken the muse?"

He rubbed at his forehead again. The fogginess with which he spoke suggested that he was either drunk or was battling a hangover of disastrous proportions.

"Well, I ..." He trailed off again.

"Please. Just tell me," she prompted.

"It would be so much better if I didn't have to worry about the day-to-day things, like cooking, and ..." He waved a hand to encompass the destruction that had fallen upon the defenseless little house.

"And cleaning," she finished for him, groaning inside.

"Yes. And the barn. The light is simply dreadful."

"The light," she said.

"It's gray."

"The light in the barn is gray," she repeated, just to be sure she had it straight.

"This is an impossible situation," he said in a tone that suggested poverty, war, famine, and possibly pestilence.

"We'll work it out," Gen said. "We'll make this work. Don't worry."

Out on the front porch of the guest house—where Kendrick couldn't hear—Gen pulled out her cell phone. First, she called Alex. It was almost time to close the gallery for the evening, and she told him to go ahead and do it without her. Then, she called Edward Dietrich, the Chicago-based art dealer who'd produced Kendrick's most recent gallery show, and explained the situation.

"Is he always like this, or is he having some kind of breakdown?" she asked, hearing the desperation in her own voice.

She heard a chuckle on the other end of the line. "Sounds like typical Gordon Kendrick to me."

Gen let out a puff of air in exasperation. "I talked to you months ago about bringing him out here. Why didn't you tell me?"

"You didn't ask," Dietrich said.

"Well … Well, what am I supposed to do now? He's drinking, he's trashed the house where I'm putting him up, he's not painting …"

"You've got to hold his hand," Dietrich said.

"What?"

"Think of him as a toddler on a playground. If you take your eye off of him for a second, he's going to fall off the jungle gym."

"I … I … Oh, Jesus."

"Indeed. Good luck, Genevieve." She heard him laughing lightly as he hung up.

She stared at the phone for a moment before replacing it in the pocket of her sleek black trousers. She took a deep breath, smoothed her hair, and went back into the cottage to begin cleaning up.

Chapter Twelve

Gen had to reassess her situation in light of this new information. She considered reassigning Alex to babysitting duty, but figured it would be only a short time before Alex decked the guy. After all, Gen wanted to, and she was the more patient of the two of them.

She considered hiring someone else—a housekeeper and personal assistant for Kendrick—but she'd spent so much bringing him out here, renting the house, hiring limousines, and buying $250 sheets that she didn't have the budget for it.

And even if she could afford it, she had too much riding on this. He had to work. He had to produce artwork that was, if not a breakthrough, then at least up to the standard he'd set so far. If he didn't, she couldn't repay the McCabes with a painting, as she'd promised them in their contract. She couldn't present a gallery show of Kendrick's work at the end of his residency. She wouldn't have the artwork that had been promised to her in the contract Kendrick had signed. And most importantly, the horse she'd bet on to win or at least place would never get out of the starting gate.

Gen grumbled to herself and wondered what the hell she'd gotten herself into as she washed dishes, wiped counters, and swept floors in the little cottage. At least the size of the place meant it wouldn't take her long to put things in order. She put a load of dirty laundry into the stacked washer and dryer unit that was tucked away in a closet off the bedroom. As she added detergent and started the load, she thought with distaste about men's dirty underwear. Here she was washing Gordon Kendrick's boxers. She'd never washed the underwear of a man she was having sex with, let alone one she wasn't. It seemed a shame that she was putting in the effort of maintaining a man without the benefit of regular orgasms.

When the cottage was in a respectable state, she ordered Kendrick into the shower. He protested, but then shuffled off into the little bathroom. He really was like a toddler. Once he was in there, she went into the kitchen and picked up the partial bottle of Jack Daniels. Funny, he couldn't manage to get his own yogurt or his own sheets, but he had no problem procuring alcohol. Priorities, she thought.

She sighed heavily and considered pouring out the whiskey. He'd gotten this bottle somehow; he'd get another. If she dumped it, that might slow down his drinking. On the other hand, if he was busy finding a way into town to buy more, then that was time he wouldn't be painting.

In the end, she decided he was an adult—though he didn't behave like one—and it wasn't her job to monitor his Jack Daniels intake. Still, she stuck the bottle into the back of the cupboard behind the bran flakes and the herbal tea. No reason to make it easy.

Gen made a pot of strong coffee and had it ready when Kendrick came out of the shower wearing a pair of sweatpants and the same T-shirt he'd put on when she'd arrived. His wet hair, now freed of the man bun, was mussed and hung limply to his shoulders.

He slumped down on the sofa, and Gen placed a mug of coffee on the table in front of him. She'd considered asking him about his cream and sugar preference, then decided that he could damn well drink it black.

When he'd had a bit of the coffee, Gen sat on the edge of the sofa, crossed her legs carefully, and folded her hands in her lap.

"Mr. Kendrick …" she began.

"Gordon," he corrected.

"Of course. Gordon. It seems to me that you're …" She searched for a tactful way to say it. "…You're getting off on the wrong foot here in Cambria. Let's talk about what we can do to get things back on track."

He looked at her miserably, and for a moment she really did feel sorry for him. While she mostly thought of the suffering artist archetype as self-indulgent bullshit, she supposed there might be something to it for some people. Maybe Gordon Kendrick really was a tormented genius.

She really hoped the *genius* part was in there somewhere.

"Well …" he began.

She leaned forward expectantly.

"I'm simply going to need a skylight in the barn."

The following day, Ryan perched his hands on his hips and tipped his head back, looking up at the roof of the barn. Gen stood off to the side, looking out of place in the sleeveless black sheath dress and high heels she'd worn when she'd come here straight from the gallery. She also looked embarrassed.

Kendrick—who'd obviously been drinking, Ryan could smell it on him—was going on about the gray color of the light and the angle at which it came in through the barn's few windows.

"Can't you just open the doors?" Ryan asked, not unreasonably. The barn doors were huge, and it seemed to him they'd let in enough light to perform surgery, let alone splatter a little paint on a canvas.

Kendrick was shaking his head sadly. "I need light from above. Light coming from the side just won't create the same effect."

"Huh," Ryan said. "What if I add some track lighting right over your work space? Would that do it?"

Kendrick winced. "It has to be natural light. Artificial light …" The expression on his face indicated his lack of regard for all manufactured sources of illumination. "I need to create the illusion that I'm painting outdoors."

Ryan looked out the barn doors, which were standing wide open. "Move your set-up twenty feet to the left, and you *are* painting outdoors."

"There's a breeze," Kendrick said.

"A breeze."

"Yes. Part of what I do involves literally throwing pigment at the canvas. With a breeze …" He shook his head to indicate the hopelessness of such a situation.

"So, a skylight," Ryan said.

"Please," Kendrick answered.

Ryan rubbed at the stubble on his chin.

"Of course, I'll pay for the work," Gen offered. Something in the tone of her voice suggested it was money she couldn't afford to spend.

He considered his options. Installing a skylight in the barn would be much easier than installing one in a house. The barn was a simple structure, and it didn't have a ceiling; he'd only have to cut through the roof and then redo the shingles around the skylight. He figured he could get it done in one day, once he had the supplies he needed. On the other hand, it was an asinine request. Why the hell did the barn need a skylight? With the myriad other options Kendrick had for lighting, ranging from artificial to the abundance of sunlight gushing through the doors, it seemed ridiculous that the one source of light he didn't have was the only one he wanted. Ryan got the un-comfortable feeling that he and Gen were being asked to jump through hoops just to see if they'd do it. Kind of like circus dogs.

"Ryan? Could I talk to you privately for a moment?" Gen looked at him pleadingly. "Please?"

He nodded and stepped outside, where they stood under the shade of an old oak tree, out of Kendrick's earshot.

"A skylight?" he said, perching his hands on his hips and peering down at her with skepticism.

"Look," she said. "I know this is stupid. This is really, really stupid. But he's not painting. He won't paint." She looked over her shoulder toward where Kendrick stood inside the barn, bathed in the miserable grey light he was so worked up about.

"I don't see how that's your problem," Ryan said, squinting at her.

"But it is," she insisted. "It really is. I spent a lot of money to bring him out here, Ryan. And if he doesn't paint, I can't … I can't give the McCabes the painting I promised them. And I can't have a gallery show at the end of the residency. And I won't get the art that I was promised as part of the contract. And then I won't make any money, or build any prestige, and if I don't have money or prestige, I can't move back to New York. So, if a skylight is the thing that's going to make him get off his ass and throw some paint on a canvas—which, I've got to tell you, doesn't sound like the hardest job in the world to me—then I have to stand here and ask you to put in a skylight even though it's such an idiotic thing to ask for that I can't even believe I'm asking." She paused and took a breath.

Ryan looked down at her and couldn't help grinning. Her pale cheeks were flushed with emotion, and her wild red hair—worn loose today—was in a glorious cascade over her shoulders. He had a lot to do. Spring was a busy time on the ranch, and he couldn't afford to waste a day sawing a hole in the roof of the goddamned barn so this pain-in-the-ass painter, whom he would never see again after the guy left here in a few months, could have the *illusion of painting outdoors*. Especially when the real outdoors was available in abundance.

But looking at her, the way her eyes pleaded with him, the way her curls fluttered in the breeze, the way the dress she was wearing hugged her curvy little body, he didn't quite see how he could say no.

He looked away from her, out to where a pale strip of ocean outlined the horizon, and sighed.

"I'll see what I can do," he said.

"Oh, God. Thank you!"

Before he knew what was happening, she leaped forward and threw her arms around his shoulders. He blinked, then laughed a little and hugged her back. "You're welcome."

He should have let go right away—he knew he should have. But the surprise of her, the solid warmth of her body pressed against his, stirred him up in a way he hadn't expected. He held on and found himself closing his eyes and smelling the clean shampoo scent of her hair.

"Well." She put her hands against his shoulders and pushed back from him. She was blushing in a way he found magical, enchanting. "I'd better ..." She pointed wordlessly toward Kendrick, then turned and picked her way through the grass on her pointy high heels.

Watching her go was both a loss and a pleasure.

Chapter Thirteen

"*A skylight?*" Sandra demanded in disbelief.

"That's what he wants," Ryan confirmed. He'd gone back to the house at the end of the day to wash up for dinner, and had apprised his mother of the situation. Her shocked outrage didn't surprise him; it nicely mirrored what he'd felt when he'd first heard.

"Well, that's just stupid," she announced with her usual diplomacy.

"I can't argue with that."

"He wants natural light, why can't he just go outside, for Christ's sake?"

"That's what I asked him," Ryan said.

"And what did he say?" Sandra was standing with her hands on her hips in her usual combat pose.

"There's a breeze."

"A breeze."

"That's right."

"Oh, of all the …" After that, she grumbled some things that Ryan couldn't quite make out.

Everyone was starting to gather around the big dinner table as Sandra brought out steaming serving bowls. Orin came in and found his seat, then Redmond lumbered in after him. Breanna and the boys were the last to find their seats before the bowls and platters started making their way clockwise around the table.

"What's this about a skylight?" Orin asked, putting some pot roast on his plate.

"That pain-in-the-rear artist out there in the cottage wants a skylight in the old barn," Sandra filled him in. "Because there's a breeze."

Orin screwed up his face into a mask of puzzlement. "Well, that's just …"

"That's what I said," Sandra told him.

Breanna was putting food onto the boys' plates, reasoning with them that yes, they did need to have some of the broccoli, and no, they couldn't just eat rolls and butter. Having done that, she joined the conversation.

"Lighting *is* important to an artist," she put in.

"It's a barn," Redmond observed. "It's not supposed to be some fancy artist's studio. He wants to use it that way, okay, but it's still just a barn."

"What'd that Gen Porter say when you told her no?" Orin asked, a forkful of mashed potatoes poised in front of him.

Ryan looked down at the food on his plate. He had the same mashed potatoes, broccoli, and roasted carrots as everyone else, but he had a pile of quinoa pilaf where the pot roast should have been. "Well … I told her I'd see what I could do."

"You *what*?" Sandra boomed.

He poked his fork at his food and shrugged. "It's just a skylight. It's one day's work."

"Can I help?" Lucas asked, his face alight.

"Me too!" Michael said.

"That's a pretty dangerous job, because you have to get on the roof," Breanna told them. "You'd better let your uncle Ryan do it."

"I could get on the roof," Michael said. "I did it before."

"What? When did you get on the roof?" Breanna demanded.

"With Grandpa Orin," he said brightly.

Breanna gave her father a pointed look.

"Well …" Orin said.

"It may be one day's work," Sandra said, getting the conversation back on track, "but it's one day's work during calving season."

"It's not like we can't afford to lose him for one day," Redmond said, pointing his fork in Sandra's direction. "The new hands we brought in for the calving are pretty much up to speed."

"Whose side are you on?" Sandra demanded.

"Look. I'll just put in the skylight, make the artist happy, and that'll be that," Ryan told her.

"Why are you so keen on making this artist happy?" she wanted to know.

"Well, I …" Ryan fidgeted and shrugged.

"I think it might be Gen Porter he wants to make happy," Breanna supplied.

Ryan looked up, started to say something, then stopped and looked back down at his plate.

"Is that so?" Sandra asked. Ryan didn't answer her.

"I can just tell her to forget the skylight," Ryan said to his mother after a lengthy pause.

She cocked her head for a moment, considering.

"No. I figure we can spare you for a day. You just go ahead and put in a damned skylight."

Breanna grinned, and Ryan went back to his quinoa.

Ryan told Jackson, Daniel, and Will about the pain-in-the-ass artist and the skylight that night at Ted's, a bar off Main Street where they sometimes gathered after work to play pool or have a few beers and blow off the steam from their day.

They were seated around a small, round table with a pitcher of beer between them, a pile of peanut shells growing in the middle of the table as they shelled and munched nuts.

"And the thing is, I don't even know how to put in a skylight," Ryan said. "I guess I could Google it."

"You need some help?" Will offered. "It'll give me an excuse to put off working on my dissertation." Will was working on a doctorate in evolutionary biology, and he worked as a caretaker at a mansion up the coast because it allowed him time to study a particular species of sea bird that lived in and around Cambria.

"How's that coming, anyway?" Daniel asked Will. "We any closer to having to call you Dr. Bachman?"

Will shook his head sadly and looked into his beer mug. "I don't think you'll have to get used to that phrase anytime soon." He pushed his glasses farther up on his nose. "So, yeah. A skylight would give me something else to think about."

"Appreciate it," Ryan said. "It'll be good to have someone there to call 9-1-1 when I fall off the roof."

Ryan was sitting in a straight-backed chair with his long legs stretched out, his feet propped up on another chair, legs crossed at the ankles. He shelled peanuts and popped them into his mouth.

"Surprised you could make it tonight," he said to Jackson. "What with you being all coupled up. Why aren't you at home with the missus?"

"We're not married. Yet," he said.

"Oh ho!" Daniel said, leaning forward in his chair and gesturing toward Jackson with his beer mug. "Yet!"

Will raised his eyebrows at Jackson. "Is there an imminent development we should know about? You getting ready to pop the question?"

"No, no." Jackson waved them off. "Nothing like that. It's just …" He ran a hand through his auburn hair. "Yeah. I can see it, you know? A future. Kids, the whole bit. I don't think we're ready yet, but …"

"Huh," Ryan said.

"Yeah." Jackson nodded thoughtfully, then took a slug from his beer. "Anyway. Kate's having a girls' night. The four of them are probably sprawled all over the living room right now, drinking margaritas and watching some weepy chick flick."

"Ah, jeez. Sympathies," Daniel said.

"No, no. It's good." Jackson nodded. "Kate's friends make her happy, and if she's happy, I'm happy."

Ryan shook his head. "You're gone, all right."

"Yeah," Jackson agreed. He grinned. "And you know what? I wouldn't change it."

"That's sweet," Daniel said. "Really. I think I'm tearing up a little bit." He made a show of wiping imaginary tears from his cheeks.

"Ah, shut up. Asshole," Jackson said mildly.

"So, I guess Gen's at your place, then," Ryan said.

"And Lacy," Daniel added, waggling his eyebrows at Ryan.

"I notice he didn't ask about Lacy," Will observed. "He asked about Gen. What's up with that? I thought you had your sights on our lovely blond barista."

Ryan shrugged and looked at his beer. "Ah, that's never gonna work out."

"Finally," Daniel said.

" 'Finally' what?" Ryan asked.

"Finally, you can see what's been obvious to the rest of us," Daniel said. "Lacy just isn't going there. Sorry, dude."

"That's okay," Ryan said. And it was. He found that he'd been thinking of Lacy less and less often, with less and less longing. It was peculiar, really. All of the energy he'd put into it over the years—the strategizing, the one-sided flirting—and his desire for her was fading like the sunlight at the end of a cold winter day.

"So, Gen, then," Will said.

Ryan shrugged one shoulder. "Let's not make a big deal out of it. I was just wondering if she was over there at Jackson's place."

"She is," Jackson said. "Probably wearing little pajama shorts and one of those camisoles girls like." He wiggled his eyebrows at Ryan.

"Hey. Shouldn't you be thinking about Kate instead of Gen and her … her pajama shorts and her …" He gestured at his own chest to indicate a camisole.

"Ha! That settles it," Daniel said, smacking Ryan companionably on the back. "Our boy has a thing for Gen."

"I wouldn't call it a *thing*," Ryan said.

"What would you call it, then?" Will asked.

"More like a … a *yen*."

"Is a *yen* greater or lesser than a *thing*?" Daniel pondered.

"Lesser than a *thing*, greater than an *itch*," Jackson supplied.

"Oh, shut up," Ryan said.

Back at Kate and Jackson's house, the girls weren't drinking margaritas—it was chardonnay—but they *were* watching a weepy chick flick, and they were sprawled all over the living room, just as he'd said.

Gen wasn't wearing pajama shorts and a camisole, mainly because it wasn't summer yet and it still got chilly at night. She'd opted for sweatpants and a hoodie instead.

The Notebook was just wrapping up on the TV, and Lacy was blowing her nose noisily into a wad of tissues.

"Jeez, Lacy, you've seen this, what? A dozen times? How can you still cry?" Rose asked, shaking her head.

"How can you *not* cry?" Lacy demanded. "Your heart must be made of stone. Wait, not stone. Ice. You're a cold, icy-hearted woman."

"Aw. I think it's sweet that she cries," Kate said from her spot under a fuzzy blanket on one end of the sofa.

"Thank you!" Lacy said.

"Of course, she also cries when we watch *The Simpsons,*" Gen observed.

"I do not." Lacy, who was on the floor next to Gen on a pile of pillows, kicked at Gen with one sock-clad foot.

Kate turned off the TV, got up from the sofa, and started gathering up everybody's popcorn bowls. "Anybody need more wine?"

"I better not," Gen said. "I have to get up early. I need to get out to the Delaney Ranch and make sure Gordon Kendrick gets out of bed." She sat up and started replacing pillows on the sofa.

"So now you're babysitting this guy?" Rose asked. Her hair was alternating shades of green and purple. She had it pulled up into a stubby ponytail on the back of her head.

"I'm afraid that's what it's come to," Gen confirmed. "I was already doing his grocery shopping and buying his damned sheets. Now I'm cleaning for him and making him take showers and … and literally making him get out of bed. I don't know how he even lived before he had me to do everything for him. God, this guy's an asshole." She shook her head in disgust.

"How's the gallery doing if you're over at the ranch spoon-feeding the artist?" Kate asked.

"Oh, it's okay." Gen waved an arm dismissively. "Alex does a good job. And things aren't too busy right now anyway. And I've got to make this thing work—I've got to make *Kendrick* work—or this whole investment will be for nothing."

"And you won't get back to New York," Rose said. Her voice held a hint of hard judgment.

"I guess," Gen conceded.

Rose's expression softened, and she reached out to rub Gen's shoulder. "Listen, honey. I'm sorry I've been giving you a hard time about moving. If going to New York is going to make you happy, you should go. I'm just going to miss you."

Gen squeezed Rose's hand. "I'll miss you too."

All of the talk about people missing each other got Lacy going again, and she honked into her tissues. "Can we stop talking about people leaving? I'm already a mess as it is."

"She's right. Let's talk about something more fun. How's the eye candy over at the ranch?" Kate said, waggling her eyebrows at Gen.

"The eye candy has to install a skylight in his barn. For the asshole artist. I mean, jeez. A skylight? I felt like an idiot asking Ryan to do it. I hope he doesn't think that I think that's a reasonable request. Because then I'd be an asshole by association. I don't want to be an asshole by association. I'm not an asshole!"

"Of course you're not," Kate said, soothing her.

"It's interesting how much you care what Ryan thinks of you," Lacy said, peering at Gen over the rim of her wineglass.

"Well, of course I do. I care what everybody thinks."

"I can't live like that," Rose said, shaking her head. "I am who I am. If people don't like it, screw 'em."

"Well, sure," Gen said. "Okay, I get that. But it's Ryan."

"Still nursing a yearning for the handsome rancher," Kate observed.

Gen got up and padded into the kitchen to rinse her wineglass in the sink. "God. It's even worse now that I have to go out there to the ranch all the time. He's just there, with his nicely fitting jeans and his Bambi eyes and his …" She gestured with her arms to indicate height and broad shoulders. "God, the lust. I can't even tell you about the lust I feel for that man. I just want to *lick* him."

"You should," Rose said.

"What, just walk right on up and lick him?"

"Well, not without some preliminary flirting. But, yeah." Rose raised her eyebrows, causing the little silver ball pierced into the left one to bob.

"I haven't … you know … *licked* anybody in a really long time," Gen said. She put her clean wineglass upside down next to the sink to drain and leaned against the counter, a hand on her hip. "I don't know if I even remember how."

"It's like riding a bike," Kate said. "You'll remember. I did. And my dry spell was even longer than yours."

"How's all that bike riding going, anyway?" Lacy asked Kate. "You've gotta have thighs of steel by now."

Kate grinned at her. "The bike riding," she said, "is awesome. I love bike riding. And Jackson really knows how to ride a bike."

"God, I want to ride a bike," Gen said wistfully.

"You need to climb up on Ryan's handlebars," Rose said.

Gen snatched a dish towel from the counter and flung it at Rose. "I think this metaphor is getting out of hand."

"Seriously, though." Lacy got up from the sofa and went into the kitchen with Gen. "You should ask him out or something. You two would be good together."

"Maybe," Gen said. "I'll think about it."

"Don't think," Rose said. "Just get on the bike, and maybe ring the little bell."

Chapter Fourteen

Ryan bought the parts for the skylight—Gen had said she would reimburse him—and arranged with Will to meet him at the ranch to help him put the thing in. They met at the house on a Thursday morning and then went out to the old barn together hauling a ladder, a power saw, and a toolbox.

The morning was bright and clear, the sky so blue it almost hurt to look at it, a cool breeze ruffling Ryan's hair and making the grass ripple.

"You ever done one of these before?" Ryan asked Will.

"Not exactly. But I researched it last night on the Internet. Should be pretty simple."

It was just like the college boy to do his research. Probably a good thing, too, since Ryan's style would have been to get up there and start cutting and hammering and hope something good came out of it. Usually, it worked out.

Will explained what they had to do, then they leaned the ladder against the side of the barn and climbed up.

"Is it just me, or does this seem not entirely necessary?" Will asked.

"It's not just you," Ryan said as he ascended the ladder. Will was already up on the roof.

"Why are we doing this again?" Will asked. "I mean, I'm not complaining. I volunteered. I'm just wondering."

"We're doing this so Gordon Kendrick can pretend he's outside, instead of actually *going* outside, where there is, apparently, a breeze."

Will nodded. "That's what I thought."

They were both up there, almost thirty feet above the ground, contemplating the placement of the skylight, when they heard a voice calling Ryan's name.

"Hey, Ryan! Are you up there?"

Gen. Her voice did unpredictable things to him. First it sent a quick hit of adrenaline to his chest, and then it made him feel unaccountably warm. The roof was steeply pitched, so he had to crawl on his hands and knees to the edge of it to look down at her.

"Hey," he said companionably.

"Oh, God, it's a long way up there. Be careful. Don't fall and break a leg or anything. I'd feel really guilty if I asked you to do something stupid and you ended up killing yourself."

"Well, it is stupid," he agreed.

"I know. I know it is. Have I thanked you for doing it?"

"You have."

"Well, thank you again. Really."

He found that he enjoyed her gratitude, enjoyed making her happy. He also enjoyed the view from up here. She was wearing a low-cut top, something black and clingy, and the angle gave him enticing scenery that had nothing to do with the rolling hills or the ocean off in the distance.

"Happy to do it," he said.

He was just starting to head back toward Will when she said, "Ryan?"

"Yeah?" He turned back toward her.

"After this is done, I'd like to take you to dinner. You know, to thank you for the skylight. Which is a stupid job you shouldn't have to do. But you're doing it anyway. And I'd really like to … you know. Do something. For you."

She sounded nervous, and he was aware that she wasn't just asking about a thank-you dinner. His heart started to beat a little bit faster, which struck him as a non-manly kind of response. Still, there it was.

"I'm not about to say no to that," he said, trying to sound casual. It sounded casual to his own ears, but there was no accounting for hers.

"Well, good then." She nodded in a *that's that* kind of way. Her hair was loose today, and the sunlight made it glimmer like new copper. "Okay. I'll let you get back to it."

She started to walk away, then turned back as though she'd forgotten to say something. Then she nodded again, and turned again, and then she really did walk away.

It was Ryan's effort to watch her walk away—to see the sway of her hips and the bounce of her hair—that caused him to lose his balance and slide toward the edge of the roof and the thirty-some feet of air beneath. He splayed out flat like a starfish, and that, thankfully, stopped him. The fact that he'd narrowly averted broken bones, head injuries, and possible paralysis caused his pulse to pound so hard he could hear it thump in his ears.

"You okay there?" Will asked from a few feet to Ryan's left.

"Holy shit," Ryan said. He tried to steady his breathing.

"That was Gen Porter down there, wasn't it?" Will asked mildly.

"Uh … yeah. It was."

"Distracting." Will grinned.

"Holy shit," Ryan said again.

"What am I doing? Why did I do that? What the hell was I thinking?!" Gen was back at the gallery, which was empty except for her, and she waved an arm for emphasis as she ranted into her cell phone.

"You asked a man you're attracted to out on a date," Kate said. "It's the kind of thing adults do."

"It's the kind of thing idiots do," Gen said. "Idiots, when they get all hot and bothered and take leave of their senses."

"He said yes," Kate reminded her.

Gen plopped into the chair behind her desk. "Yeah, but I told him it was a thank-you dinner for the skylight, and so now I don't even know if he knows it's a date."

"He knows," Kate said.

"How do you *know* he knows?"

Kate sighed. "He's not stupid."

"No, but he's a man. Men don't have a clue about this stuff. Emotions, and expectations, and ... and subtext."

"That's true," Kate admitted.

"But I couldn't very well say, 'Hey, Ryan, you want to go out with me on a date that I'm calling something other than a date because I'm too big of a wuss to admit it's a date?'"

"Well, I guess you could, but it's a mouthful," Kate observed.

"So now I don't know what to do," Gen fretted.

"Yes you do."

"No, I don't. Tell me. What should I do?"

Kate's voice was patient. "You take him out to dinner, say thank you for the skylight, then run your hand up his thigh during the soup course."

Gen didn't say anything.

"Gen?"

"Sorry. I was visualizing."

"You'll be okay," Kate said. "You know how to do this. You've dated men before."

She had. But those men weren't Ryan. Just thinking about her hand and his thigh and the soup course made her palms damp.

"Right. I have. I can do this," Gen agreed.

"Just, the licking thing?" Kate said. "You should probably save that for after dessert."

They met at Neptune, the restaurant where Jackson worked as head chef, on a Friday night. Gen wondered whether the fact that they were doing this on a Friday night would tip off Ryan that this was a date-date, and not a thank-you date. It might, but then again, they'd met at the restaurant rather than someone picking someone up, and *that* said friendly rather than romantic. Given all of the conflicting input, she was left uncertain about what, exactly, the impression was that she was giving him.

As they sat in the crowded dining room perusing their menus, it occurred to her that the soup course might be a little early for the thigh-groping move Kate had suggested, especially if Ryan didn't know this was a date-date. And timing was only one concern. If she ran her hand up his thigh, an event she now couldn't stop herself from imagining in vivid detail, it was entirely possible she'd burst into flames of desire. And that wasn't the sort of thing you wanted to do in public.

Ryan looked handsome—but then, he always did. He was wearing a light blue button-down shirt open at the neck, with a dark blazer, his dark hair neatly combed. As she tried to focus on the wine list, she couldn't decide what was more distracting—his eyes, or his voice. Listening to Ryan's voice was like wrapping yourself in a soft, warm blanket while eating dark chocolate. At the moment, he was talking about the wine, but he could have been talking about anything. He could have been reciting a dishwasher repair manual, and it still would have made her hot as hell.

"… the cabernet?" he said. She hadn't heard the rest because she'd been fixating on the timbre of that voice rather than the content of what he'd been saying.

"Uh … sure," she said. It must have been the right answer, because he nodded as though his thoughts had been validated.

They ordered their wine, and when it came, she lifted her glass in a toast. "Seriously, Ryan, thank you for the skylight. That was above and beyond. I'm glad you didn't break your neck trying to install it."

"I almost did," he said mildly.

"You did?"

"I did." Amusement made the corners of his eyes crinkle, and she wondered if he looked like that in the morning when he first woke up, all sleepy and warm. "At one point, I lost my balance and started plunging headlong toward the edge of the roof. I wouldn't say my life flashed before my eyes, but I was thankful my insurance is paid up."

Her eyes widened. "Oh crap. What happened? Why did you slip?"

"I was distracted." He took a sip of his dark red wine and peered at her over the rim of the glass.

"By what?"

That look of amusement deepened, and he hesitated. Then he said, "Well, let's just say it's not a good idea to talk to a pretty girl when you're thirty feet off the ground."

Gen's first thought was that Lacy must have been visiting the ranch while Ryan was on the roof. How had that happened? Then it hit: He was talking about her. A shot of adrenaline made her pulse spike. She let out a gasp and pressed her fingertips to her mouth to suppress a giggle. "Oh, jeez. Are you saying that I almost killed you?"

"Almost." He grinned at her. "Will wouldn't stop ribbing me about it."

She could feel the blush rise to her cheeks, and she busied herself straightening the napkin in her lap and lining up her flatware in neat parallel lines so she could avoid his gaze.

"Well. It's good that you're not dead," she said.

"My mother thinks so," Ryan agreed.

The waitress, a pretty blond woman Gen knew from the book club she attended at Kate's shop, came and took their order. Gen ordered the bacon-wrapped filet mignon, and Ryan chose the gnocchi with wild mushrooms. When the food came, Gen offered him a taste of her steak.

"This is fabulous," she said. "Here, try it."

"Nah, thanks." He waved her off. "I don't eat meat."

At first, that seemed like a normal enough thing for someone to say. Then she remembered what he did for a living, and her eyebrows shot skyward. "You don't eat meat?"

"Nope."

"You're a vegetarian," she stated again, just to be sure.

"Six years now."

"But ..."

He lowered his fork, and the look he gave her told her he'd had this conversation many times, with many people, and his explanation remained the same.

He pointed at Gen's steak. "That fillet you're eating?"

"Yeah?"

"I probably knew her."

"Oh." She looked at her plate, feeling uneasy. "I never thought of that."

"My parents think I'm nuts," he went on. "Especially my mom. She thinks every time I eat a bite of tofu I'm passing moral judgment on her."

"But you're not?" Gen ventured.

He waved a hand to dismiss the notion. "Ah, hell no. I mean, where would my family be if people stopped eating meat? But for me ..." He shook his head. "I raised 'em. I probably was there when they were born."

When she hesitated to resume her meal, he laughed. "I don't mind if you eat that," he reassured her. "If I were bothered by other people eating meat, I'd have to get a new line of work."

"I guess you would," she said. She considered that for a moment. "But it bothers you enough that *you* don't do it. So how is it that you can do what you do when you feel that way?"

He paused long enough that she believed he was trying to give her a real answer, one that wasn't easy or glib. Finally, he said, "We—my family—have been ranchers for generations. It's what we do. More than that, it's who we are. It's a connection to my grandfather, and his father, and his father before that. It's what makes me a Delaney."

She wondered what it would be like to feel that kind of connection to family, that kind of meaning, that sense of belonging.

"My mother and father are divorced," she said. "My father is an accountant. My mother is a professional bride. She's on her fifth husband. I haven't even met the most recent one. They live in Palm Springs." She wasn't sure why she'd blurted all of that out. She felt the quick sting of tears in her eyes and blinked them away.

"You know ..." He tilted his head to look at her. "There's more than one way to form a family. You can have your own.

You can join somebody else's. Or you can make one out of spare parts. That's what you've done with your friends. The four of you—you're family."

How could he understand that so fully when he was looking in from the outside? How could he know? But he did know. Somehow, he did.

"Yeah. They're my family. Kate, and Rose, and Lacy … and even Jackson now, too. I'm lucky to have them."

He reached out and put a hand over hers on the table, and a gentle flurry of wings fluttered in her belly. Right then, there was no longer any doubt about what kind of date this was.

They talked about Ryan's family, and their childhoods— his on the Delaney Ranch, hers in a series of different schools as her mother moved from one husband to another—and his nephews, and the things he wanted to do to improve the operation of the ranch. By the time they finished dessert, it felt at once as though they'd been talking forever, and that no time had passed.

When the bill came, he tried to pay, and she playfully smacked his hand away and reminded him that it was a thank-you dinner for the skylight that had almost killed him. If a skylight had almost killed *her,* well, then he'd be welcome to pick up the check.

He walked her out to her car, and she didn't want to get into it and drive away. She wanted to stay with him, even if they were doing nothing. Even if he were going to the post office or the DMV, even if he were planning to clean out the rain gutters. She just wanted to be with him.

"It's still early," he said. "Do you want to take a walk?"

"Sure."

He reached out to her, and she put her hand in his. They walked down Burton Drive and then, because the full moon lit up the night well enough that they could easily see their way, they climbed the stairs that led up a woodsy, fern-covered hill to the Cambria Pines Lodge. They opened a little white gate and entered the lodge's gardens, a fantasy world of manicured hedges, heirloom rose bushes, stone fountains, and delicate little flowers in a riot of colors.

They sat on a bench beneath a trellis covered in flowering vines. The moonlight bathed everything with a silvery glow that made the garden look enchanted, as though a tiny troupe of elves might dance by at any moment.

Ryan was holding her hand again, and she felt the delicious tension hovering between them like the memory of joy, like a miracle.

When he kissed her, she melted, and everything inside of her dissolved into him with the sweetness of warm honey.

They parted, and she sighed his name. His earthy, manly smell mixed with the scent of flowers and lush greenery. He tasted like comfort—like the sanctuary of home.

She slowly opened her eyes. "I haven't kissed anybody in a long time," she said.

"Why not?"

She shook her head and didn't answer.

"You should kiss people. You should always kiss people." He put a hand on her face and slowly ran a thumb over her cheek.

If he'd taken her home, she would have asked him in. She wouldn't have been able to stop herself. But they'd met at the restaurant, so he walked her to where her car was parked at the curb in front of Neptune.

"Ryan ..." She started to say something, but then she didn't know what to say. There was so much going on inside her head. She wanted to kiss him again. She wanted to tell him not to toy with her if the one he really wanted was Lacy. Most of all, she wanted to tell him not to hurt her, to be careful with her heart. She didn't have the words, though, and so she just looked up at him and stayed silent so he wouldn't hear the catch in her throat.

"Thank you for dinner," he said. He took her hand in his and kissed her, just briefly, before opening the car door for her and seeing her safely inside.

She shut the door, rolled down the driver's side window, and leaned out toward him. "I had a really good time," she said.

"I did, too. Will you be coming to the ranch tomorrow?"

She gave him a wry grin. "I'll have to. Now that Kendrick's got his skylight, he's damned well going to use it."

He nodded and smiled, and gave the hood of her car a friendly tap before walking down Main Street toward his truck.

Chapter Fifteen

"So, you and Gen Porter, huh?" Jackson was throwing darts over at Ted's, and he'd hit two out of three bull's eyes, making Ryan glad they weren't playing for money.

"We had a date," Ryan said. He wasn't sure he wanted to admit to anything further, at least not yet.

"That's what I heard. Lindsey at Neptune said you two came in, had dinner. She was the bacon-wrapped fillet, you were the wild mushroom gnocchi." His turn over, he stepped aside and handed the darts to Ryan.

"It's so interesting being identified as a menu item," Ryan said. He stood at the line taped on the bar's matted-down carpeting, lined up his shot, and threw. He missed the center circle by a mile.

"So? What's going on with you two?" Jackson prompted him. "I figure I have a right to know. She's practically my sister-in-law."

Ryan wanted to protest the point, but found he couldn't. Gen and Kate were sisters in spirit, if not by birth, as he himself had pointed out to Gen during dinner. And Kate and Jackson, if not married, were certainly headed in that direction. So, yeah, he guessed Gen *was* practically Jackson's sister-in-law.

He aimed and took another shot, this one two inches closer to the bull's eye than the last one had been. Progress.

"I don't really know what's going on yet," Ryan said after thinking about it a little. "We had a date. It was a really good date." His third shot went high and to the left for five points. "Shit."

"You going to ask her out again?" Jackson said.

"I didn't ask her out the first time. She asked me."

Jackson glared at him. "You're avoiding the question."

"You noticed."

With the dart game over, they got two fresh mugs of beer from the bar, made their way to a small, round table in the center of the room, and sat down. It was past midnight—Jackson got off work at the restaurant late on Friday nights. After Ryan had taken Gen back to her car, he'd called Jackson and asked if he wanted to meet up. Ryan had felt restless—at loose ends—and he wasn't ready to go home.

The bar was busy, with a clientele of mostly locals drinking, playing pool, and listening to the loud music being pumped through the speaker system. The crowd at Ted's was generally loud, generally obnoxious, but also generally harmless. The place smelled like beer and sweat, and Jackson had to raise his voice to be heard over the commotion.

"So, back to the question," he said.

Ryan didn't want to answer it, but he didn't know why. It wasn't that he didn't know the answer. He knew. He wanted to see Gen again, and again after that. But something about the subject made him feel raw and exposed, and he wasn't willing to let Jackson get near it just yet. He didn't quite know how to approach it himself.

"Is it okay if we don't talk about this?" he asked.

"Why not?"

"Because we're not girls, that's why not." He was aware that the answer was stupid and childish. As though men didn't have feelings, or weren't in touch with those feelings. As though women were somehow silly and frivolous for knowing how they felt and being unabashed about it. It occurred to him that he was being an ass.

"Look," Ryan tried again. "There's something there. Between me and Gen, I mean. But I'm not ... I guess I just don't know what it is yet, so I don't know how to talk about it."

Jackson nodded. "Fair enough."

A minute or two later, Lacy Jordan came into the bar with a guy—some stiff who taught English at the high school. They went to the bar and the stiff said something to the bartender. Ryan glanced at them briefly—only briefly—and then turned back to Jackson. "Gen is ... I don't know. I'm not good at talking about this stuff. But I definitely need to see her again."

Jackson looked at Ryan with interest, then looked at Lacy and the high school teacher. Then he raised his eyebrows at Ryan and grinned.

"What?" Ryan said.

"Lacy's here."

"What? Oh ... yeah." Ryan shrugged.

Jackson laughed and shook his head.

"What?" Ryan said again.

"Welcome to the club, man." Jackson looked deeply amused.

"What are you talking about? What club?"

"The *hopelessly in love with one of the four sisters* club. The dues are high, but it's worth it." He reached out with his beer mug and clinked it against Ryan's.

"I still don't know what the hell you're talking about," Ryan insisted.

"Dude. You just saw Lacy Jordan with another guy, and you couldn't have cared less. This thing with Gen? If she decides she wants you, it's a done deal. Might as well just go with it."

Ryan thought about that, and he felt a little stunned.

"Well, shit," he said.

❖

"Ryan kissed me," Gen told Lacy on the phone just a few minutes after she got home from her date. Lacy passed the word on to Rose. Kate, who'd been Gen's first stop moments after she'd parked her car, already knew.

The four decided to meet for breakfast on Saturday morning to deconstruct the events of the evening. They were sitting in a big wooden booth at the Redwood Café, big plates of eggs, pancakes, and bacon in front of Kate, Lacy, and Rose, and an egg white omelet with fresh fruit sitting mostly untouched at Gen's place. She didn't seem to have an appetite.

"So, the kiss," Rose prompted Gen after they all were settled in with their food. "I need details. Setting first. Where were you?"

"We were in the gardens at the lodge. You know the bench with the big trellis over it? The one across from the stone fountain?"

"Oh, sweet," Lacy said with a dreamy look on her face. "That's a great spot for a first kiss."

"It really was," Gen agreed. "There was a lot of moonlight last night. Everything was all silvery and pretty, and there was the smell of flowers …"

"And the sound of the fountain," Kate supplied.

"And Ryan looking the way Ryan looks," Rose said.

"I know! Jeez," Gen said. "It's not fair for one guy to be that sexy. I mean, just for the sake of balance, there's gotta be five guys out there with no sex appeal at all just to average him out."

"I've dated those guys," Rose said.

"We all have," Lacy agreed.

"And then he just … kissed me," Gen said. Just saying the words caused a rush of heat through her belly.

Rose held a forkful of pancakes aloft. "So, does he still like Lacy?"

"I don't know."

"Is he looking for a relationship?" Kate asked.

"I don't know!" Gen picked up a forkful of omelet, looked at it, and put it back down.

"Maybe you should ask him," Rose suggested.

"Ask him?" Gen said.

"Yes."

"You mean, like, just *ask* him?"

Rose tilted her colorful head and peered at Gen. "Well, you could send him a message in code, but what if he deciphers it wrong?" She batted her eyelashes in a parody of innocent inquiry.

"You're funny." Gen's tone suggested Rose was anything but.

"Look. You don't have to have the answers right now," Kate said, pointing her fork at Gen. "Just ... see where it goes. Be open to whatever happens."

Gen took a deep and shaky breath to steady herself, and then nodded. "Right."

After the kiss, Gen started finding more and more reasons to drop by the ranch—especially the main house.

When Kendrick wanted to rearrange the furniture in the cottage—to improve the feng shui, he said—Gen dropped by the main house to ask whether anyone would mind if she and Kendrick put the sofa on a different wall and moved the dresser two feet to the left. When Kendrick clogged the toilet, Gen went to the house to ask if she could borrow a plunger.

She wasn't even fully aware that she was doing it; she simply found herself going to the Delaneys' front door more and more often, for more and more reasons. Sometimes Ryan was there, and sometimes he was busy out at the new barn, or checking fences in distant pastures, or keeping watch over a sickly calf.

When Sandra was there, she'd invite Gen inside and they'd chat for a while about this and that—the gallery, whatever was happening at the ranch, the minutia of Sandra's day—before Gen got the information or the item she needed and went on her way. When Ryan was there, he gave her his slow, sexy smile and helped her with whatever it was that she'd come for.

The problem was, the thing she'd really come for was to see whether, given multiple opportunities, he would ask her out on a date that wasn't shadowed by the thank-you specter, the way the last one was. It seemed like he might. She could feel the unasked question in the pauses before he spoke, in the quiet hesitation of his body in relation to hers.

But he didn't ask.

The fact that he didn't made her wonder whether she'd been the only one to feel the electricity in the kiss, whether she'd built a story in her head based on imagination and longing.

The hope of the kiss, followed by the letdown in its wake, left her feeling out of sorts whenever she saw him. But seeing him, even as a reminder of a desire left unconsummated, was better than not seeing him. The ache in her chest that came from wanting him was better than the emptiness that came from his absence. So she kept going to the ranch, and when Kendrick didn't need anything, she invented things for him to need.

It was the best she could do.

Chapter Sixteen

"Why the hell haven't you gotten off your ass and asked that woman out?" Sandra demanded of Ryan one morning at breakfast.

"Well, good morning to you too, Mom," Ryan said mildly.

"Don't change the subject." She slammed his bowl of whole grain cereal down on the kitchen table. "If you're too big an idiot to notice that the Porter girl is crazy about you, then I didn't raise you right."

Ryan blinked. He didn't know what had brought on this scolding, what spark had been added to what accelerant to set off this particular explosion. He knew only that he was unfortunate enough to be in its path.

"You raised me fine," he assured her. "What's this about?"

"What the hell are you waiting for?" she barked at him, slamming down a bowl of fresh-cut fruit.

"I haven't even had my coffee yet," he said, scrubbing at his face with his hands.

"Good God, Ryan. Just ask Gen out," Breanna said as she came into the room wearing her getting-the-kids-ready-for-school uniform of sweatpants, socks, and a T-shirt. "So we don't have to hear about it anymore." She rolled her eyes and gestured toward their mother.

Ryan poured himself a cup of coffee, added sugar, leaned against the kitchen counter, and turned toward his mother. "Mom? You mind telling me how this is any of your business?"

"It's my business because that poor thing is so desperate to see you that she keeps coming around here asking for things she doesn't really need, taking up all of my precious time because she thinks she might run into you. I'm a busy woman, Ryan! I don't have the luxury of entertaining your would-be girlfriend!"

"I thought you liked talking to Gen," Breanna said to her mother. "I see you two in here having tea, laughing like teenagers."

"You mind your own business," Sandra told Breanna.

"*She* should mind her own business?" Ryan said.

This was the first Ryan had heard of Gen and his mother having tea and laughing. What were they talking about? Were they talking about him? What were they saying that was so damned funny? He found the whole idea disturbing.

"What the hell is wrong with Gen Porter, anyway?" Sandra went on. "You think you can do better?" She grunted. "That'll be the day. She's not Tara, you know. You think she is, but she's goddamned well not."

"I don't even know what's happening here," Ryan said. His head was starting to hurt. "It's like I came in here in the middle of an argument I didn't know we were having. Puts me at kind of a disadvantage, don't you think?"

Orin came into the room, pulling on the light jacket he wore every day during the spring months. "What argument are we in the middle of that Ryan didn't know we were having?" he inquired.

"We're not arguing about a damned thing," Sandra said. "I'm just pointing out that your son's an idiot."

"Oh," Orin said. He sat down at his place at the table and Sandra put a plate of eggs and bacon in front of him. "Ryan, right?"

"Of course, Ryan." She shot Orin a dirty look.

"Son," Orin said, stabbing a piece of bacon with his fork, "you're probably better off just doing whatever your mother's telling you to do."

"Goddamned right," Sandra said, plunking a carton of milk down on the table.

"Is Uncle Ryan in trouble?" Lucas said, running into the room with his brother close behind him.

"No, I'm not in trouble," Ryan told him.

"Yes, you are," Breanna said. She turned to her son. "He is." Then she chuckled under her breath and started on her breakfast. "Better him than me."

The thing was, Ryan wasn't entirely sure why he hadn't asked Gen out yet. He knew it was kind of an asshole move to kiss her and then fail to make any kind of follow-up. And he knew she wasn't Tara. He'd never thought she was. The fact that his mother had even brought her up baffled him. What did that have to do with this?

Ryan thought about it as he rode Annie out to the northeast pasture to check out how the new calves and their mothers were doing. The sun was warm, with a hint of a breeze off the ocean. Annie huffed and picked along the trail, in no hurry. Neither was he. He had a lot on his mind, and being alone out here gave him time to let it all roll around in his brain, changing shape until—one would hope—it eventually made sense.

Ryan had met Tara when he was about twenty-six. He was out of college and back here working the ranch, and she'd come down here with her parents, a couple of upper-middle-class suburbanites who, amid their midlife crises, had decided to try their hands at winemaking. They'd bought a winery near Paso Robles and opened a tasting room in Cambria, and Tara had run the storefront for them until a fungus on the wine grapes had ruined their crop. Then they'd decided that maybe winemaking wasn't as easy as they'd thought it would be.

Tara had asked Ryan to bail them out. With his trust fund, he could have done it easily enough. He might have given them the loan they wanted if they'd been a different sort of people, but Tara's parents were the kind who blew through money carelessly. In the time they'd owned the winery and tasting room, they'd learned little about wine, grapes, or how to run a business. It was just a lark for them, something to tell their friends about on their next Caribbean cruise. So Ryan had said no, and they'd closed the shop, packed up their crap, and moved back to the suburbs.

For some reason, it had never occurred to him that she would go with them. He'd thought he loved her. He'd thought she had loved him. He'd been having visions of building a new house on the ranch property, of kids running around in the yard, of Tara waiting for him when he came home all dirty and exhausted, smelling like hay and horse. But when he'd refused to give her parents the money, things had changed between them. Money always changed things.

Everybody needed to have one great heartbreak in their lives, and that was his. When she'd left, he'd felt raw and fragile for a long time, so long that the rest of his family had looked at him with concern when they thought he wouldn't notice.

Eventually, he'd just had to get on with his life.

Eventually, he'd healed.

And Gen wasn't Tara.

Tara had been cool sweetness, and Gen was all fiery heat. Tara was peace; Gen was vibrant life. He could just see her out there in New York, charging up Fifth Avenue in her towering heels and her clingy black dresses, confident and purposeful. The thought made him smile.

She'd own the place.

New York.

Ah, Jesus.

It hit him so suddenly that he stopped, climbed off of Annie, and paced around in the grass, his head down, his hands planted on his hips.

Shit.

Was he really this dense? Gen wasn't Tara, no. But Gen was talking about leaving town, just like Tara had.

That had been fine when they'd just been flirting, when he'd just thought of her as a sexy woman he liked, someone he could spend some time with.

But then there was the kiss, and the kiss had mystery and promise and longing in it, things he hadn't felt since …

… since Tara had ripped his heart out and stomped on it.

He was an idiot.

His mother had seen what was happening, but he hadn't. He shook his head at the thought that he was just another stereotypical male, so out of touch with his feelings that he couldn't even see what was happening in his own mind until a woman pointed it out to him.

The breeze ruffled his hair, and Annie made a chuffing noise as Ryan stood there and looked out at the ocean. He mounted up again, turned Annie around, and headed back home.

Ryan marched into the house, looked around for his mother, didn't find her, and then finally tracked her down in her garden, where she was weeding rows of peas. She was down on her knees on a foam mat, gloves on her hands, one fist full of prickly weeds, when he stormed up to her.

"I have feelings for Gen Porter, and I'm afraid I'm going to fall for her and she's going to leave for New York," he said without introduction.

Sandra peered up at him with a half smile on her face, using her free hand to shade her eyes from the sun.

"I guess the penny finally dropped," she said with a hint of triumph.

"Well," he said.

"Get down here and help me with these weeds." She tossed a spare pair of gardening gloves his way. Obediently, he got down there and started plucking weeds from among the peas.

"I'm not wrong," he said after they had worked side by side for a while. "She told me herself she wants to move back to New York. If I start seeing her, and we hit it off, and she leaves …" He left it open, because the rest was understood. If she left, he'd be moping and brooding for months in the wake of her departure, just like he had with Tara. The other thing he didn't say was that he suspected this time would be even worse, that the blow to his hopeful heart would be dire enough that he wouldn't recover as easily. He wasn't sure how he knew that, since he and Gen had only been on one date. But his instinct told him that once the idea of her settled into him like the smell of the grass or the feel of the sun on his skin, she would persist in his heart in ways he wasn't sure he could handle.

"Ry," his mother said in a tone that was uncharacteristically patient, "you can't be afraid of things because you don't know if they'll work out. How are you ever going to find what you're looking for that way?"

"I don't know that I'm looking for anything."

"Of course you are. I see how you are with Lucas and Michael. You want kids, you want a family of your own. That's obvious. What's also obvious is that you're never going to get it if you're so scared of being hurt that you don't take any risks."

It irritated him that she was right, and he felt that irritation like a burr under his skin.

"That Lacy Jordan was never going to be the one," Sandra went on.

Ryan looked up from the peas in surprise—first at the very mention of Lacy, since she'd been absent from his thoughts for weeks now, and second at the fact that his mother knew about the crush he'd harbored. A crush that seemed silly and distant now.

Sandra chuckled. "You thought I didn't know about that torch you were carrying for Lacy Jordan?" She waved him off. "Of course I knew. And I'll tell you what else I know: The biggest attraction for you—aside from the fact that she's pretty—is that she's lived here her whole life, same as you. You were playing it safe, but that's just stupid, because she and you aren't a match. The two of you ..." She shook her head. "It'd never be right."

He plucked at the weeds and wondered whether she was right. Had he been interested in Lacy just because she was as anchored in Cambria as he was? Maybe, he had to concede. But it was more than that. He'd thought of Lacy as a safe bet not only because she wasn't likely to move away, but also because she wasn't interested in him and never had been.

It was hard to crash and burn when things never got off the ground in the first place.

I'm a wuss, he thought. Then he said it out loud: "I'm a wuss. Aren't I?" He didn't look up from his work with the weeds, and in a way, his reluctance to meet his mother's gaze further proved his wussiness.

"You sure are, son," she said, chuckling.

Ryan wondered why she couldn't just be comforting and reassuring like other mothers.

Chapter Seventeen

Gen was about to give up on Ryan. She'd put herself in his path so many times he was lucky he hadn't tripped over her, and still—nothing. No phone call, no invitation to dinner, no suggestion that they take a sunset walk on the beach. It hurt, no question. There was no sense pretending she wasn't disappointed, after longing for him and then, finally, kissing him, and finding that kiss to be everything she'd imagined.

Who wouldn't feel the sting of rejection?

She'd just about decided that he was a lost cause when she got a call at the gallery on a Monday morning and was surprised to hear his voice.

"How's the artist like his skylight?" he asked without a greeting, and without preamble.

"Ryan?" she said.

"I was just wondering," he went on. "It was my first skylight. I wanted to know if it was working out okay."

And goddamn it if her heart didn't speed up just hearing his dusky voice. *Stop it. You are not going to get all moony over a guy who doesn't want you. Screw that.*

"It's fine," she said, keeping her voice as businesslike as possible. "The light in the barn is much better now. Thank you again."

To her own ear, she sounded like a telemarketer, or maybe a pollster.

"Well, good," he said. "You're welcome."

He didn't say anything else for a while, and she stood behind her desk, wiping her clammy palms on her dress and scolding herself for her physical reaction to him. As though she could control it.

"Well. I'm expecting a client in a few minutes, so …" It was a lie, but she needed to get off the phone because, might as well admit it—it hurt to talk to him knowing that he didn't want her.

"Ah. Okay. I won't keep you," he said. But he still didn't hang up. After a few more seconds of awkward silence, he said, "Um, Gen. I … ah … I was just wondering if you'd like to go out again sometime."

"Really?"

"Yeah. Another dinner, maybe. Or we could go riding again—you were really good at it for a first-timer. Or … I don't know. Whatever you'd like to do."

Now she was the one who was silent for an awkwardly long stretch.

"What took you so long?" she demanded finally.

"What?"

She'd gone from cool and businesslike to confrontational in a heartbeat. She hadn't planned it, but her emotions were seesawing.

"We went out," she said. "We kissed. You kissed me. And I thought it was a very good kiss. And then … nothing. Do you know how many lame excuses I made to show up at your house, thinking that if you saw me, if I were right there in front of you, then you'd make a move? Jeez. What the hell was your problem?"

At first, she was horrified by the words coming out of her mouth. She'd intended to play the part of Cool Woman Who Couldn't Care Less, but she'd ended up portraying Vulnerable Woman Carrying a Torch. Then she thought, screw it. This is who I am. This is how I'm feeling. He can take it or leave it.

"I'm sorry," he said.

"Okay."

"I should have called you."

"You're right. You should have."

"But I'm calling now. I guess I just … I had to figure out where I was going with this, what I wanted to do."

"And did you?" she demanded.

"Yeah. I figured out that I really want to see you."

Still in offensive mode, lips pursed, one fist planted on her hip, Gen nodded. "Well, it's about time. Pick me up tonight at seven." She hung up on him before he could answer.

She looked at the phone in her hand and smacked it down onto the desk.

"Goddamn right," she said.

Ryan didn't pick Gen up at seven. He didn't pick her up at all, though he wasn't to blame. The blame lay squarely with someone else: Gordon Kendrick.

Gen was right in the middle of primping for her date—fluffing up her hair, choosing an outfit, picking out the right shade of lipstick to complement her skin tone—when Kendrick called her, panic forcing an edge into his voice.

"It's all wrong!" Kendrick wailed into the phone, obviously already well into a bottle of whatever it was he was drinking these days. "I can't do it. Not out here, in the middle of nowhere. It was a mistake to come here. I'm going home."

"Wait. What?" Gen said in disbelief. "You can't do what?"

"I can't paint!"

"Of course you can," Gen insisted. Her pulse started to pound. "I've done everything you've asked. I got you the yogurt you wanted. I got you the sheets. I even got you a damned skylight!"

"It's not that," Kendrick moaned. "It's not … Yes. You've done everything I've asked. But it's not working! Everything I do is shit! I can't fucking paint!"

Gen held the phone to her ear and pressed a hand to her forehead to make sure her brain wasn't going to come flying out. She'd busted her butt for this asshole, and this was what she got?

"Gordon," she said in a tone that was deliberate, calm, and serious as hell. "You signed a contract. I promised you living quarters and a stipend, and you promised to produce art work. I've held up my end of the deal. I've *more* than held up my end. You are not going to … to have some kind of *tantrum* so you can renege on your contractual obligation."

"Do you think I *want* to paint insipid crap? Do you think I *want* to lose every last ounce of my creative inspiration? Do you think this is all about *you* and your damned contract?"

She heard some ragged breathing and realized with horror that he'd started to cry.

"Gordon …"

"I want to go *home,*" he wailed like a kid at an ill-fated slumber party.

Gen looked at the clock on her bedside table. Ryan was scheduled to pick her up in less than twenty minutes.

"Gordon, just don't do anything, okay? Just relax tonight, get some rest. And stop drinking. I'll come over tomorrow and we'll talk this out."

"I want you to come get me," he said. "I need …" She heard some rustling sounds.

"What are you doing?"

"I'm packing."

"*What?!*"

"I need you to come get me and take me to the airport."

Gen took some deep breaths and closed her eyes. "We can't do anything tonight," she tried again. "There won't be any flights out this late." She had no idea if that was true. "I can come over tomorrow, and we'll talk."

"Fine. I'll get a cab." She heard more rustling, and she imagined him cramming heaps of clothing and other detritus into his suitcase.

"No. Wait. Just … just sit tight," Gen said, cursing under her breath. "I'll be right there."

She hung up the phone and looked at herself in the mirror, in her date outfit and her nice hair. All of that hotness, just so she could talk Gordon Kendrick off the ledge.

Shit.

She picked up the phone again and called Ryan. She hoped he'd pick up, and that he wasn't already on his way here.

"Gen," he said, and he sounded so pleased to hear from her that she felt awful about canceling their date. She felt awful about it anyway, because it meant she definitely wouldn't be getting laid.

"Something happened," she said, and filled him in on the details.

"I'll meet you at the guest cottage," he told her.

"You will?"

"Sure. Somebody's gotta make sure he doesn't leave before you get here, right? I'm already here." The way he said it made it seem like simply the logical thing.

"Thank you," she told him. "Really, thank you. I'll be right there."

She hurried out to the ranch still in midprep for her date; she was wearing eyeliner but had not yet applied mascara, and she was carrying the big, clunky purse she used for work rather than the sleek little bag she'd planned to bring to dinner. And she hadn't yet put on the accessories she'd chosen. Her necklace and earrings still sat on her dresser, waiting for her.

None of that mattered, though, if Kendrick was going to flee the ranch. The money she'd spent, the time she'd put into the artist-in-residence' program—all of it would be gone, wasted, if he got into a cab or a rental car and scurried back to Chicago before the residency was over. She'd have to sue him for breach of contract, and the very thought of that caused a knot of stress to form in her chest. She might spend thousands on a lawyer and never get back her investment.

When she pulled her car up to the guest cottage, Kendrick was hauling a suitcase out onto the front porch, and Ryan was talking to him, trying to calm him down.

"Let's just go back inside and talk about this," Ryan was saying as Gen got out of her car. "The cab's not even here yet. We've got time to just settle down, think this through."

Oh, shit. If Kendrick had called a cab, this might not be simply a show of drama, a display of fragile artistic tempera-ment. He might really intend to get the hell out of here. Gen went into damage control mode. She took a moment to calm herself before she got out of the car and walked purposefully toward the cottage.

"Gordon," she said in the most soothing tone she could muster. "What's going on here?"

Kendrick looked disheveled, his clothes askew and his hair sticking up in all directions, his man bun flopping pathetically. Gen could smell the alcohol from here. "I told you on the phone," he said. "I'm leaving. I can't work here. I feel trapped. There's no air! I can't breathe!"

Kendrick turned away from her to go back into the cot-tage and retrieve more of his belongings, and Gen looked at

Ryan and rolled her eyes extravagantly to indicate the depth, the sheer size, of Kendrick's absurdity.

Wordlessly, she pointed to Kendrick's suitcase, which was sitting on the porch, and then made a sweeping motion with her hands to indicate that he should put the case back inside the cottage. Ryan grabbed the handle of the big Samsonite and hauled it back in the door, Gen following close behind.

Inside the little guest house, Kendrick had an armload of his things and was carrying them toward the door. Apparently, he planned to take his shampoo, razor, spare shoes, and umbrella back to Chicago without the benefit of a bag to contain them.

"Gordon, please. Let's just sit down on the sofa and talk," Gen said in a soothing voice she imagined police used to calm hostage-takers.

"There's nothing to talk about," Kendrick said. "It's over. I can't paint. My career is finished. I'm going home." A stick of deodorant fell from his arms and clattered onto the floor, and he made no move to retrieve it.

"Your career isn't finished. Here, let me take this." Gen reached out and started taking the collection of random belongings out of Kendrick's arms and setting them on the coffee table. "There. That's better," she said when he'd been relieved of his burdens. "Now, sit down. Let me make you a cup of tea." Kendrick had tea, Gen knew—he'd insisted on a particular brand that she'd had to have shipped from India.

She went into the kitchen and started rooting around through the cupboards for the tea. When she found it, she filled a kettle with water and turned on the stove. Ryan came into the kitchen and whispered to her.

"I heard a car pulling up outside. It's the cab. What do you want me to do?"

"Get rid of him!" Gen hissed at him.

"We can't hold this guy prisoner," Ryan shot back.

"Just get rid of the cab! Tell him we changed our minds! Tell him … tell him Kendrick got another ride! Just get rid of him! And get out there before he rings the doorbell!" Gen shoved at Ryan's shoulders, pushing him toward the front door.

With Ryan gone, she continued with the tea, using the task to stall for time so she could think about what to do. She poured hot water over the tea bag and thought about artists and their egos. She thought about Gordon Kendrick and his particular ego. By the time the tea was ready, she had just about settled on a strategy.

"Here we go," she said brightly to Kendrick as she set the cup of hot tea on the coffee table in front of him.

"Oh," he said, frowning at the tea, looking crestfallen.

"Is there something wrong?"

"You forgot to add the milk and sugar."

"Of course." Gen wanted to throttle the guy, but instead, she hurried into the kitchen to get milk and sugar.

"Make sure it's the soy milk," Kendrick called after her. "And the raw sugar. Lumps, not loose."

She briefly considered searching in the cabinet under the sink for rat poison she could substitute for the sugar—lumps, not loose—but dismissed the idea, because Kendrick couldn't paint if he were dead. She gathered the items he'd demanded and returned to the living room, where she prepared the tea to his specifications.

"There," she said, when he finally sipped the tea and pronounced it acceptable. "Now, let's talk about this."

Ryan came back in through the front door, and Gen shot him an inquiring look. He raised one eyebrow at her, and she took it to mean that the cab was, indeed, gone, but that he was questioning the wisdom of keeping Kendrick here rather than just letting him flee like his ass was on fire.

She questioned it, too. There was a certain appeal to the idea of just letting him go, writing off the expenses, and pretending none of this ever happened. Then, the only sheets and yogurt she'd have to worry about would be her own.

But as she looked at Kendrick huddled on the sofa with his tea, his hair disheveled and his clothes rumpled, with dark circles under his eyes and the smell of bourbon drifting up from him, she realized this was about more than her business investment.

Arrogant or not, a pain in the ass or not, the guy was having a genuine crisis. She knew what it was like to feel as though your entire career was bursting into flames and burning down to a heaping pile of ash.

She sat down on the sofa next to Kendrick and her voice softened.

"Gordon. Just take a few deep breaths and tell me what's going on." She put a hand on his arm, and he seemed taken aback by the one small gesture of compassion.

He told her.

With Ryan leaning a hip against the kitchen counter listening in, Kendrick told Gen about his efforts out in the barn, his attempts to paint, his endless, fruitless sketches of concepts and ideas, and his ultimate, deep conviction that everything he'd produced since he'd been here had been a hot, steaming pile of shit.

He cried—not loud, showy boo-hooing, but quiet tears that slipped down his face and plunked wetly onto his shirt— and her heart hurt for him.

"I think Chicago is my muse," Kendrick concluded, snuffling into a tissue that Gen had handed him. "I think I need to go back."

"Gordon," Gen began. She leaned toward him with conviction and enthusiasm. "The work you did in Chicago was good. It was very good. But you haven't had your big breakthrough yet. You know I'm right. And as long as you keep doing what you've always done, you'll keep getting the results you've always gotten."

"The blender," Ryan said from where he stood observing them with his arms crossed over his chest.

"Yes!" Gen said. "The blender!"

She explained the blender concept to Kendrick—how if he kept putting the same ingredients into his blender, the result would be an acceptable but bland smoothie that would keep his career on its same flat trajectory.

"But this …" Gen gestured to the world around her. "…The ranch, Cambria, California … It's all new ingredients. If you put new stuff into the blender, you're going to get something new and fresh and exciting!"

She found herself pumped up by her own motivational speech. She wondered if it was all bullshit, and she decided it probably was not. There probably was something to the blender concept.

"But …" Kendrick rubbed at his face with his hands, folded over onto himself, his knees splayed. "It's not working. It's not … blending. I think the blender's broken."

"The blender isn't broken," Gen said soothingly, putting a hand on his back to comfort him. "This is all perfectly normal! It's a well-known fact that creative people sometimes have a big emotional crisis right before a breakthrough. You don't get new growth without some pain, Gordon. It's like …" She scrambled for a simile. "It's like birth!" she finally concluded. "Birth is a painful, bloody process, Gordon, but at the end of it, you get new life. You get new creation. Freshness, and ... and infinite potential!"

Gordon looked up from where he'd buried his face in his hands, and she saw a glimmer of something there, a hint of something in his eyes that said she was reaching him. It was time to close the deal, time to bring this train into the station.

"Here's what we're going to do," she said. "We're going to get you out of that barn, for one thing. The barn is great—especially with the new skylight." She shot an apologetic look toward Ryan. "But working indoors, simulating outdoor light—it's what you've always done."

"It's the same old ingredients in the blender," Gordon put in, and she knew she was getting somewhere.

"Right. Exactly. So, starting tomorrow, we're going to get you outside."

Kendrick made a snuffling noise and sat up straighter. "I don't know. I don't think I'm ready for that. It just ... It doesn't feel right."

"Will you at least think about it?" Gen rubbed Kendrick's back with her palm in tight little circles.

"I suppose so."

"And, Gordon? You need to stop drinking."

"But ..."

"Just while you're here," Gen reassured him. "Just while we're working out your creative issues. You might have a muse in Chicago, Gordon, but I know you've also got one here. And you can't hear her talk to you if you're ..." She hesitated, not wanting to choose a word that would offend him.

"If you're lit up like a goddamned Christmas tree," Ryan put in.

She wondered if that last part might have taken it too far, but Kendrick nodded at her, and she felt buoyed.

"Okay, then," Gen said. She gave her thighs a prim little pat, as though she were a first-grade teacher saying it was time for recess. "Let's just get you unpacked."

Chapter Eighteen

Gen and Ryan unpacked and put away Kendrick's things and got the cottage back in order while Kendrick lolled around on the sofa, looking frazzled and depressed but more or less resigned to staying. When they were done, Gen coaxed Kendrick up from the sofa and shooed him into the bedroom to get ready for bed. It was early still—not quite nine p.m.—but Kendrick needed to sleep off the alcohol and the self-doubt so he could start fresh the next day.

Once Kendrick was asleep—he was snoring loudly less than fifteen minutes after being nudged into the bedroom—Gen leaned limply against the back of the bedroom door and sighed.

"That was a close one," she said.

Ryan was leaning his hip against the kitchen counter, his arms folded over his chest, in the position he'd adopted since arriving here earlier this evening. "Is it true all that stuff you said about artists having a crisis before a big breakthrough?"

"I have no idea." Gen ran a hand through her loose curls. "It could be. It sounded true."

He raised his eyebrows at her. "Nice improvisation."

Gen went into the tiny kitchen and picked up the partial bottle of bourbon that was sitting on the counter. "I guess this has to go." She opened the bottle and started pouring the remainder of the bourbon into the sink. A second or two into it, she stopped pouring.

"Wait a minute," she said.

She opened a cabinet and rooted around, then brought out a couple of glasses. She poured two fingers of bourbon for herself, then looked questioningly at Ryan. At his nod, she poured some for him as well.

She held up her glass and clinked it against his, then took a sip and felt the liquid burn down the back of her throat.

"Jesus," she said, scowling at the bedroom door and Kendrick behind it. "After all this, he's probably just going to leave tomorrow when he sobers up."

Ryan shrugged. "Well. You can't exactly keep him here against his will."

"I know." She went over to the sofa and slumped down onto it with her glass in her hand. "I just really wanted this to work."

"So you can go back to New York?" He brought his drink to the sofa and sat down next to her.

"Not even that," she said. "I just wanted to achieve something. In the art world, I mean. I wanted to redeem myself, I guess."

"Redeem yourself from what?" He stretched out on the sofa and looked at her with interest.

"That's right. You haven't heard the full story."

So she told him about Davis MacIntyre, about the sexual harassment and the fraud, and how she'd fled the city with a payoff from MacIntyre and a black mark against her name in every gallery in the city.

She shook her head and polished off what was left in her glass. "I guess I just wanted to prove something."

Ryan took the last sip of his bourbon and put the glass down on the coffee table. "I guess I don't see why you want to prove something to people who treated you so badly in the first place."

She regarded him. "No, you wouldn't."

"What's that supposed to mean?"

She shrugged. "You just seem so confident. So self-assured. You know your place in the world. I can't imagine you feeling like you need to prove anything to anyone."

Ryan let out a low laugh and rubbed at his eyes with one hand. "That's because you don't know Sandra Delaney."

"Your mom? I know your mom."

"You know her," Ryan said, "but you don't *know* her."

Gen considered that. The bourbon was seeping into her system, and she was beginning to feel warm and relaxed.

"I can see that she's a little ... rigid, maybe," Gen allowed.

Ryan nodded slowly. "She is that. Look, I don't want to give you the wrong impression. She's a great mom. As steady and constant as the earth. Always there for me and my brothers and sister."

"But?" Gen prompted.

"But, there was always that feeling that if you weren't doing things the Sandra Delaney way, you were a disappointment. And the Sandra Delaney way is never the easy way." He gave her a wry smile.

She regarded him, all tall and strong and at ease with himself. "I seriously doubt you're a disappointment."

"No, I don't think I am," he said. "But there's always that worry, that fear of not quite measuring up."

She shifted on the sofa, turning to face him more fully. "Look, Ryan. About that time at Kate and Jackson's party, when I got so drunk ..."

He grinned. "That was months ago."

"I know."

"You don't have to be embarrassed." He shrugged. "People get drunk sometimes. It happens. I've been known to do it once or twice myself."

"Yeah. But ..."

"But what?"

Her pulse sped as she weighed whether she should go ahead with what she was about to tell him. Part of her said she should keep the walls she'd erected intact, keep him at a safe distance, protect her heart. But another part of her said that nothing was ever gained without risk. Especially when it came to love.

"But, I never told you why I got drunk."

He waited, and she plunged forward with the heady, reckless abandon of a gambler laying all of her chips on a soft seventeen.

"Part of it was because of Davis MacIntyre dying, and what that meant to my future, my career. And part of it was about Kate moving in with Jackson, which I thought meant she didn't need me anymore. But the rest of it ..."

He raised his eyebrows, listening, waiting.

"You couldn't stop talking about Lacy that night. About how much you wanted to be with her. You kept asking me about her, what she liked, what she didn't like, what kind of men she dates." Gen swallowed hard. "And I was jealous. I wanted you to want *me*."

The tension filled the air between them like a gathering storm.

He eased closer to her on the sofa. He put his palm against her cheek and ran his thumb over her skin. Then he leaned in and gently touched his lips to hers. She closed her eyes and felt a pure, crystalline rush of happiness and need.

She put her arms around him and deepened the kiss. Her blood rushed faster and her senses were heightened, as though this moment were more real, more present, than those that had gone before.

She knew she should hold back; this wasn't the place for this, and whatever existed between them was so new. But the longer they kissed, the greater the urgency she felt as she pulled him to her and ran her hands over his back, his arms, before entwining her fingers in his hair.

"Gen." His voice was husky and rough.

She pulled back just a little, her mouth a hair's breadth from his. "Ryan. I want this. I really want this. But I can't do this if …"

"Tell me."

"I can't do this if Lacy is the one you really want."

He looked at her for just a moment, those dark eyes alight with desire. Then, with breathtaking suddenness, he scooped her into his lap and picked her up from the sofa, standing with her in his arms.

She let out a little yelp. "What are you doing?"

"Kendrick's in the other room," he said simply. Then he carried her out the front door and kicked it closed behind him.

Outside, the temperature was mild and the tang of sea air filled her senses.

"Your house?" Gen said.

"Whole family's there," he answered.

"Car?"

They both looked at Gen's car, a tiny little two-door. Ryan was six-foot-three.

They looked at each other and they both said, at the same time, "Barn."

Gen giggled and he gave her a little toss to seat her more comfortably in his arms. Then he set out with long, confident strides toward the old barn, with its new skylight that she imagined would let in silvery strands of moonlight.

The barn wasn't far, but it was far enough. Far enough that she'd have thought carrying a one-hundred-and-twenty-pound woman there would be out of the question. But he hardly seemed to notice her weight—he made carrying her seem effortless, and his strength, his pure manly force, turned her on even more. Snuggled up so close to him, she could feel his heartbeat against her chest.

By the time they got inside the barn with its pale, shimmering light and its smells of hay and earth, the blood was pounding in places she'd neglected for far too long.

He set her down inside the barn and she looked up at him, breathless. Then he tangled his fingers in her waves and waves of glorious hair and kissed her.

She'd imagined this for so long. Had a raging crush on Ryan Delaney for so long. How many times had she wondered how his mouth would taste? How many times had she wondered how his body would feel pressed against hers? There was, of course, the potential that the reality—when it finally came—could pale in comparison with the fantasy. That the fact of him could let down, disappoint. But the way he kissed her, the way he handled her—all firm, manly confidence, forceful in a way that made her feel as feminine and delicate as a flower—was so much better than what she'd expected. So much *more*.

She gave back everything, and more. Her hands roamed his chest, his arms, his face, taking in the feel of him, of everything. The kiss, the long, passionate kiss, the claiming of her mouth by his, sent shivers of need through her body. She unbuttoned his shirt, then pulled it off of him. She grabbed the T-shirt she found underneath and yanked it over his head.

And oh, God, the glory of his naked torso was so much better than what she'd pictured in her mind. Sculpted muscles, hard planes. Skin golden from time spent in the sun.

"Ah, Gen," he murmured into her ear, and it was *her* name he said, all breathy and rough, not Lacy's. No one else's but hers.

They kissed again and she nipped at his lips with her teeth. She wanted to devour him.

She was wearing the dress she'd planned for their date—the date that hadn't happened—and he reached around her and drew down the zipper, slowly, all the way to the small of her back. He put his hands on her shoulders and eased the dress off of them, down her arms, until the fabric pooled on the floor at her feet.

"You're beautiful," he whispered in a voice made rough by desire.

Suddenly, he picked her up again and she wrapped her legs around his waist as he carried her further into the barn.

Ideally, he should have thrown her down onto a soft pile of hay, but this was the old barn, and it hadn't been in use for a few years except for storage, and—most recently—Gordon Kendrick. So there was no pile of hay, and instead he had to grab a thick, wool blanket from the boxes of stuff piled up in one corner of the cavernous space. Still carrying her in one arm, he shook out the blanket with his free hand and tossed it on the floor, spreading it out with his foot while she giggled.

"That would probably be easier if you put me down," she said, laughing at his efforts to arrange the blanket while holding her.

"Like hell," he said. "I'm not letting go of you."

She looked into his big, dark eyes. "Oh."

He went down onto his knees with her still wrapped around him, then lowered her onto the blanket. He looked at her lying there, with her smooth, white skin and her flaming red hair spread out around her.

"You're gorgeous," he said. "God. Just look at you." He ran his hands down over her, her throat, her belly, her legs, and she shivered in the wake of his touch.

"I want you so much, Ryan," she whimpered. "I've wanted you so much …"

"Shh."

He lifted her up just a little, so he could unclasp her lacy bra and slip it off of her shoulders. Then he lowered his mouth to her breasts, tasting one of the pink peaks and then the other. She groaned and squirmed beneath him, impatient with the force of her arousal.

"I love your breasts," he murmured, his mouth so close to her skin that she could feel the tickle of his warm breath.

Then he slid her panties off of her hips and down her thighs.

Lying naked beneath him, with him still partially dressed, was so erotic she almost had an orgasm right then. She tugged at his belt. "Now you."

She unbuckled him, undid the snap, and slid his zipper down with the same teasing slowness he'd used with hers.

He groaned at her touch, then pulled away from her long enough to free himself from his jeans.

When they were both naked, both clothed in nothing but the moonlight filtering through the skylight, he used his mouth on her again, kissing the hollow between her breasts before moving downward, making a hot trail down her body with his tongue.

"Ryan. Please. I need you, right now. Please."

"In a little bit," he said, a hint of a tease in his voice. He kept working his way downward with his mouth until he was between her silky legs. He kissed the insides of her thighs, increasing her torment, until finally using his tongue on her warm folds.

"Oh. Oh." She tangled her fingers in his hair, her entire body on fire with urgency. "Ryan. Oh."

When he'd brought her right to edge of the abyss, he stopped, rose up her body, and knelt before her.

"I ... shit," she murmured. "I didn't bring a condom. I'm on the pill, but ..."

"Shhh." He hushed her, and reached over to where his jeans had been discarded. He pulled a little foil packet out of one of the back pockets.

"Oh, thank God," she said.

When he was ready, he lowered himself onto her and she felt the delicious sensation of his body pressing into hers. It felt so right, so perfect, that her body sang with the joy of it. As he moved inside her, he ran his hands over her round, heavy breasts, the delicious curves of her ass. She thrummed with pleasure, and she wondered briefly if it were possible to be driven insane by sexual bliss. The pressure, the tension of her passion rose and rose until she cried out with her release.

"Oh, Gen." The words were soft and warm in her ear. He buried his hands in her hair and groaned as his own pleasure peaked.

Afterward, they lay wrapped in each other's arms, damp with sweat, breathing hard.

"God," she said and laughed, a low, throaty sound. "I knew it would be good if we ever did this. I knew. But this ... So much better than the fantasy."

He ran a finger gently across her face, moving a curl of hair away from her eyes. "You fantasized about me?"

"I might have." She grinned. "Once or twice."

"Hmm." He planted light kisses on her neck, her shoulder.

"We were supposed to have a date first," she said, teasing.

"We did."

"We did not."

"Of course we did." He said the words as he moved his head down toward her belly, teasing the skin with his tongue. "I don't know about you, but I always take my dates to talk crazy artists off a ledge. So much more stimulating than dinner and a movie."

She felt his breath as a tickle against her damp skin as he spoke.

She laughed.

"Well, I feel stimulated."

"Me too."

She watched his face in the moonlight as he held her, and she thought that no matter what happened between them, she never wanted to forget this moment, right here, right now. The way he looked at her, the way his voice sounded as he murmured her name.

Chapter Nineteen

"You did it in the *barn*? You had barn sex?" Rose looked at Gen with interest, her pierced eyebrow arching skyward. "Barn sex with an actual cowboy. God. I am so jealous right now."

Gen, Rose, Kate, and Lacy were gathered at Kate's house the next morning. They sat around the dining room table with mugs of coffee in front of them while Jackson worked in the kitchen, making omelets.

"Ah, jeez, I should *not* be hearing this," Jackson muttered as he flipped a mushroom and onion omelet.

The kitchen timer dinged, and Jackson pulled a tray of blueberry muffins from the oven.

"Man, it must be nice living with a chef," Lacy commented as they all got a whiff of warm muffins.

"It is," Kate commented, "but then you have to deal with a guy hovering around when you're trying to talk about barn sex."

"As soon as the food is done, I'm out of here," he said, sounding distinctly uncomfortable.

"I could have cooked," Kate said to him. "You didn't have to do this."

"You burn your omelets," Jackson said. "And you make muffins from a boxed mix."

"True," Kate acknowledged.

"You've got to admire a man with standards," Rose said.

"Thank you," Jackson replied.

"So. The barn sex," Lacy said to Gen. "How was our rancher friend? Did he meet expectations?"

"Ah, jeez," Jackson groaned.

"Whatever I say, Jackson is going to repeat to Ryan," Gen said, cutting a piece of omelet with her fork.

"Goddamn right I am," Jackson said.

"Ah. Good point. We'll wait," Lacy said, batting her eyelashes at Jackson over the rim of her coffee mug.

"There." Jackson put the last of the food on the table, looking relieved that he could now flee the scene.

"Thank you for doing this," Kate said warmly, pulling him down toward her for a kiss.

"You're welcome."

"I'll clean up. You can escape now."

"Thank God."

He ducked into the bedroom, and within a few minutes he was in his running clothes and had gone out the front door for a jog.

"This omelet is fabulous," Gen said. "Jackson's a really good guy."

"He is," Kate agreed.

"The good guy is gone now, so spill about the barn sex," Rose demanded.

"Yes, spill," Lacy agreed.

So she told them about the ruined date, and persuading Kendrick not to leave Cambria, and talking about their lives over the last of Kendrick's bourbon. And when she got to the part about Ryan scooping her up in his arms and carrying her to the barn, her three friends swooned.

"Oh, God. He *carried* you?" Rose said.

"He did." Gen couldn't quite keep the smile off her face.

"Maybe you should have gone out with him when you had the chance," Kate said to Lacy.

"This is what I'm thinking," Lacy agreed.

Gen pointed one finger at Lacy. "Don't you dare. Hands off."

Lacy raised her hands in surrender. "Don't worry, I had my chance. I'd never break the Girlfriend Code of Honor. And anyway, I doubt he's thinking much about me anymore." She batted her eyelashes at Gen.

"God, I hope not," Gen said.

They ate their omelets and muffins and drank their coffee next to a wall of windows that looked out on a spectacular view of the ocean. The morning was crisp and clear. Seagulls soared in the distance over the breaking waves.

"I've never had barn sex," Kate said wistfully. "I want barn sex."

"Well, most of us have never had bookstore sex, so you're one up on us there," Rose observed.

"True," Kate said.

"So, you never said," Lacy prompted Gen. "How was it? Was it fun?"

"No." Gen looked at her plate, avoiding their eyes.

"No? Oh, honey." Kate reached out and put a hand over Gen's on the table.

"No. It wasn't fun. It was …" Gen shook her head. "Fun is too small a word for what it was."

"Oh," Rose sighed.

"I think I might be in trouble now," Gen said. "I mean … I've had a crush on him for a long time. But now …"

"Oh, no. You're in love," Lacy said.

"I think I might be, yeah." Gen had barely touched her food, and now she'd lost her appetite entirely.

"Is that a bad thing?" Kate asked gently.

"It is if he doesn't feel the same way," Gen insisted. "It is if, for him, it was just ..." She waved her hands vaguely, looking for the right word. "Fun."

Lacy put down her fork and looked at Gen. "I've known Ryan Delaney for a long time. We went to high school together. And I have never known him to use women just for the hell of it."

"Unlike Jackson," Kate put in wryly.

"Jackson's changed. You changed him," Rose said.

"My point is," Lacy said, getting back to the topic, "Ryan was never like that. Back in school, he didn't date very often, but when he did, he'd be with the same girl for a really long time. He was never looking for fun. He was looking for a relationship."

"Huh," Gen said.

"It's been a while since I've heard about him dating anybody," Rose put in. "And you know how word gets around in this town. We'd have heard. I think Lacy's right. He's not going to play with your emotions just to get laid."

Gen poked at her food with her fork. "Well, then I've got another problem, I guess."

"The am-I-really-ready-for-a-big-relationship problem," Kate supplied.

"Exactly," Gen said.

"Well, are you?" Lacy asked.

"And what happens if you really are going back to New York?" Rose said.

Gen sighed. "That sums up the problem, all right."

Ryan was grappling with a similar issue as he rode out to the southwest pasture to check on the cattle. Only he didn't have a group of friends handy to talk it out—if men did that sort of thing. He only had the cows, and he didn't think he'd get any sound relationship advice there.

No, he hadn't been toying with Gen. He hadn't been using her just for pleasure. He had feelings for her. Real feelings. Why else would he have put a damned skylight in the barn? He sure as hell hadn't done it for Kendrick.

But Gen had been straight with him that she didn't plan to stay in Cambria. She'd made no secret of that. The whole reason she'd brought Kendrick out here was to drum up the money and the clout she needed to relocate to New York.

He'd be a fool to think she'd change her mind about staying just because of him. And he couldn't kid himself that going to New York with her would be a simple thing. His family had been on the ranch for generations. His brothers had left to pursue other things. His parents were counting on him to run the operation here. What would happen if he left? Who would his parents turn to? Breanna would be the only one of his siblings still here, and she had never had much of an interest in ranching. If she suddenly decided to take on a big role working the ranch—which seemed unlikely—she'd have a lot to learn before she could take Ryan's place.

That was the practical side. The emotional side—which, to him, was just as compelling—was that the Delaney Ranch was so much a part of who he was as a person, so much a key element in his soul, that he doubted he could successfully make the adjustment to a life elsewhere. And that was assuming she would even want him to come.

What about a long-distance relationship? He pondered that as he dismounted Annie and went to check on a calf and its mother near the northwest corner of the pasture. The grass swished between his legs as he walked.

Ryan approached the cow and her calf slowly, speaking soothing words to them. When the calf had been born, the mother had initially rejected him. It happened sometimes. After a few days of forced nursing—Ryan had enclosed the mother in a pen and immobilized her to allow the newborn to feed—she'd warmed up to the calf some, but Ryan was still keeping an eye on them to make sure everything was going smoothly.

He examined the calf, looking for signs of weight loss and checking its abdomen for indications that it hadn't been eating and drinking properly. He observed its breathing, and checked its face for discharge from the nose or eyes. That done, he simply stood back and observed the calf for a while to see how it was eating and moving. When the calf raised its tail and released a steaming pile of manure, Ryan ambled over and took a look at the pile. That was one of his least favorite parts of the job, but you could tell a lot about an animal's health from the look of its manure. He drew the line at sifting through it, though. A man had to have some boundaries.

"He looks pretty good," Ryan said to no one.

Ryan wondered if Gen liked animals.

There she was, in his head again: Gen. He sighed.

Ryan didn't do casual hookups, he didn't look at sex as simple recreation, and he didn't hold his heart in check when he cared about someone.

When he was in, he was all in.

But he also knew that the ranch was his home—always had been, always would be. And he didn't hold any illusions about the idea of persuading Gen to stay. If he tried that, and it worked, she'd resent him—maybe not right away, but eventually. He couldn't live that way.

He briefly wondered whether he should sabotage the whole Kendrick deal so she couldn't go, but then laughed at himself, knowing that he'd never do such a thing.

The calf looked at him like he was an idiot. The calf was probably right.

"Well, shit," he said.

Chapter Twenty

If he were a different kind of guy, he probably would have gone ahead and sabotaged the Kendrick deal to get Gen to stay. But he was Ryan—for better or for worse—and so he checked on Kendrick later that day to make sure he was doing okay.

It was around midmorning by the time he finished with the calf, met with some of the ranch hands to assign tasks for the day, and rode Annie to the guest cottage. When he got there, he knocked on the door, but Kendrick didn't answer. Had Kendrick fled after all? And what would that mean to Gen? But then he remembered the old barn—the site of such happy recent memories—and found Kendrick there, bathed in the illumination of the skylight, doing something unidentifiable to a big, rectangular canvas.

"Mr. Kendrick," Ryan said in greeting.

Kendrick looked up suddenly and blinked, as though waking from a sound sleep. "Oh. Hello." His tone was not unfriendly, but he went right back to doing whatever it was he'd been doing with the paint.

"You're working," Ryan observed.

"I'm ... Well, yes. I had an idea," Kendrick said. He didn't expand on the thought. He just went back to mixing paint on a palette and flinging it onto the canvas with the tip of his brush.

Ryan went outside, and when he judged that he was far enough away to be out of Kendrick's earshot, he pulled out his cell phone and dialed Gen.

"Ryan," she said. She sounded pleased to hear from him, and that made him happier than he would have expected. A little bloom of warmth spread across his chest.

"Kendrick's painting," he said.

"He's what?"

"I'm out here at the old barn. Thought I'd better check and see whether he took his crap and ran away during the night. And there he was, painting. At least, I think you'd call that painting. Didn't look like anything but blobs of color to me."

"Oh, thank God," Gen said, the relief in her voice almost palpable. "Did he seem drunk?"

"No. Now that you mention it, he didn't."

"Okay. Okay, that's really good news. I was going to come out there anyway, because I thought I'd have to talk him down again. As soon as Alex gets here to take over at the gallery, I'm on my way. I want to talk to Kendrick … see the lay of the land, so to speak."

The thought that Gen was coming to the ranch—and coming soon—made Ryan stupidly happy. He chided himself. He had things to do—a lot of things. The ranch wasn't going to run itself. He had a full day ahead of him, and would have had a full day, in fact, even if that day were far longer than twenty-four hours. And yet, here he was pondering how he could wait around for her without it seeming like he was waiting around for her.

His mother would laugh at him if she knew.

He considered his options. He could find something to work on at the guest cottage, so he'd be there when she arrived. Or he could find something to work on at the old barn. Or there were the various areas of the ranch within sight of the road she would use to drive in—he could just happen to be replacing a fence post near the gate that led to Kendrick's place.

Then he realized that was stupid. He pulled his phone out of his pocket and dialed Gen again. When she picked up, he said, "Call me when you get here. I want to see you."

"I will," she said, and he could hear the smile in her voice.

"Good."

He disconnected, shoved the phone back into his pocket, and nodded. There. Much easier than replacing a perfectly good fence post.

Gen made the drive to the Delaney Ranch feeling optimistic. Kendrick was painting. She was riding on a cloud of afterglow from last night's impossibly good sex. And Ryan wanted to see her, making her wonder when that impossibly good sex might happen again.

She might even have been singing as she drove through the gate and up toward Kendrick's guest cottage. Though she would never admit to such a thing, should anyone ask.

She parked her car by the cottage and got out. The sky was so blue it almost hurt her eyes to look at it, and she heard the murmur of crashing waves in the distance. A light breeze rippled the grass, and birds chattered over her in the trees.

Jesus, the only things missing were some animated birds and some Disney music.

She leaned against her car and pulled her phone out of her purse. She texted Ryan:

I'm here.

He texted back:

So I see.

She looked around her, and there he was, walking up the road with his phone in his hand, doing that sexy Ryan swagger, a lazy smile on his face.

Oh God, she thought. *I am in so much trouble.*

"Hey," she called to him.

"Hey."

"So, Kendrick's painting?"

"He is."

There was the thrill of seeing him, all dark-haired and tousled from work, his espresso-colored eyes roaming over her, taking her in. But there was also the awkwardness of having slept with him without really knowing the status of their relationship. What should she do? Should she run to him and throw herself into his arms, like she wanted to? Or should she play it cool, pretend last night never happened, and see where he went with it?

When he reached her, he ran one hand slowly down her arm, on a leisurely trip from her shoulder to her elbow. He looked down at her with a half-grin, his eyes crinkling at the corners in pleasure, and she simply melted. She tilted her face toward his, and he kissed her as easily as if they'd been doing it their whole lives.

That settled the issue of whether to pretend last night hadn't happened; it sure as hell had. She felt as warm and languid as a cat napping in a patch of sunlight.

"Well, hi," she said, her eyes fluttering open after the kiss.

"I've been thinking about you all morning. All night, too."

There was that smile again. How was it that somebody so goddamned gorgeous had stayed single this long?

Time to get her head back in the game, though.

"So. Kendrick." She said it less resolutely than she'd intended.

"Right," Ryan said. "I don't know if I'd call it painting, but he's out there in the barn doing some damn thing with some paint and a canvas."

She sighed deeply. "That's so great. God. Really. I have to see."

They walked together out to the old barn, holding hands. It felt right to have her hand in his. It felt like her hand was where it belonged.

When they got out to the barn, Gen could see what Ryan had meant about Kendrick doing some damn thing with paint and a canvas. Gen was experienced with art and artists, and even she wasn't sure what Kendrick was doing. As she walked into the barn, he was holding a brush filled with drippy paint in front of his face and blowing on it, sending a fine spray of droplets onto the canvas in front of him. Because he was getting so close to the brush, and because the barn was somewhat breezy with the doors open, little drops of blue had gathered in the vicinity of Kendrick's mouth. He didn't seem to notice.

Considering Kendrick's long period of inactivity, and considering his unusually delicate artistic temperament, Gen considered it prudent to stay silent rather than announcing her presence. While she stood there, he scowled, whisked the canvas off of its easel, tossed it aside, and put a fresh one in place.

After a moment, Gen and Ryan retreated.

"Well, that's promising," Gen said when they were out of Kendrick's earshot.

"If you say so." Ryan sounded skeptical. "He didn't seem too happy with it."

"No, but he's *doing* it. Which is more than I could say for him yesterday."

They walked at a leisurely pace away from the barn and came to a stop under the leafy canopy of an oak tree. Ryan's fingers were still entwined in hers.

"Seems kind of a shame you drove all the way out here just to look at Kendrick for two minutes," Ryan observed.

"Well. I didn't necessarily come out here just to see him," she said.

Ryan's eyebrows rose, and his mouth quirked into a grin. "Is that right?"

"There might have been other factors," Gen said, grinning right back at him. He was so tall in comparison to her five-foot-two frame that she had to crane her neck to look at him. "Ow," she said playfully. "You're too tall. I'm gonna hurt my neck."

"Come here, shorty," he said. With no warning, he lifted her up into his arms and pressed her back against the trunk of the oak. She squealed with surprise. With nowhere else to put them, she wrapped her legs around his waist, feeling grateful that she was wearing slacks instead of a dress. Sandwiched between him and the tree, she was now pretty much level with him.

"That better?" he said.

"Much."

He kissed her, and oh, God, her entire body came alive. The taste of his mouth, the feel of his body pressed against hers, the gentle brush of the breeze on the delicate flesh of her neck.

When he pulled away from her, just slightly, she sighed.

"Too bad the barn's occupied," she quipped.

"I was just thinking the same thing." Gently, he set her back down onto the grassy ground.

"Well. Listen." She was flustered, and she worked to make her voice sound calm and smooth. "As delightful as this was— and it really was—I'll bet you have work to do. I don't want to keep you from … herding cows or … or … whatever it is that you do." She realized that she had, in fact, little to no idea of what he did.

"I can spare some time if you can," he said.

"What did you have in mind?"

He peered down at her shoes—gallery shoes. Pointy-toed black pumps with slim three-inch heels.

"I was gonna say we could take a walk, but you're not really dressed for it."

"I've got other shoes in my car. Hang on."

The car was about a hundred yards away, so with Ryan by her side, she picked her way back to it, walking carefully in her pumps so she wouldn't turn her ankle or drive one of the spiky heels into the soft ground.

At the car, she opened the back door and plopped down on the back seat while she pulled off the pumps and put on a sturdy-looking pair of track shoes.

"You keep running shoes in your car?" he asked.

"Sometimes I go to the gym after work," she told him. "I like to be prepared."

The shoes weren't the best fashion complement to the black slacks and scoop-necked black top she'd worn to the gallery that morning, but sometimes a girl had to be practical. She tucked her purse into the back seat of the car and closed the door.

"I'm ready."

They held hands and walked up a path that led past the old barn, through a grove of oaks, and up onto a hill over-looking the ocean.

Little wildflowers dotted the grass on either side of the path, and butterflies alighted on the blooms.

"It's incredibly beautiful here," Gen said, and realized she was stating the obvious. "I'm surprised some developer hasn't

170 CAMBRIA SKY

come in and bulldozed the whole thing, putting up rows and rows of identical stucco houses. That's what they do here in California, isn't it?"

"That's what they'd like to do," Ryan agreed. "We've had offers. Big offers."

"I'll bet. But this …" She gestured to encompass the grass, the trees, the air, and the world around them. "Covering this up would have been a crime."

"You're not going to get a view like this in Manhattan," he commented.

He was aware that he was treading on delicate territory. They'd gone out once, slept together once, and so it was way out of line for him to suggest—even obliquely—that she should abandon her plans to return to New York. He didn't want to be clingy and possessive just because they'd had sex. Even if it *was* really great sex.

But it was more than the sex. It was the way her copper-colored hair spread out around her in the breeze, catching the sunlight and gleaming. It was the way her firm, compact body fit in his arms. It was the way she smiled when she saw him, like a light had been turned on inside her, brightening everything around her. It was all of that, and other things he couldn't name, things he wasn't sure he could live without now that he'd found them.

Knowing that she ultimately planned to leave—knowing that she didn't intend to make a life here in Cambria—he never should have gotten involved, never should have become attached to this idea of her, this idea of the two of them together. But it was too late for that now. He supposed it was possible she'd change her mind and stay. He wasn't self-centered enough to believe she'd stay just because of him—not this soon into something that couldn't even be called a relationship—but maybe because of everything. She had friends here, good friends. And now she had him, too, and he hoped that would add another weight onto this side of the scale.

He knew what it was to be a man. He knew men were not supposed to make themselves vulnerable, to leave themselves open for heartbreak. But he had an idea that maybe part of what it was to be a man was to love fearlessly, to have that kind of courage. He hoped he was up to that challenge.

"Tell me about it," he said after a while. "About New York. What was your life like there?"

She squeezed his hand and then paused, as though the subject were too large for her to approach without steeling herself first.

"New York," she said finally. "Well. It's so different from here. Have you visited there?"

"Once, when I was in college. A friend and I took a trip out there for a week during winter break. See the Statue of Liberty, go to the top of the Empire State Building. That kind of thing."

She nodded. "Okay, then you have some idea. There's a power, there's a—oh, I don't know—a *life force* pumping through everything. Like you really are at the center of the universe. That thing about it being the city that never sleeps— that's so true. There was always somewhere to go, always something to do. I used to stay out until four a.m. and then work at the gallery all day." She smiled and shook her head at the memory. "Looking back, I don't know where I got that kind of energy."

He considered that. "Being that busy, staying out all night … did you enjoy that kind of thing?"

"I did." Then she seemed to reconsider. "Well. Sometimes I did. But there were other times when it seemed really … exhausting."

"I can imagine." What she was describing was a life so foreign to his own that the very thought of it tired him. He was no stranger to staying up all night, but it was usually to nurse a sick calf or to help a cow give birth. Bars and nightclubs, parties … he'd done some of that in college, but it had grown old fast.

"What about friends?" he asked.

She frowned. "I had a lot of people I knew. A lot of acquaintances. And I thought I had a lot of friends. But not like this. Not like I have here."

That was what he'd hoped she would say—he'd hoped to remind her that she had good, close friendships here—but now he felt manipulative having led her there. And being manipulative made him feel like a dick.

"Look, Gen." They paused on top of a ridge with a view of swaying grass and a horizon of blue water. Some birds flew overhead that might have been sandpipers. "I've got to admit something. I asked about friends because I don't want you to leave. I thought if I reminded you about your friends here in Cambria …"

She looked up at him and gave him a half grin that made him feel soft inside. "You don't want me to leave?"

"Well, no."

She turned to fully face him. "That's interesting."

"You think so?"

"I do."

He shifted uncomfortably. "I know we don't have a relationship yet, not really, but I hope we will, and if we do, and then you decide to go …"

He left it hanging there. If she decided to go, then what? He'd be hurt. He'd miss her. Or perhaps he'd leave the only life he'd ever known to build a new one three thousand miles away. The fact that he was even thinking that way left him confused and worried. Okay, scared. Screw it. He could admit that.

She put her hands on his shoulders, went up on the tips of her toes, and pressed a quick kiss to his lips.

"It's not a sure thing, me leaving. And if I go, it won't be for a while," she said.

"All right."

"And in the meantime … you're hoping this will be a relationship?"

He'd said those words, there was no point in taking them back now. "Well … yeah. I don't want to rush anything, but … yeah."

She grinned at him and lowered herself back onto her heels. "I'm so glad we're not still talking about Lacy."

He pulled her into his arms so suddenly that she gasped.

"Lacy who?" he said, and then silenced her with a long, deep kiss.

Chapter Twenty-One

S ince their date hadn't worked out—or, more precisely, it
had worked out so well that they hadn't actually gone
anywhere—they rescheduled for that weekend.

They'd already been to Neptune, and Ryan wasn't sure
where to take her this time. He wanted to do something
special, though, something fun. He was still pondering it when
he, Jackson, Will, and Daniel gathered at Shamel Park, down by
the beach, for a pickup basketball game. They hadn't played in
months, and Ryan worried that his skills would be lacking from
disuse. He worried that he would embarrass himself.

He did embarrass himself, but not because of his
basketball ability. It was more because he was so distracted by
thoughts of seeing Gen again that he wouldn't have noticed if
the ball had smacked him square in the face.

Which it did, once.

"What the hell's goin' on with you?" Jackson asked after
Ryan completely missed a ball Jackson had passed to him.
"These two jokers are kicking our asses."

"Sorry," Ryan said. Will and Daniel shouldn't have been
kicking their asses; it should have been a pretty fair game. Ryan
had played varsity basketball in high school, and Will was an
excellent baseball player, which seemed to translate to
basketball better than one might expect. With one jock on each
team, it should have worked out, and it would have if Ryan
hadn't been so distracted.

"Seriously, man," Jackson pressed. "Your head's not in
the game. What's going on?"

They'd been playing for about a half an hour, and they
were all starting to breathe hard and sweat. They moved over

to a bench next to the court, where they toweled off and drank some water.

"I went over to the gallery yesterday morning," Daniel said mildly, running a small hand towel through his hair. "Gen wasn't there. Alex said she was at the ranch." He said nothing more, but he looked at Ryan and raised his eyebrows in question.

"Aha," Will said. He hadn't worn his glasses during the game because of the safety hazard, so now he was squinting a little as he looked at Ryan.

"What the ... there's no 'aha,'" Ryan insisted. He busied himself with rooting around in his gym bag.

"That's not what I heard when Kate had Gen and the others over for breakfast the other morning," Jackson observed.

Will and Daniel made a variety of hooting and catcalling noises that Ryan would have found more appropriate if they were fifteen.

"Okay. Look." Ryan faced the three of them. "I'm not going to talk about Gen like that. About ... what might or might not have happened between us."

Jackson nodded appreciatively. "Respectful. I can admire that. Especially since she's my sister-in-law. Practically."

"And my friend," Daniel put in.

"Yeah, well," Ryan said, "whatever she told her friends, that's hers to tell. But I will say this. We've got a date this weekend and I don't know where the hell to take her."

"Hm. You've already been to Neptune," Jackson said.

"Right. A town this small, it's hard to think of a place she hasn't been a thousand times. And I want ... I need ... to impress her."

"Aha," Will said again.

"Shut up," Ryan told him.

"There's The Sandpiper," Daniel offered, suggesting a restaurant with a view of Moonstone Beach.

"Yeah, yeah," Ryan said, blowing off the idea as too ordinary, too pedestrian.

"You could do something outdoorsy," Jackson suggested. "Go kayaking over at San Simeon."

"Hm. Maybe," Ryan allowed.

"Or you could just bring her to the Cooper House," Will said.

All three heads turned toward him.

"The Cooper House?" Ryan said.

"Sure."

Will was the caretaker of an enormous estate just up the coast, not far from the ranch. The Cooper House, a twenty-two-room behemoth atop a hill with a stunning view of the Pacific, was named for Eustace Cooper, the logging tycoon who had originally built the place in the late 1800s. Now it was owned by a tech billionaire who only used the place two or three weeks of the year. The rest of the time, Will tended to the property, bringing in gardeners, painters, plumbers, housecleaners, and others as needed. He lived in a small guest house there while he worked on his dissertation—a study of a particular type of bird that made its home on the Central Coast.

"Are you allowed to let him do that?" Daniel asked.

"Would there be sneaking involved?" Jackson wanted to know. "Not that that would be a bad thing, necessarily. Could add to the overall flavor of things."

"No sneaking." Will shrugged. "Christopher says I can use the main house every now and then. Might as well. It's just sitting empty."

The "Christopher" in question was Christopher Mills, whose invention of a wildly popular dating website had rendered him so obscenely wealthy that it allowed him to be indifferent to what people did with his coastal mansion. Will had met him when they were both undergraduates at Stanford. They'd become friends, and that was what had led to Will's admittedly cushy position at the Cooper House.

"Huh," Ryan said. "Well … how would that work?"

Daniel was warming to the idea. "You get Jackson here to make the two of you a picnic dinner. You take that and a nice bottle of wine or two up to the Cooper House, set it up at a table next to the infinity pool, have a nice intimate meal …"

"There's no infinity pool," Will said. "There's a regular pool."

"Well, that's disappointing," Daniel said.

"But there's an observatory," Will offered.

"The guy's got his own observatory?" Jackson wanted to know.

"Yep. Top-quality telescope, retractable roof, the whole bit."

"Holy crap." Jackson looked impressed.

"Okay," Daniel said, warming to a new and improved script for the evening. "You take a picnic dinner, you eat it by the regular, non-infinity pool. Drink some nice wine, maybe sit in front of the fireplace. Then you go upstairs and retract the roof."

"You made that sound obscene," Ryan said. "Retracting the roof. What's that code for, exactly?"

"You'll have to figure that out for yourself," Daniel said.

Ryan thought about it and nodded. "That sounds great. Thanks, Will."

Will waved him off. "Somebody ought to use the place. Christopher hasn't been there in months."

"Any chance he might drop in unannounced?" Ryan asked uncertainly.

Will scoffed. "When he's coming, he lets me know a week in advance so I can have people clean stuff that's already clean, bring in groceries, things like that. He's not coming. At least, not this weekend."

"Okay." Ryan nodded. "Okay. This could be really good."

"Jeez. Now I want to ask somebody out so I can take them up there," Daniel said.

"Who'd go out with you?" Jackson demanded.

"That's an excellent question," Daniel said. "Sadly."

"Can we play now?" Will insisted. "I think you guys are stalling because you're losing."

"We're not losing," Jackson said. "We're giving you guys a false sense of security."

"Well, it's working," Daniel said. "I feel secure."

Jackson did agree to make a dinner that Ryan could pack up and take to the Cooper House. He also suggested a particular wine that he thought would go well with the food. Well, he might have done more than "suggested." Jackson pretty much informed Ryan that he'd be a wine-ignorant fool to serve anything else.

Ryan bought the wine Jackson told him to get, arranged with Will to get a key to the place, and talked to Will about a few of the particulars of the Cooper House. Ryan asked Will again if he was sure this was okay; he worried that he was pulling something underhanded by using some other guy's house for his own romantic ends. Although Will had gotten his job through his friendship with Mills, Ryan knew he took the work seriously, and he didn't want to get Will in trouble.

"Yeah, it's fine," Will reassured him. "I e-mailed Christopher and asked him. All he said was, don't touch his action figures."

"His action figures?"

"He's got a collection. Early Marvel Comics, mostly focused on the Stan Lee characters. You'll see."

"Huh."

With all of that worked out, there was nothing to do but worry about the whole thing until date night. Ryan didn't think of himself as someone who worried about dates; he didn't date much, but when he did, he was usually fairly confident. If a woman liked him, she liked him, and if she didn't, then she probably wasn't the right one anyway. His longstanding crush on Lacy—now thoroughly extinguished in the wake of his earth-shattering lovemaking with Gen—had been an exception.

But this was different somehow. He worried about what impression he would make on Gen. He worried about whether she would have a good time, whether she would think it was odd to be using the Cooper House, whether she would like the food Jackson made for them. Essentially what it all boiled down to was that he worried about whether she would want to see him again. Because he needed to see her, not once, not a few times, but over and over again.

When Friday night came, he picked up the food from Neptune—Jackson had packed it carefully in an insulated carrier—and went down to Marine Terrace to get Gen. He'd dressed carefully for the evening, in charcoal slacks, black leather loafers, and a blue cashmere V-neck sweater with a hint of a white T-shirt peeking out from underneath. He went down the steps to her door feeling butterflies. It had been a long time since he'd felt butterflies. He liked it.

On Friday night, Gen was a little bit frustrated because Ryan wouldn't tell her where they were going for their date. How was a girl supposed to pick out clothing for a date if she didn't know where they were going or what he had planned? Of course, last time, her date clothing had been wildly inappropriate for what they'd actually ended up doing—rolling around on the floor of the barn—so she supposed she could argue that it didn't make any difference.

It made a difference to *her,* though, because she wanted to feel pretty and confident, sexy and self-assured.

She surveyed the contents of her closet, and then, having decided that she didn't have anything suitable for a date of indeterminate destination, she went up the stairs to Kate's place and banged on the door.

"What? What?" Kate threw open the door. "Is the house on fire?"

"Sorry. I may have pounded."

"You did. What's going on?"

"I'm going out with Ryan, but I don't know *where* we're going, and how the hell am I supposed to plan what to wear when it might be a nice dinner or it might be … camping! Or … or fishing!"

Kate opened the door wider to let Gen in.

"Did he tell you he was taking you camping or fishing?"

"No! That's the problem! He didn't tell me anything!"

Kate closed the door behind Gen and leaned back against it, her arms crossed over her chest. "If he takes you on a surprise date and it turns out to be camping or fishing, you've got bigger issues than your wardrobe."

"Well. That's true."

"You'd better have a glass of wine," Kate said, heading for the kitchen. "You're freaking out."

"I'm not …"

"You are."

"Okay. Maybe. A little bit. I might be freaking out a little bit."

Kate pulled a wineglass from a cupboard over the sink and poured Gen a glass of pinot noir. "Here. You need this."

"Okay. Okay." Gen took a deep breath, had a sip of the wine, and closed her eyes for a moment in an effort to find her inner serenity. When she opened them again, Kate was looking at her with a combination of amusement and sympathy.

"I don't know why I'm freaking out," Gen told her. "I mean, Ryan and I have already slept together. The hard part is over, right? It should be easy now."

"Except that you like him," Kate observed.

"Well, of course I like him. I wouldn't have had barn sex with him if I didn't like him."

"You know what I mean," Kate said.

And she did. She meant that this was more than like, more than attraction, more than something fun and easy that could be dismissed quickly when it was over. It was too early to think in terms of the future, too early to think in terms of love. But this was more than like. They both knew that.

"Yeah," Gen admitted. "Could you maybe help me?"

If they'd been closer to the same size—if Kate hadn't been four inches taller than Gen with what the designers would call a straight figure in comparison to Gen's hourglass—they might have shared clothing. As it was, they had to settle for Kate coming downstairs with Gen to root through her closet.

"This is nice," Kate said, pulling out a red sheath dress that would emphasize the color of Gen's hair.

"It's nice for a fancy dinner or a cocktail party or something," Gen complained, "but this is a mystery date! How can I know if it's nice for a mystery date?"

Kate replaced the dress in the closet and gave Gen a stern look. "You've got to wear something. Unless you intend to greet him at the door naked. Which, now that I think of it, might be a good plan."

"Ugh." Gen groaned and flopped down on the bed.

"Okay, look. What's your happy outfit?"

Gen looked at her blankly. "My happy outfit?"

"Yeah. You know. The one outfit that, whenever you wear it, you feel good and you know you look good. We've all got one."

Gen thought about it, and then her face lit up. "I've got a top that makes my boobs look great."

"Good. Get it."

They paired the top with jeans and boots, and a leather motorcycle jacket Gen loved but that she hadn't worn in a long time because she usually dressed more formally for work.

When they were done, Kate kissed Gen on the cheek and gave her a companionable pat on the shoulder. "You look great. I'm gonna get out of here before he shows up."

"Okay. Kate?"

"Hmm?" Kate looked back on her way out the door.

"Thanks."

"You're welcome." She started to go out, and then hesitated. "It's kind of awesome that he's worth freaking out for, don't you think?"

Gen thought about that. "You know, it really is."

Chapter Twenty-Two

Ryan came to the door on time, to the minute. It made Gen wonder whether he'd arrived early and then waited out the clock before knocking. If so, that was pretty cute; it indicated that he was as nervous as she was.

She opened up and let him in, and he looked so handsome she would have swooned if that sort of thing were still done by smitten women. Kind of a shame that it wasn't.

It would have been so tempting to scrap this whole date business and just pull him inside and tear his clothes off, but, with some variation, that's what they'd done last time. This time they were going to have a real date, by God, one not interrupted by drunk artists or made somehow lesser by the suggestion that someone was thanking someone for something.

And, she wanted to know what the big secret was.

"So? Spill. Where are we going?" Gen asked as soon as she got him through the door.

"It's a surprise," he said with that sexy grin.

"Well, jeez. At least tell me if I'm dressed okay."

"You're perfect," he said, and she had an idea that he might have meant something more than her clothes.

As they drove north on Highway 1, the Cooper House appeared atop a rolling hill that was carpeted in green grass. It was early evening, but the sun was still fairly high in the blue, cloudless sky. They turned into the driveway in Ryan's truck, and Gen wiggled in her seat in curiosity and excitement.

"What are we doing here?"

"We're having our date."

"At the Cooper House?"

"Yeah." He shot her a look and grinned at her.

Gen tried, for a moment, to make sense of it, and then she realized what was going on. "Wait. Will Bachman works here, right? That friend of yours who was at Kate's party?"

"Yeah." He nodded. "Will's the caretaker. Christopher Mills is a friend of his from college. Will arranged for us to use the house for the evening."

Gen squealed. "That is so cool. What are we going to do up there?"

Ryan shrugged. "I brought some food that Jackson made for us. Some wine. We'll just get up there and see what happens."

Gen drummed her feet against the floor of the truck in excitement. "This is so much better than dinner and a movie."

"I'd hoped you would think so."

The driveway was a long and meandering affair that went past a stand of pine trees, over a low hill, and past a creek before leading them to a tall, wrought-iron gate. Ryan stopped at the gate, leaned out the window, and pushed a security code into the keypad. The gate slowly rolled open.

"You've got the security code?" Gen wanted to know.

"Will gave it to me."

"So you could just drive in here anytime you feel like it? You could burgle the place if you wanted?"

Ryan laughed. "Nah. Will recodes the gate every week or so."

Gen nodded sagely. "Me too. I recode my gate every week or so. It's one of the burdens of wealth."

The flavor of the place changed once they were inside the gate. Manicured lawns stretched for what appeared to be acres. A formal garden stood to the right, with a marble fountain, rose bushes, and towering trees that bathed it all in shade. Off to the left and down the hill a short distance were two fenced tennis courts with a lighting setup that looked like it belonged on a Major League Baseball field. A little farther up, they passed a cottage that Ryan identified as Will's guest house before they came to rest in a big circular driveway in front of the main house.

Gen had seen the Cooper House in magazines and on the Internet, and of course she'd seen it from Highway 1 as she'd passed on the way to Hearst Castle or Big Sur. But seeing it in pictures or from a distance was very different from seeing it in person.

The house was a hulking, three-story Victorian with gables set into a steep roofline, a large, wrap-around porch, gingerbread trim in shades of blue and red, and a circular turret topped with a roof shaped like an onion dome. The highest point of the third-floor roof was crowned with a widow's walk, its iron railing pointing to the heavens.

Stepping out of Ryan's truck, Gen craned her neck to look up at the house. "There should be a horror movie set here."

"You think?" Ryan came to stand beside her. "I kind of like it."

"Oh, I do, too," Gen said. "I just think a horror movie would up the cool factor. Which is already pretty high."

Ryan retrieved the key he'd gotten from Will and let them in the front door. In anticipation of their arrival, Will had already disarmed the security system.

Gen wanted to take a tour before doing anything else, so they roamed around the house for a while, through the oak-paneled foyer that led to a grand staircase; into a formal dining room with a marble fireplace; through a library with floor-to-ceiling bookcases filled with books of every description; into the parlor that was situated inside the turret, arching bay windows reaching out toward the porch and the landscape beyond.

They peeked out into the backyard and found more gardens and a mammoth swimming pool. Upstairs were innumerable bedrooms and a couple of bathrooms—one including an enormous claw-foot bathtub that had Gen aching to take a hot, bubbly bath.

They found the action figure collection in the third bedroom they checked. In a glass case that filled one wall, tiny superheroes amassed for the coming showdown with the forces of evil.

Naturally, Gen recognized some of the characters. Everybody knew Spider-Man, the Hulk, and Iron Man. But the array of figures was so vast and varied that she found it remarkable that anyone, other than their creator, could possibly name them all.

"Who's this?" Gen pointed toward a figure in shades of orange and red, his hair rising upward in frozen plastic flames, licks of fire emerging from his wrists and feet.

"That's the Human Torch," Ryan answered without hesitation. "He's part of the Fantastic Four."

She looked at Ryan with interest. "You know comic books?"

He shrugged. "Sure. I used to read them when I was a kid. I wasn't into it like some people, but … yeah. I liked them."

Gen had an image of Ryan at nine or ten years old, lying on his belly on his bed at the ranch, poring over comic books, his hair askew, his room and explosion of toys and clothes. The idea made her smile. Quite unexpectedly, she wondered if that was how their son would look. She was shocked by the thought—it was far, far too soon to be thinking such things—and she pushed it out of her head.

"You getting hungry?" Ryan asked. Grateful to have been pulled out of her kids-with-Ryan reverie, she smiled and nodded.

"Yes. Absolutely."

"Great. I'll go out to the truck and bring in the food Jackson packed for us, and we'll figure out the best spot to set up. Daniel said we should eat by the pool."

She peered up at him. "You talked to Daniel about our date?"

"Well, yeah." He shifted on his feet, looking uncomfortable. "Does that bother you?"

"No, no. I just didn't think guys did that. I thought when guys talked about their dates, it was usually bragging. You know, after the fact."

He shrugged. "I don't know what other guys do, but I find bragging—after the fact—to be ungentlemanly."

The sweetness of that—the rightness of it—made her feel warm inside. "You would, wouldn't you?"

He shrugged again and his face colored slightly. "Let's go set up for dinner."

They took Daniel's advice and had dinner by the pool. The evening was mild, the skies clear and the breeze a gentle caress. The pool—a large, formal affair with turquoise water, marble statues standing sentry at intervals around it—overlooked a view of the azure ocean as the sun descended toward the horizon. Gardens of deep green grass with trimmed hedges and rose bushes surrounded the pool area. They set up their meal at a table to one side of the pool, next to a fountain that sent plumes of water skyward.

Jackson had thought of everything. He'd packed plates and wineglasses along with the food, as well as flatware wrapped in white linen napkins. Ryan set everything up and then opened a bottle of wine and poured.

The menu, carefully chosen foods that could be served cold—all vegetarian for Ryan—included an appetizer of red pepper dip with crusty bread; a colorful salad with radishes, beets, carrots, sweet potato, and escarole; fusilli with spinach and sun-dried tomato pesto; and a dessert of coconut raspberry cookies.

"This looks amazing," Gen said when it was spread out on the table.

"I'd like to take credit, but this was all Jackson," Ryan informed her.

"Kate's a lucky woman," Gen said, digging into the red pepper dip.

Ryan looked at her with that smile that made her heart go all liquid and soft. "You know, I felt a little stab of jealousy when you said that. Made me want to go punch Jackson in the face."

"It would be a shame to do that when he's been so good to us," she said. Then: "You really felt jealous?"

"I did."

Something about that made her ridiculously happy, so much so that she giggled, and she did not consider herself to be a giggling woman.

The food was delicious—she'd expect no less from Jackson—and as she ate, she reflected that this date was not at all what she'd expected. Dinner, she'd thought, maybe a drive down to the next town for a movie. This—coming to the Cooper House—was a twist she could not have predicted. *So this is what it's like to be filthy rich,* she thought, taking in the gardens, the fountain, the endless expanse of the pool, the beauty of the sky as the sun lowered itself toward the ocean, bathing the horizon in oranges and reds. But then she thought, no. If she were filthy rich, she probably wouldn't even notice this. The beauty would be all around her, but she'd be so used to it that she wouldn't even see it. This was better.

"So you said Christopher Mills rarely even comes here?" It was hard to believe that someone could have this and take it for granted.

"That's what Will says. He's here maybe two, three weeks out of the year. The rest of the time, it sits empty."

"That's such a shame."

"It is."

"What would you do if you had this kind of money?" she asked, sipping her pinot noir.

Ryan didn't say anything. He avoided her gaze, poking at his food.

"Did I say something wrong?"

He shrugged. "Not exactly. It's just …"

"What?"

"Well. I do."

"You do what?" She was confused. What was happening here? What had she stepped in?

"I do have this kind of money."

Gen was thunderstruck. Her fork fell onto her plate with a clatter.

"You do?"

"Well …" He cleared his throat. "Yeah."

Gen thought back to her visits to the Delaney Ranch. The main house was roomy and comfortable but shabby. She remembered the old linoleum on the kitchen floor, the countertops that were cracked at the edges. She thought of Breanna and her kids, and how Gen had assumed she lived with her parents because of financial struggles. She thought about how

Ryan did all of the hard work on the ranch—including putting in Kendrick's skylight. *He* did all of that, not some workers he'd hired. She never would have guessed that there was money there, other than the land itself, which had to be of immense value.

"Wait, wait, wait. Back up." She pressed her fingertips to her temples, feeling a pressure there, like the information she'd just received was struggling to get out of her head.

"All right, here's the thing." He leaned toward her, his wineglass in his hand, and warmed to the story. "My great-grandfather's great-grandfather got some acreage of land as part of a Mexican land grant in 1846. The Delaney Ranch, it's only maybe ten percent of the land he was given."

She blinked at him. "Ten percent?"

He nodded. "Right."

But the Delaney Ranch was huge. "Well … what happened to the rest of it?"

"Mostly it was sold off over the years. My grandfather was the one with the real head for business. He sold some land—a lot of land—and put the profits into real estate. The ranch … Well. We do it because we love it. Because it's what our family has always done. But it barely makes a profit. Our real business is real estate."

"Real estate." She realized that she was blindly repeating him, but she didn't know what else to say.

"Yeah."

"How … How much real estate?"

He rubbed at the back of his neck, looking uncomfortable. "A lot. Mostly commercial properties."

"So … how wealthy are you exactly? What … what exactly are we talking about here?"

"We're, I think, fourth? Or maybe fifth now. I can't remember."

"Fourth or fifth what?"

"*Forbes* puts out a list of the wealthiest families in the state. I think last time, we were fourth. Or fifth."

"The Delaney family is the fourth richest family in the state."

"Or fifth, right. I don't remember which."

"I don't … I can't … Shit." She was rubbing at her temples more vigorously now. It was as though the words he was saying were in some foreign language that was a lot like English but that lost some meaning in the translation.

"Sorry to lay all that on you. It's a lot to take in, I know. But I didn't want you to find out later and feel like I was keeping things from you."

"But … but … nobody ever said anything. Nobody ever told me."

"I'm not even sure they know. It's not the kind of thing we talk about. And … you know. Do you think Jackson and Daniel read *Forbes*?"

"You don't talk about it." There she was with the repeating thing again.

He shrugged. "No. Not when I can avoid it."

"But why?" She was struggling to make sense of this, of the revelation.

He cocked his head and looked at her, and there was something in his eyes that she couldn't quite identify. "When people find out you've got money—more than a certain amount, I mean—then you become that to them. You become the money. You're not a person anymore. You're just … wealth."

As he said it, she knew what it was she'd seen in his eyes. It was worry.

"You didn't tell me because you were worried that I'd see you as wealth."

He shrugged again, and his discomfort with the entire subject was both puzzling and endearing. "Well, yeah, but once you asked the question—what would I do if I had this kind of money—I had to tell you, because if I didn't, it would be lying. And I don't want to lie to you."

The revelation of the Delaney family's vast wealth was shocking and overwhelming. Gen didn't know what to do with the information—how to process it. "But … your family. Your house."

"What about them?"

"I just mean …" She struggled with how to put it. "It just seems like a regular house. They just … they just seem like a regular family."

"It is a regular house, and they are a regular family."

She shook her head as though to clear it. "I meant …"

"I know what you meant."

He looked at her with those chocolate brown eyes and she could see from the expression in those eyes, from the set of his jaw, that he'd had this conversation before.

"The house doesn't look like a rich person's house," he said, filling in her thoughts. "And my family—my mom with the football jerseys and the fuzzy slippers—she doesn't look like a real estate tycoon."

"Well … yeah."

"We're just regular people, Gen. We like to live simply. Who the hell needs all of this?" He gestured to encompass the Cooper House, the garden around them, the pool, the grounds. "I mean, it's fun to visit. I'm enjoying this, being here, as much as anybody would. But to live like this?" He shook his head. "I don't need it. My parents don't need it. Breanna doesn't need it. And I've got to think Lucas and Michael will grow up more well-adjusted without it."

Yeah, she could see that. They probably would.

She took a deep drink from her wineglass—she needed it.

"So you … you run a big real estate empire? On top of running the ranch?"

He shook his head. "Nah. I just run the ranch. At least, I will when my dad finally decides to retire. My brother handles the real estate stuff."

"Your brother." There she went repeating things again.

"Colin. He's a lawyer, lives down in San Diego. He handles the real estate. I handle the cattle. Me and my other brother, Liam."

"Liam? He works on the ranch, too? I haven't met him."

"He has a ranch in Montana. Part of the family holdings."

"The family holdings."

He cocked his head at her. "You keep repeating the things I say."

"I know. I'm just making sure that I really heard them."

A trio of birds flew overhead, and the breeze rustled the leaves of an oak tree that stood sentry in the garden. The horizon was flaming orange as the sun dipped into the water.

"Look. I know this is a lot to take in," he said. "You wouldn't be the first woman not to take it well."

She wondered what that meant, and as she thought about it, it became clear why Ryan was still single in his early thirties. She'd wondered about that. He was smart, sweet, kind-hearted, and handsome as hell. Plus there was the added sexiness factor of the whole cowboy thing. And yet here he was, still dating, still looking for his match. Why? It had to be hard, with the money added into the mix, she realized. The baggage the money represented.

"I'll bet it complicates things, with dating," she said. Now that the initial shock had passed, she realized she was still quite hungry, and she picked up her fork again and began to eat the garden salad.

He let out a puff of air in a way that suggested frustration and even disgust. "You could say that. The ones who are only interested in the money are pretty easy to spot. But the ones who are a little more complicated are the women who really do like me, but who think I should be living like a rich guy. 'Why don't you have a nicer car?' and 'You know, you should really tear down the house and build something new.' That kind of thing." He shook his head, clearly troubled by the memories. "It's a pretty common reaction, and I can understand them wondering. But when they won't let up about it, well, that's when it starts to become clear that they think dating me is going to bring a certain kind of lifestyle. And they really want that lifestyle."

"That's got to be hard."

"It is." He nodded. "Well. Anyway. Now you know. So let's talk about something else. Anything else."

And so they did. They talked about Kendrick, and what it was like to run a ranch, and Gen's gallery. At first it was weird, because the information about his wealth seemed to change who she thought he was, and the dynamic between them. But the more they talked, the more relaxed she became, and the more he seemed like just Ryan. They ate Jackson's food and watched the sunset, and when the food was gone—including the cookies—they drank some more wine and held hands. Then, after they'd put away the remains of the meal—the leftovers, the plates, the napkins—they got up from the table and Gen stepped into his arms.

"What now?" she said.

"Well." He pressed a quick kiss to her lips. "I was thinking that pool looks pretty good."

"I didn't bring a bathing suit."

"I was kind of counting on that."

She'd never skinny-dipped before, in anyone's pool, let alone in a tech tycoon's pool, with marble statues of Aphrodite and Neptune looking down on her, probably with judgment and scorn. But who gave a crap what they thought? She felt giddy and free as she splashed nude through the water under the darkening sky. The pool was heated to a comfortable eighty degrees, and the night was warm.

"I hope Will's not around," Gen said, slicking her wet hair back from her face, bobbing at the surface of the water.

"Will needs to get his own date." Ryan ducked under the water and swam toward her. He glided under her and playfully grabbed onto her thigh, and she squealed and laughed.

They swam and splashed, dove, and then floated with their backs to the water, soundless, staring up into the starry sky.

When they both were tired and breathing hard, they swam toward each other and embraced, their feet kicking gently to keep them afloat.

"This is fun," she told him. "Really fun. I can't remember ever having a date this cool."

"It's not over yet." He kissed her deeply, his tongue caressing hers, and she could feel his arousal against her body.

"You're really good at this," she said when he broke the kiss, his lips just a breath away from hers.

"Money can't buy this kind of skill." He gave her the half grin again.

"How do I know that? How do I know you don't have … I don't know. Some kind of expensive coach or something." Her words were playful but she was breathless with desire, with her need for him.

"If I did, would that be a problem for you?"

"God no. Results are results."

He laughed, a low and husky sound that she felt through her entire body. Then he kissed her again and she clung to him in the water, tiny waves lapping against them, the scent of chlorine and warm man surrounding her.

Her body felt loose and hot, her heart pounding, the erotic center of her pulsing with urgent longing.

"You want to continue this inside?" he murmured. He kissed her mouth, her jaw, the soft, tender skin of her throat.

"Yeah." Her voice sounded rough. "I really do."

They climbed out of the water and wrapped themselves in the plush towels Ryan had retrieved from the house before their swim. With their clothes gathered up in their arms, they went inside, where he made a fire in the big marble fireplace of the library. Clothed only in the towels, they sat together on a rug a few feet from the flames, watching the fire and letting it warm their wet skin.

When he reached for her and pulled her to him for a kiss, she thought, *Yes.* They let the towels fall and held each other, touched each other, their bodies bathed in the warm glow of the fire.

The kiss was deep and delicious and Gen savored the feel of it, the way it made her body hum. His warm hands explored her back and the tender hollows of her throat before coming to caress the sensuous curves of her breasts.

She couldn't get enough of him. It was as though she were starved for him, desperate for something only he could give her. When his mouth lowered to cover her breast, she threw back her head and gasped in delight.

She wasn't inexperienced when it came to sex. There had been men. But never like this. There had always been a self-consciousness, a calculation to the giving and receiving of pleasure. But this was pure instinct, a warm river of bliss running through the center of her, and she didn't think, didn't know, only felt.

He held her against him as one hand roamed lower, until he found her warm, wet core. He eased a finger into her and caressed her firm little button with his thumb. She let out an animal sound and pressed herself closer to him, closer to the magic he was performing on her. Her pleasure was climbing higher, higher, the pressure rising.

Too soon.

"Not yet," she whispered. She didn't want this euphoria to end.

He withdrew his hand and she breathed, bringing herself back to the center, before focusing on him. She wrapped her hand around him, and he let out a growl. She caressed him, stroked him, kissing the firm planes of his jaw.

She wanted to know all of him, wanted to taste him, so she lowered herself to take him into her mouth. His fingers plunged into the tangles of her wet hair and he gasped. "Oh God. ... Gen ..."

She tasted, explored, licked, bringing sounds from him that made her feel powerful, desirable, until finally he gently pulled her away from him.

"I need you now. Please," he murmured.

"Yes. God, yes."

He pulled her up toward him and turned her, leaning her over the low table that stood in front of the sofa. She heard him rustling around in the pile of clothing they'd discarded, heard him tearing open a condom wrapper.

"Hurry," she said. "Now, Ryan. Oh …"

He moved behind her and brought his hands around to caress the weight of her breasts. Then he reached around between her legs to caress her there until she thought she'd scream with need.

When he pressed into her, when she felt the delicious sensation of him inside her, she lost all ability to think. She bucked back against him with his rhythm, driving her own pleasure, the pressure inside her building with each glorious thrust.

"I … Oh." She grasped at the edges of the table for purchase as he sped his rhythm. Once more he reached around and caressed her nub with his fingers. Her body tightened, tightened—and then exploded. She cried out once, twice, as her body pulsed with satisfaction.

He moved his hands back to her breasts and sped his pace, increasing in intensity before he stilled and trembled with his own release.

Sated, he rubbed his hands over her back, her sides, her ass. Finally, he separated from her.

She lay limp against the table. She could hear him moving around, removing the condom, but she couldn't move. She'd be perfectly happy never to move again.

She was pleased to still be alive, still breathing.

In a moment he came to her with a blanket he'd found tossed over the back of the sofa. He wrapped her in it and pulled her into his arms.

"Oh, holy … Wow," she said. "I thought the barn sex was good, but this …"

He laughed his sexy, low laugh and pulled her closer to him, holding her in front of the fire. He kissed her earlobe gently, softly.

"Maybe sometime we'll try doing this in a bed," he said.

"What for? Why mess with success?"

"You've got a point."

She wanted to stay there forever in his arms.

"This was Will's idea, you know," Ryan said. "Coming to the Cooper House. I probably would have taken you to The Sandpiper."

"Was it? I'll have to thank Will. And Jackson. Come to think of it, I've got a lot of people to thank." She kissed him. "Especially you."

"I think you already thanked me just a few minutes ago."

She smacked his arm and giggled.

Later, when they'd relaxed in front of the fire for a while, they showered in the big master bathroom, got dressed, and then climbed up to the third floor to check out the observatory. Will had given Ryan some basic instructions on how to open the roof and how to use the telescope, so it only took him a little bit of fumbling around before a panel in the ceiling slid open, leaving them blinking and exposed beneath a blanket of stars.

"This is amazing," Gen said. "I can't believe he's got this in his house."

"Just … hang on a minute. Let me see if I can get this going." He entered something into a screen, and the short, squat telescope moved a fraction up and to the left. Ryan peered into the eyepiece, and then stepped back so she could look. "There."

She looked, and she gasped at a view of the moon that was so sharp, so crisp, that she could count the craters in its surface. "Oh, wow."

She stepped back. He thought for a minute, entered something else into the display, and the telescope shifted its position again. He looked, and saw a group of stars like a pentagon with a long tail. "Try this."

Gen peered into the eyepiece. "What is it?"

"Pisces. The fish."

"Are you interested in astrology?" she asked.

"Nah. But it does happen to be my sign. March 17."

"Oh." She backed away from the telescope. "I just missed your birthday. It happened before we started seeing each other."

"Ah, well. You'll make it up to me next year." The thought that she might be here next year, that they might still be together, pleased him and made him feel a gentle peace at the center of his soul.

"Maybe I will. Can you find Aquarius?"

"You?"

"Yeah. January 21."

"Hmm. Let's see." He fiddled with the screen. "Yeah. Hey, look at that. They're right next to each other."

"Yeah." She slid a look at him and gave him a slow smile. "Look at that."

The thought of them together in that limitless sky seemed right to him somehow. When the world ended some day, however it would end—in a fiery explosion or in a slow, cold, final exhale—they'd still be up there, the two of them, side by side in the heavens.

Chapter Twenty-Three

"**D**id you know Ryan was rich?" Gen was standing at the counter at Jitters the next morning, waiting for her skinny vanilla latte. Lacy was bustling around behind the counter, making espresso and steaming milk. The crowd was light this morning, just a few locals chatting over muffins and cappuccinos.

"Sure," Lacy said, as though it were the most normal thing in the world.

"You knew?! Why didn't you say anything?"

Lacy shrugged. "I didn't think of it."

"You didn't *think* of it? How does one not think of something like that?!"

Lacy paused in her work and cocked her hip, one fist planted on it. "I guess I just don't think of him as this rich guy. I think of him as … as a guy I went to high school with. I think of him as this nice guy who's good at algebra but crap at chemistry."

"I wouldn't say he's crap at chemistry," Gen mused. "Quite the opposite, in fact."

"Ooh." Lacy waggled her eyebrows at Gen. "So you had a good time last night?"

"I had a very good time last night. I had such a good time that …"

"That what?"

" … That it might … God." She blew a lock of hair away from her eyes. "It might change everything."

Lacy stopped what she was doing and focused all of her attention on Gen.

"What kind of everything?"

"Just … everything!"

"You're talking about the move back East, aren't you?"

"I don't know," Gen said miserably. "Maybe."

Lacy finished making Gen's drink and then, latte cup in hand, she came out into the seating area, took Gen by the arm, and led her to a table. They sat, and Lacy leaned in close to Gen and spoke in a lower voice to avoid being overheard by the other customers.

"You can't change your career plans for a man," Lacy said. "Especially Ryan Delaney."

"What do you mean, especially Ryan? I thought you liked him."

"I do. He's sweet, he's good-looking, he's nice to his mother. I mean, he wasn't for me, but he's great."

"Then what?" Gen heard the whiny quality in her own voice, but she couldn't help it. Why *especially Ryan*?

Lacy clutched Gen's forearm and leaned toward her. "It's just … *the money*."

Gen pulled her arm out of Lacy's grasp. "What about the money?"

Lacy got a look on her face that suggested that Gen was either dense or deliberately obtuse. "You have a lot of plans for your career. Plans you've gone to great lengths to realize by bringing the artist here. Then you start dating Ryan, and he's part of the Delaney family." She said the last part with air quotes. "You think people are going to say, 'Oh, she changed her plans for the sake of true love'?" She looked at Gen point-edly.

"They're going to say I abandoned my plans for a shot at the Delaney fortune," Gen said as the truth of it dawned on her.

Lacy sat back in her seat and raised her eyebrows.

"Oh, hell," Gen said. "*You* don't think that, do you?"

"Of course not." She waved an arm to dismiss the idea. "I know you. I know you'd never be with a guy if you didn't have honest feelings for him. I mean, jeez … I know you've had a thing for Ryan since long before you knew about the money. But … Look. Let's forget about what people will think. Okay? What do *you* want? I thought what you wanted was to rebuild your career—in New York."

"It was. It is."

"Then you can't just turn your back on that."

Gen looked down at the latte in her hands and blinked back tears.

"But …"

"But what?" Lacy's voice was gentle now.

Gen plucked a napkin out of the metal dispenser on the table and started shredding it with her fingers. "I'm going to sound like a cliché, but nobody's ever made me feel like this before."

The look on Lacy's face was one of surprise, and, Gen thought, maybe a little bit of jealousy. Not because Gen was with Ryan, surely—Lacy and Ryan had just never connected, had never clicked—but because Gen had found that thing, that spark, while Lacy was still looking.

"I see," Lacy said. "But, Gen, you've just started seeing him. You don't know yet where it's going to go."

That was true, Gen couldn't deny that the relationship was in its infancy. But it felt like so much already. It felt so substantial, so real.

"What if … What if it's love?" Gen's voice was barely more than a whisper.

"If he loves you, he won't stop you from building your career. If he loves you, he'll go with you." Lacy's features were set, her voice determined.

But would he? Knowing what Ryan had here in Cambria—his family, the ranch, the land that had been the Delaney home for generations—she wasn't sure. And she wasn't sure if she could even ask him to.

Gen felt low for the rest of the day, which pissed her off, because a girl should not feel low after the best date—and the best sex—of her life. She thought that Lacy had a point about the money, and about how people would see her if she decided to stay in Cambria to be with Ryan. But who the hell cared what other people thought?

She did, she realized. She cared what other people thought, and she especially cared what Ryan thought. Yes, she'd started dating him before she understood what it meant to be dating one of the Cambria Delaneys. But now that she did understand, would he think she was staying with him because of the family money?

Ryan had admitted over dinner that women had feigned interest in him in the past just to get at the wealth he represented, and she could see that it had hurt him. She knew she wasn't like that—she didn't think she was capable of pretending to love a man she had no feelings for—but did *he* know that? And if he didn't, how could she make him sure?

She wondered if he was the type to make a woman sign a harsh and restrictive prenup. And if he asked her to, would she do it?

That line of thought made her realize that she was pondering marriage only three dates into what couldn't even be called a relationship yet. And that realization made her think that somebody really should slap some sense into her.

Who better to do that than Rose?

On her lunch break from the gallery, Gen walked over to De-Vine, where Rose was pouring two-ounce portions of wine for a pair of tourists who were tasting a selection of local offerings. The woman—who appeared to be in her early thirties—was making oohing and aahing noises over a chocolate wine, which, to Gen's mind, wasn't really wine at all. Gen knew that Rose agreed with her, but she also knew that the novelty wines—the chocolates, the flavor-infused sparkling wines—paid the bills at De-Vine with an efficiency a good oaky chardonnay never would.

"Hey," Rose greeted her when she came in. Today, Rose's hair was hot pink with streaks of purple, and it was hanging loose in a blunt-cut bob.

Gen sat on a barstool a few seats down from the tourists.

"Get you anything?" Rose offered.

"Just water, thanks."

Rose poured a wineglass full of water for Gen, told the thirty-something woman and her boyfriend about the origins of the port they were about to enjoy, and then came back to Gen.

"So? How was the date?"

"Ugh," Gen said, and her upper body slumped down onto the counter.

"That bad? Oh, sweetie. I'm surprised. I had high hopes for Ryan."

"No. Not bad. Good. Earth-shakingly good. So good that the angels in the heavens wept with joy."

"That's a good date," the woman to Gen's right said as she sipped her port.

"I'll say," Rose agreed. "So what's the problem?"

"He's rich."

"Horrors!" Rose said.

"I'm serious, Rose." Gen pulled herself up off the bar and took a drink of her water. "He's really, really rich. Not just kind of rich, but … you know. Filthy."

"Well, this is getting interesting," the tourist said.

"I think I heard something about that." Rose leaned against the bar. "About him being filthy rich."

"And you didn't say anything?! Jeez! Lacy knew, too. You two are supposed to be my friends. You'd think somebody would have mentioned that the guy I'm dating is some kind of goddamned Bill Gates!"

"I think Bill Gates has more," Rose mused. "Quite a bit more."

"That's not the point!"

Rose crossed her arms over her chest. A tattoo of a rose peeked out from beneath the cap sleeve of her T-shirt. "Then what is the point?"

"The point is …" Gen hesitated, because even she wasn't sure. "The point is, now I'm that woman!"

"What woman?"

"That woman who dates a guy because he's rich! God! Are you not following the conversation?"

The tourist leaned toward Gen, wineglass in hand. She came off as a natural, granola-eating type with her flowing sundress and her long, straight hair. "But you started dating him before you knew."

"Right. Right. But people won't know that."

"But the guy knows that, right?" The tourist's boyfriend, a guy in his early forties wearing a blue polo shirt and jeans, was getting into the conversation.

"Yeah. He does. But what if he thinks I'm only staying in it because of the money? What if ... What if he thinks that, yeah, I started seeing him when I thought he was just a guy, but I *kept* seeing him because ... because ..."

"Because he's Bill Gates," the woman said.

"Right!"

"He's not going to think that," Rose said. "And who cares what other people think? If they have a problem with it, it's jealousy, pure and simple. I mean, what woman wouldn't want to snag a hot, rich cowboy? It's every girl's fantasy from the time we hit puberty."

"A cowboy?" the woman tourist said. "A real one? Ooh."

"See?" Rose pointed at the woman, who had just proven her point. "What are you going to do? Give up the fantasy because somebody might gossip?"

"It does sound kind of stupid when you put it that way," Gen said.

The man who'd come in with the hippie chick looked glumly into his wine. "I don't see what's such a big deal about a cowboy. Guy probably stinks, shoveling cow shit all day."

"Well, that's just sour grapes," Rose said. She looked at the wine bottle in her hand, and at the grape displays all over the store. "So to speak."

"You're right," the hippie chick said sarcastically. "Bank teller is a much sexier job than cowboy." She rolled her eyes.

"Hey. My job has good benefits," the man said, his tone heating up.

"Here. Try this port. It's one of our best," Rose said, pouring miniscule servings of the syrupy wine to forestall any further arguments.

"You're right," Gen said when the tourists had been tend-ed to. "I'm not going to stop seeing Ryan just because of the money, and what people will say. It's just freaking me out, is all."

"That's because you're a good person," Rose assured her. "If you weren't, you'd be out looking at designer wedding dresses right about now."

"I guess."

"Donna Karan," the hippie chick said.

"What?" Gen asked.

"If I were going to marry a gazillionaire cowboy, that's what I'd wear. Donna Karan."

"Huh," Gen said. It was something to keep in mind, if it ever came to that.

Chapter Twenty-Four

Kendrick moved his easel outside a couple of weeks later. The move followed an intense period of work inside the old barn, during which he splattered paint on canvases, discarded them, and then covered them over to reuse later. To Gen's eye, he was furiously doing a whole lot of nothing. But the lack of a completed painting was only part of the story. The other part was the fact that he was getting up early and working every day with an enthusiasm she hadn't previously seen from him. And he wasn't drinking.

Maybe Gen couldn't see any progress in whatever it was Kendrick was doing, but she knew from his demeanor that *Kendrick* could see it, and so she felt a giddy optimism that he was on the verge of something good. And moving outside—that would be part of it, whatever this thing turned out to be. Going out into nature, into the fresh air, was a new ingredient in the blender, and it was what she'd envisioned for him all along.

"Hey. Did you see Kendrick out there by the creek?" Gen asked Ryan as she approached him outside of the main house one day in mid-July. She was walking up the driveway, and he was replacing an aging railing on the front porch. He smiled when he saw her.

"Yeah. He was already there when I passed by that way early this morning." He got up from where he'd been squatting on the porch and wiped his hands on a rag he'd pulled from his toolbox.

"That's got to be good, right?" Gen said.

"I dunno. You tell me. You're the art expert." He came down the stairs and onto the driveway, striding toward her.

"I think it's got to be good."

"Then it probably is."

When he got to her, he wrapped an arm around her waist and pulled her to him with a swiftness that left her breathless. They'd been dating for a few weeks now. He'd slept at her house a number of times, and they'd revisited the barn as well as making some choice new memories at some of the more picturesque spots at the ranch. But still, after all that, his touch made all thoughts fly out of her head like birds heading south.

"My question is," Ryan said, grinning at her with amusement, "what's Kendrick doing out there looking at the trees and the rocks and the creek, when his paintings are just splotches on a canvas?"

"It's all inspiration," Gen said. "He can be inspired by the creek and the trees and the rocks, even if he's not actually painting those things." She thought it was a pretty good answer, given the fact that she couldn't think straight with him holding her.

"I guess that makes sense." He kissed her then, so thoroughly that she felt her knees grow soft and watery, and after that all thoughts of Kendrick were forgotten.

"Well," she said, her voice weak and breathy. "I'm glad I stopped by."

"I'm glad you did, too."

This wasn't supposed to be a visit to Ryan. She was supposed to be out here checking on Kendrick, and then she was supposed to get back to the gallery to plan a show that was coming up next week. But right now, the things she was supposed to be doing paled considerably in comparison to standing here and being kissed.

She had to keep her head, despite the feel of his arms around her, the taste of his mouth, the way he looked at her ...

"Enough of that." She pushed him away. "Now that I've checked on Kendrick, I've got to get back to the gallery. Alex is expecting me. We've got a show opening next week, and I can't just …"

His dark-chocolate eyes were looking at her with a mixture of amusement, desire, and affection. She couldn't think. She lost track of what she'd been saying.

"Okay." She started again. "I really have to go."

"All right." He ran one hand up her arm in a gesture that she found immensely soothing and comforting. "But, listen. My mom wanted me to ask you over for dinner."

She blinked at him. "You mean … here? At the house? With your family?"

"Well, this is where we usually have dinner, so, yeah."

He was laughing at her. Not outwardly, but she could see it in his eyes.

"Well, that's …" Terrifying, is what it was. He wanted her to meet his mother? Of course, she'd already met his mother, on numerous occasions, but that was informal, unofficial. This was different. He wanted her to Meet His Mother.

"You don't have to be nervous." He was looking down at her with his amused gaze, and it pissed her off that he could read her expressions so easily.

"I'm not nervous."

"Okay."

"I'm not!"

"Whatever you say."

She smacked him on the arm, and he laughed.

"Look. It's not a big deal. It's not like you've never met my parents." He sat down on the top step of the porch, and she sat beside him.

"Right, but that was before we were dating."

"And they liked you before we were dating. There's no reason they shouldn't like you now that we *are* dating." He reached out and took her hand in his.

"But ..." Oh, God. The thought of the money entered her head again. Not only were she and Ryan dating, but now the whole issue of the Delaney fortune was on the table as well. She could only imagine that Ryan's parents would be suspicious of anyone he took a romantic interest in. They had to be looking for ulterior motives. What if they thought she was a user? What if they thought ...

"Gen," Ryan said gently. "I know it's a big deal when the guy you're dating wants you to have dinner with his parents. I know that. It means you're not just dating anymore, you're in a relationship."

They sat so close that her arm was pressed against his, the length of her thigh kissing his. She felt a nervous, giddy tingle in her center. "Is that what this is? Is this a relationship, Ryan?"

"I hope so."

Her heart sped up at the thought of that.

"But if you're not ready ..." he said.

"I might be." Her voice was barely more than a whisper. "But it's complicated."

"I know." He avoided her gaze. The hammer he'd been using to fix the porch sat beside him atop his toolbox, and he picked it up and started fiddling with it. "You're still planning to go back to New York once this thing with Kendrick is done."

She swallowed hard. Was she still planning that? It was hard to think with him so close to her.

"That's been my plan."

He nodded, still not looking at her.

"Okay."

"Okay?"

"Well. I won't pretend that I want you to go." He fiddled with the hammer some more. "But that's not a decision I can make for you. You've got to do what's right for you."

"Maybe … if I do go … would you ever …" She wanted to ask if he'd ever consider going with her, moving to New York to be with her. But she was afraid to ask the question, because she was afraid of what the answer would be.

"Would I go with you? Is that what you want to ask me?" She nodded.

"Well. That's complicated, too."

"I know."

They were silent for a while, sitting side by side, considering the weight of the choices before them.

"Listen," he finally said. "All of this … it's all going to work itself out. Dinner is just dinner. Will you come?"

She doubted that the dinner would be *just* anything, but nodded. "Of course. I'd love to."

"Great. Sunday?"

Of course they had a big Sunday family dinner. Of course they did. That figured. "Sure," she said. "Tell your mother thank you for inviting me."

She got up from the porch, dusted off her butt, and gathered herself to return to the gallery. She turned to him, where he was still sitting on the step.

"Ryan?" Her heart was pounding.

"Hmm?"

"I …" She took a deep, steadying breath. "Nothing. I'll see you later, okay?"

❖

She'd been one word, one breath, from saying *I love you.* She'd come so close before she'd stopped herself. Why hadn't she said it? Did she mean it? Was this love?

Back at the gallery, she dragged herself glumly through the front door and to her desk. She stowed her purse in the bottom drawer and plopped down onto her chair.

"Something go wrong with Kendrick?" Alex had emerged from the back room when she came in, and now he was studying her mood.

If they'd been in New York, Alex would have been a trim metrosexual with an expensive haircut and sleek black clothes, probably with an eyebrow wax. But here in Cambria, Alex was just Alex, a medium-sized, brown-haired twenty-something in jeans, scuffed boots, and a flannel shirt. He hadn't known anything about art when Gen had hired him, but he was earnest and hard-working, and he had learned fast.

"No, Kendrick's fine. He's good, in fact. He's working outside today."

"That's new."

"It is. I think it might be really positive."

"So what's wrong, then?"

She looked at him miserably. "Ryan wants me to meet his parents."

"But you've already met his parents."

"No. Alex. Ryan wants me to Meet His Parents."

Alex's eyes opened wider as the full meaning of her implied capitals sank in. "Oh. But you two have only been dating for a few weeks."

"I know."

"Must've been a pretty good few weeks." He raised his eyebrows.

"It was! But! This is a step! When a guy asks you to have dinner with his parents? It's a big step, right?"

"Yeah. I dated my last girlfriend for two years before I brought her to meet my parents."

"Two years!" She stretched out her arms to him in triumph. "Why don't I get two years? I want the full two years!"

Alex shrugged. "Well, then again, that wasn't a very good relationship. There was a reason I didn't want to take The Step." He could do implied capitals, too.

Gen considered this. "Huh."

"So? What are you going to do?"

"I don't know. It's a lot to think about."

"Especially when you consider the Delaney fortune," Alex added helpfully.

"You know about that? And you didn't tell me?"

"I thought you knew. I thought everyone knew."

"Future reference?" She pointed a finger at Alex. "When your boss is dating a gazillionaire, don't assume she knows he's a gazillionaire."

Alex nodded. "Duly noted."

Chapter Twenty-Five

In the end, Kate was the one who persuaded Gen to go. Over coffee one morning in Gen's apartment, while Jackson was sleeping in upstairs, Kate told Gen she was being a coward for avoiding the invitation. Though she said it much more politely.

"You're good with people. I don't see why this has you so freaked out," Kate said. They were sitting on the Adirondack chairs on the patio outside Gen's sliding glass doors, sipping from steaming mugs and looking off toward the ocean, which glowed a soft, silvery blue in the morning light.

"How can you not see? Ugh. Weren't you freaked out when Jackson wanted you to meet his parents?"

"Not really. I thought it was sweet that he wanted to take that step."

"See?! See?! It's a step! That's my whole point! It's a step!"

"Well, of course it's a step," Kate said, scowling slightly. "And it's sweet that Ryan wants to take that step, just like it was sweet of Jackson. Gen. Calm down, honey. This is a good thing."

"I know." Gen sounded miserable. She felt miserable. She knew Ryan was putting himself out there in a way that was important, that meant something, but the happiness that made her feel paled in comparison to the terror of facing the scrutiny of the senior Delaneys.

"You have to suck it up and do this," Kate said simply.

"Why? Why do I have to?"

Kate looked at her pointedly. "Because Ryan is offering to take this thing between you to the next level. And if you decide not to do it—not to go to the next level—you're making a statement about how you feel about him. And I'll tell you what: He is a kind man with a soft heart. If you don't have dinner with his parents, you're not just rejecting dinner, you're rejecting the whole next level. And that's going to hurt him."

"I ... Oh."

"You should bring a nice bottle of wine. Or maybe a pie," Kate said, closing the subject.

Later that day, Gen took a deep breath, sucked it up, and called Sandra Delaney. She accepted the invitation and asked whether she could help in any way. Sandra shooed off the offer, saying she would take care of everything.

Gen thought it was still probably a good idea to bring a pie.

By the time Gen arrived at the Delaney house on the Sunday evening in question, the butterflies in her stomach had turned into hawks, or maybe falcons, flapping their massive wings and inadvertently scratching her with their talons. She didn't know how to act. What kind of demeanor would say, *I genuinely care about your son and I'm not in it for his fortune?*

She'd carefully selected her clothing for the visit. Her usual gallery attire said *I'd rather be in New York*, so that was out. She knew the Delaneys were casual people; every time she'd seen Sandra at home, the woman had been wearing a football jersey and fuzzy slippers. So Gen opted for jeans, a pair of soft leather ankle boots, and a heather grey cashmere sweater.

She showed up at their doorstep bearing a pie she'd baked herself. She hoped that the fact she'd made the pie, rather than picking one up from a bakery, would make some sort of statement. What that statement might be, she wasn't sure.

Breanna opened the door to Gen's knock. Breanna was tall, like Ryan, with the same dark eyes and thick, dark hair. She looked slightly frazzled—probably from chasing the two boys around all day—but she greeted Gen with a smile that seemed warm and genuine.

"I'm so glad you could come," Breanna said, ushering Gen inside. She leaned toward Gen and said conspiratorially, "I'll bet you tried to think of ways to get out of it."

"What? No!" Gen said.

"Right." Breanna grinned. "The first time I had dinner with my husband's parents, I was terrified."

And there it was. That word. Husband. Is that where this was headed? Toward Ryan being her husband? The weight of it all bore down on her, and her knees almost gave out.

"You look kind of green," Breanna observed.

"What? No. I'm good. It's good." She was babbling. She handed Breanna the pie. "Here. There's pie."

Breanna peered down at the pie, which was apple crumble. Gen was a pretty good baker, but she considered the apple crumble to be her best.

"Homemade," Breanna observed.

"Um … yeah. I just … you know. Threw it together."

"Sure."

Gen entered the house and was immediately surrounded by noise and chaos. Lucas and Michael were running around the living room, playing some kind of game the rules of which probably only they knew. An older man Gen recognized as Ryan's uncle Redmond was sitting in a recliner in front of the TV, watching a baseball game and intermittently grumbling at the screen. Through the doorway that led into the kitchen, Gen could see Sandra bustling around in her fuzzy slippers. She came to the doorway to yell at the boys to stop yelling, then vanished into the kitchen once again. Ryan's father, Orin, was padding around in socks, looking for his shoes.

"Sandra? Where are my shoes? We've got company coming, and I can't find my damned shoes!"

"Well, it's not my job to keep track of your shoes! You're a grown man. Though sometimes I doubt it. I swear!" Sandra yelled back.

"Mom? Dad? Gen's here!" Breanna called out, bringing the disorder to a temporary stop.

Sandra came to the doorway of the kitchen, pressed her fists to her hips, and said, "Well, I guess you'd better come on in instead of just standing there." Then she vanished into the kitchen again.

Orin looked up from where he'd been hunting all over the floor for his shoes, saw Gen, and grinned sheepishly. "Oh. Heh heh. Don't mind my feet." He wiggled his toes inside his socks. "I seem to be having a shoe crisis."

"Oh. Um … Are those yours, over there?" She pointed to a spot next to the fireplace, where a pair of Timberland work boots were sitting askew beside the hearth.

Orin followed her finger to where she was pointing, and noticed the boots with a start. "Oh! Well." He hurried over to the boots and snatched them up.

Lucas and Michael, apparently attracted by the presence of a new person, ran over to where Gen stood.

"Michael, Lucas, this is Gen. Do you remember meeting her when she was here to have tea with Grandma Sandra?" Breanna spoke to them in a tone of love and infinite patience.

"I like your hair," Michael said. "It's all curly and bright."

"Well, thank you," Gen said.

They ran off again, chasing one another around the coffee table.

She heard footsteps on the stairs, and looked up to see Ryan coming down in jeans and a flannel shirt, his dark hair still wet from the shower. He smiled at Gen, and she marveled at how his smile always made the blood rush to certain parts of her body that she couldn't mention in front of his parents. Or the kids, for that matter.

"Hey," he said as he descended. "It's good to see you."

Any further conversation was forestalled as the boys rushed to Ryan, throwing themselves at his body. With the ease of someone who'd done it thousands of times before, he hoisted Michael up onto his shoulders, and lifted Lucas up into one arm.

Laden with boys, Ryan came the rest of the way down the stairs and kissed Gen on the cheek as the boys giggled and squirmed. "Eww! You kissed her!" Michael cried.

"I did," Ryan confirmed. "And I'm gonna do it again."

This time, he planted a quick, chaste kiss on Gen's lips.

"Ewww!" both boys cried out in unison, earning them a chuckle from Ryan.

Sandra appeared at the doorway to the kitchen again. "Well, I don't know what's taking you so long to get in here," she said to Gen.

If Gen hadn't already spent some time with Sandra, she'd have taken the comment as a rebuke. But as it was, she understood that this was Sandra's way of making Gen feel welcomed into the heart of the family—the kitchen.

Pie in hand, Gen went into the kitchen and found Sandra working over a big Dutch oven. Gen set the pie down on the butcher block table in the center of the kitchen.

"Is there anything I can do to help?"

"Well, I don't suppose that salad is going to make itself." Sandra gestured toward a collection of lettuce and other vegetables that had been set out on the table. Gen grinned and got to work.

Dinner consisted of a pot roast with potatoes and carrots, collard greens, a bulgur wheat dish with olives and tomatoes for Ryan, and Gen's green salad. When Sandra called everyone to the table, there was a flurry of hand-washing, glass-filling, and seat-finding during which Breanna had to gently scold the boys more than once.

Gen found the general disarray of things, the noise and the chaos, to be reassuring and somehow comforting. In her own home when she'd been growing up, there'd been no such happy disorganization, since she was an only child, and her mother was more occupied with the task of finding another husband than she was with Gen. Then there had been New York, where children had rarely been a part of her world. She might have expected this kind of noise and disorder to be intimidating or distasteful, but instead, she felt a warmth inside her that was wholly surprising.

Ryan took her hand and led her to a seat at the table next to his own. Her anxieties melted away, and it was as though she'd always been here, had always been a part of the loud, squirming organism that was this family.

She dug into the pot roast and potatoes as Orin talked about his day and about the business of the ranch. Redmond groused about the game he'd been watching, and Breanna chatted with the boys about an outing they were planning for the following day. Sandra asked Gen about the gallery and about "that artist you got living in our guest house," and Gen talked about Kendrick and about how she'd come to live in Cambria after her time in New York.

When dinner was done, including Gen's pie, Michael and Lucas took Gen by the hand and pulled her into the living room, where they insisted that she play a game of Sorry! with them. At only five years old, Lucas needed help reading the cards and counting spaces, but his brother, two years older, seemed to enjoy showing off his own more advanced abilities.

At first, it felt strange and awkward to Gen sitting on the floor playing with small children. She'd had such limited experience with kids that it felt like they were small aliens come to take her to their own strange and miniature-sized planet. But she was charmed by how quickly they had warmed to her, how readily they accepted her as a playmate. Before long, all three of them were laughing and exclaiming over the twists and turns of the game, yelling "Sorry!" when someone got bumped back to start.

Gen was surprised and touched when, during a rare quiet moment in the game, Lucas leaned over and rested his head against her side.

Ryan watched from the kitchen doorway as Gen threw up her hands in triumph and shouted "Sorry!" to Michael as his game piece was sent back to Start. He saw Lucas lean his head against Gen, saw her put her arm around him and rub his small back with her palm.

Sandra came and stood next to Ryan and watched with him for a while.

"If you don't hang on to this one, you're an idiot," she said in her usual blunt, Sandra way. "And I didn't raise any idiots."

"Well, I *plan* to hang on to her," he said mildly. "But it's not just my choice, is it? She's still talking about moving back East."

Sandra waved a hand and made a scoffing sound. "That's not what she wants. She thinks it is, but it's not."

Ryan raised his eyebrows. "You seem awfully sure."

"You wait and see," she said.

"Well." He shifted uncomfortably from one foot to another. "I hope you're right."

"Wait and see."

At the end of the evening, Ryan walked her to her car. When they arrived, she leaned back against the driver's side door, and he kissed her.

"That was really nice," Gen murmured, her mouth still close to his.

"The kiss, or the dinner?"

"Mmm. Both."

The evening air was mild, with a light mist from the ocean softening everything, like a photo blurred at the edges.

"They like you," Ryan said.

"I like them."

He nodded. "It showed."

"Your mom ..." she began.

"Aw, don't worry about her. She puts on a big show of being all gruff and crusty, but ..."

"I love your mom," Gen assured him.

He grinned. "You do?"

"Oh, God, yes. Coming from New York, I know so many people who are all sweet and charming to your face, but then cut you down the minute you turn your back. Your mom is refreshing."

He chuckled. "Well, I'm not sure I've ever heard anyone describe her as refreshing. But she's genuine. If she doesn't like you, you'll know it. And if she does, well, that's that. Once the decision is made, she sticks to it."

"And she likes me?"

"She does." He kissed her again, gently.

"That's ... well. I'm honored." And she meant it. Tears came to her eyes suddenly, and as hard as she tried to blink them away, a few spilled down her cheeks. She quickly swiped at them with the backs of her hands.

"What's wrong?" Ryan sounded alarmed.

"Nothing. Nothing's wrong. It's just ... Tonight was really nice."

He held her, rubbing a hand in gentle circles on her back. "I'd like to meet your family sometime."

"Oh." She gave a shaky laugh. "I don't think you'd like it as much as you think."

"Why not?"

"My family ... they're not like yours. My mother's been divorced four times. My father sends cards at Christmas and on my birthday. When he remembers."

"That's rough."

"It is." She looked up at him and into his liquid brown eyes. "You're lucky, Ryan. You're so lucky."

"I feel pretty lucky right now," he said. They kissed, and it was a long, warm kiss that made Gen feel cherished and protected. It made her feel safe.

Chapter Twenty-Six

A day or two later, Gen got a text on her phone while she was busy opening the gallery. It was Ryan:

You should come out here. It's Kendrick.

What about Kendrick? Was he packing up to leave again? On a drunken bender? Having some kind of wild artist party and tearing up the guest cottage? Frustratingly, Ryan offered no clues. She wrote back:

What? What's wrong with Kendrick?!

He responded:

Just come and see for yourself.

She got to the ranch late that morning. The sun was warm, and the day was clear and bright. A light breeze tickled her skin as she got out of her car at the guest cottage. The smell of the ocean permeated the air.

Kendrick wasn't at the guest house. She knocked on the door, but she already knew there was no one inside. The cottage had the feel of emptiness.

Knowing that she was in for some tromping around on the rough paths of the ranch, she went back to her car and traded her spike heels for her track shoes. Properly shod, she followed the dirt path to the old barn, the site of such lovely erotic memories.

The barn, like the guest cottage, was empty. Kendrick's easel was gone.

The last time she'd seen Kendrick working outside, he'd been set up next to the creek. Gen headed that way, the low buzz of the insects in the grass providing musical accompaniment to her walk.

She didn't know what she'd find when she found Kendrick. A feeling of dread in the pit of her stomach warned her that there was likely to be a crisis she'd have to fix, a dilemma she'd have to solve.

She followed the path toward the creek, rounded a bend past a grove of trees, and saw him.

Gen was prepared for him to be drunk. She was prepared for him to be neurotic, panicking, possibly angry, or ranting about leaving. She was not prepared for what she actually found.

Gordon Kendrick was standing at his easel, calmly dabbing paint on a canvas, humming something that she identified as Beethoven. And the painting he was working on made her stop short and catch her breath.

"Oh my God," she said, quietly, to avoid disturbing him.

He turned to look at her. "What do you think?"

"It's … it's …" She was sputtering, but she couldn't gather her thoughts.

"It's different than my other work," he concluded for her.

"Yes. Very."

She came closer carefully, as though she were trying to avoid startling a small woodland animal. As she approached, Kendrick stepped back from the painting so she could see.

Kendrick's previous paintings had been purely abstract— slashes of color that Gen had found appealingly raw and expressive. This one was abstract as well, with bursts of color creating the illusion that the paint had somehow exploded out from the canvas. But amid the chaotic colors, amid the riotous drips and splashes, she saw *nature*, she saw the world around him. The trees, the stream, the rocks and birds, the eternal blue sky. The painting wasn't *of* those things—not exactly—but they were there all the same. The suggestion of them. The essence of them, if not their literal form.

"God, Gordon," Gen said. It was the best she could do. She had no words for what she was seeing.

"It's good, right?" He asked the question with none of his usual Kendrick ego or anxiety. He seemed calm, at peace.

"It's better than good." She turned to face him. "It's a breakthrough." She let out a laugh of pure joy, and impulsively threw her arms around him. He patted her lightly with the hand that wasn't holding the brush.

"Oh. Ha, ha. Well," he said.

She pulled back and appraised him, and she saw that his painting style wasn't the only thing that had changed. It was as though the demon that had caused him to drink too much, worry too much, and obsess over ridiculous things like thread count and yogurt had fled his body, leaving him comfortable and at ease.

She imagined that she was going to like this Gordon Kendrick a whole hell of a lot better.

Gen was so giddy about the work Kendrick was doing that the happiness she was feeling spilled over into her relationship with Ryan. One clear benefit was that the sex was better than ever.

Since it would have been awkward for her to sleep at his place with his mother and father right down the hall, he usually came to her. Because of the absurdly early hours he kept, he was always gone by the time she woke up in the morning. Sometimes she heard him moving around in the pre-dawn darkness, showering and making coffee. He pressed a kiss to her forehead or her cheek and murmured his goodbyes before slipping out the door.

Over a period of a few weeks, Gen fell into a comfortable rhythm of working at the gallery, checking on Kendrick, spending time with Ryan and his family, and then sleeping beside him in the happy, warm cocoon of her bed.

On a day in early August, she decided it was time to make a move regarding Kendrick. He'd been working steadily, producing more paintings in the stunning new style he'd developed, and enough of his work was ready that she could present it to dealers and collectors. She knew she needed to handle it carefully to get not only the highest possible price for the work, but also the highest exposure for Kendrick. She had to think about the long game, not just the short-term profit.

The first part of her strategy had to be presenting a show of Kendrick's work in New York. San Francisco would have been more convenient, and Chicago would have made sense since it was Kendrick's hometown, but New York would lend the work a legitimacy, a cachet, that he would not get anywhere else.

After consulting with Kendrick, Gen settled on a gallery that she thought would be perfect: the Joan Whitley Gallery on 57th Street. She carefully drafted an e-mail to Joan Whitley, giving a brief history of Gordon Kendrick's career, explaining what Gen believed to be the significance of Kendrick's newly emerging style, and inquiring about the possibility of a showing of Kendrick's work at the gallery. She attached high-quality images of Kendrick's best new pieces.

When Gen didn't hear back for a week, she called the Whitley Gallery to follow up. She didn't get past Whitley's assistant. The woman, who sounded as pinched and uptight as Gen used to be, dispatched Gen quickly and mercilessly: "Ms. Porter, I'm afraid Ms. Whitley's schedule is completely full."

Gen asked if she could speak to Ms. Whitley personally, and the assistant informed her that would not be possible.

Because of the time difference, it was still early—just past seven a.m.—when Gen finished the call. Ryan was already gone to start his workday at the ranch, and Gen was hanging out with Kate, having coffee upstairs at Kate's place while Jackson made an early run to a produce supplier for the restaurant.

"Well, that's just …" Gen plunked her cell phone down on the coffee table, frustrated. "I'll bet she didn't even show Whitley the photos. Shit."

"So what are you going to do now?" Kate stood in her tiny kitchen in sweatpants and a T-shirt, stirring sugar into her second coffee of the day.

"I don't know." Gen shook her head.

"Try another gallery?" Kate suggested.

"It's probably going to be the same everywhere," Gen said. "The New York art people—they don't know me anymore. I'm just a … a nobody who owns a souvenir shop out in the sticks."

"So what are you going to do?" Kate asked again.

Gen got up from her seat on the sofa and paced around the room in her bathrobe and socks. "I need buzz," she said.

"Buzz."

"Yeah. I've got to get them talking about me, about Kendrick. Then they'll know our names, and then we won't be nobodies anymore." She turned to Kate. "That's how I get them to take my calls."

"All right." Kate nodded. "That sounds promising."

"I need a collector. Somebody with some influence."

"The McCabes?" Kate suggested.

Gen waved off the idea. "Nah. They're all money and no taste. I need somebody who's respected. I need a tastemaker."

"A tastemaker."

"Right."

"Like Oprah," Kate offered.

"What's Oprah got to do with this?"

"You know art, I know books," Kate said. "Back when Oprah still had her TV show and she was doing the book club thing, all she had to do was mention a book and it sold a gazillion copies."

Gen snapped her fingers and pointed at Kate. "Exactly. Like Oprah."

"Okay. So who's like Oprah, but with art?"

Gen thought she knew the perfect person. But getting his attention wasn't going to be much easier than getting Joan Whitley to answer her calls.

"David Walker." Gen announced the name to Kendrick later that morning at the guest cottage. Kendrick was getting ready to head out to his spot by the creek. Gen had caught him just as he was packing up his supplies.

"What about him?" Kendrick inspected a brush before placing it in a sheath to take out to the creek.

"I've got to get him to buy one of your paintings."

Kendrick gave her a look that was half amused, half incredulous. "Good luck with that."

David Walker was a self-made multimillionaire who'd earned his fortune in the office supply industry. What had started as a single storefront selling staplers and paperclips had developed into a chain of stores that spanned the United States. Once success had hit, Walker had taken an interest in art, and had started a modest collection with the help of some astute advisers and his own uncanny eye.

The modest collection had grown over the years into one of the best—and most valuable—private collections of modern and contemporary art in the world. Walker was, indeed, like Oprah—a nod of approval from him could set off an avalanche of high-priced sales and publicity that could have Joan Whitley and her ilk approaching Gen, and not the other way around.

Kendrick's skepticism about getting Walker's attention was not misplaced. Walker was several rungs higher on the art-world ladder than Whitley, and that meant Gen would probably be getting a no not from Walker himself, or even from his assistant, but from the random guy who answered his mail.

"Hmm," Gen mused as Kendrick continued to pack up his paints and brushes.

"You can't just walk up to David Walker's door and show him a painting," Kendrick said.

"Huh." She thought about that, and then thought about it some more. Walker lived in Palo Alto, just a few hours' drive up the coast.

"Why not?" she asked Kendrick.

"Why not what?"

"Why can't I just walk up to his door and show him a painting?"

Kendrick stopped what he was doing and looked at her.

"This should be interesting," he said.

Gen made the three-and-a-half-hour drive up Highway 101 on the following Monday, a clear day with temperatures in the mid-70s. She'd asked Ryan to come with her, for the company and also so they could have a date in the Bay Area, but apparently it was time to castrate the bull calves—a prospect she decided she'd rather not think about—and he couldn't afford to take the time off from the ranch.

She was hoping to come back the same day, but that was a best-case scenario. It was much more likely that she would have to stay in the Palo Alto area overnight, so she'd packed a small bag and put it in the trunk of her car.

She didn't trust the painting in the trunk—her overnight bag or some of the other random items she kept back there might roll onto it—so she wrapped it carefully in a cotton sheet and put it on the front passenger seat of the car.

The drive was going to be long, so she got an early start—though not as early as Ryan. He'd already been gone from her apartment two hours before she took a quick inventory of her things, climbed into the car, and headed east on Route 46 toward Paso Robles, where she could get on Highway 101 north toward the Bay Area.

Gen didn't know exactly how she was going to approach David Walker once she got to his house, but she had a lot of time to think about it during the drive. As she headed through places like San Miguel and Bradley, San Lucas and Greenfield, she pondered the various scenarios she might encounter.

Scenario A was that Walker would open the front door, exclaim over the brilliance of the painting, and make an offer to buy it. As appealing as that idea was, she considered it to be wildly improbable.

Scenario B was that she wouldn't get to see him at all—either he wouldn't be home, or he'd have a security gate and the voice on the other end of the intercom would decline to let her in.

Scenario C was that he would be home, and he would let her in, but he simply wouldn't like the painting.

Of course, there were infinite possible variations on each of the three scenarios; she understood that she'd have to think on her feet once she got there. She rehearsed her pitch in her head. She had long versions and short versions, polite versions and direct versions, but in the end, they all came down to this:

Mr. Walker, I know it's presumptuous of me to show up unannounced like this. But I have an artist whose work you need to see.

If all else failed, she would thrust the painting in front of his face and hope the artwork would speak for itself.

She arrived in Palo Alto around midday. She'd found Walker's address online, and she used the Google Maps app on her phone to find the house. The street where Walker lived was tree-lined and shady, a narrow two-lane road with houses that looked like they'd been built in the mid-'50s. As her car approached the address, her heart started to beat faster as her nerves ratcheted up.

When the app announced that she'd arrived at her destination, she double-checked the address to be sure. The house looked far more modest than what she'd expected, a stuccoed ranch-style home with archways and lines that had probably looked cutting-edge sixty years ago, but that now appeared hopelessly dated. The lot the house stood on wasn't large, and to her relief, there was no security gate. She parked on the street near a boxwood hedge, carefully removed the painting from the car, took a deep breath to steady herself, and walked up the driveway to David Walker's front step.

While she'd considered the idea that he might not be home—it had, of course, been one of her main scenarios—she still found it to be a big letdown when a middle-aged Hispanic woman who identified herself as the housekeeper informed Gen that Mr. Walker was at a lunch meeting in San Francisco. He wasn't expected home until midafternoon.

Standing there on the doorstep, she tried to consider what to do. The housekeeper looked at her patiently as she considered her options.

"Okay, just … Would you wait just a moment, please?" she asked the housekeeper as she rooted around in her purse for a pen and some paper.

She found the notebook that she kept in her bag, dug a ballpoint pen from among the detritus at the bottom of the purse, and began to write.

Mr. Walker,

I know it was presumptuous of me to show up at your house unannounced—she'd rehearsed this part, and didn't want to waste all that mental effort by not using it—*but I have a painting you need to see. It's by Gordon Kendrick, a Chicago artist who has experienced a remarkable breakthrough in his work over the past several weeks.*

I'll be in Palo Alto for the rest of the day, awaiting your call.

—Genevieve Porter, owner of the Porter Gallery

She thought about adding more, about herself, about Kendrick, about her interpretation of the painting and the reasons she thought it was significant. But it was likely she'd have only moments of his attention before he moved on to other things, so she added her cell phone number at the bottom of the note and hoped the painting would speak for itself.

Gen thrust the painting and the note at the housekeeper.

"Would you please make sure Mr. Walker sees these?"

The housekeeper hesitated.

"Please," Gen said again. "I've driven almost four hours to give this to him. He's going to want to see it."

The housekeeper continued to resist, so Gen gave her a pleading look and wondered if she should also try to look a little bit hungry and exhausted. She *was* hungry, as she hadn't had lunch yet, and the drive *had* been tiring.

Finally, the housekeeper nodded and reached for the painting and the note. She peered at the painting. "At least it's better than the last one," the woman quipped in a heavy accent. "That one had used cigarette butts glued to it."

Gen did a mental victory dance as the housekeeper took the painting and closed the door.

The gambit had been risky, as now that she'd delivered the painting to the Walker household, there was no guarantee she'd get it back. But she'd deal with that problem if and when it came. She wasted time in Palo Alto waiting for him to call. She ate lunch at a café on University Avenue, then strolled through the Stanford University campus, admiring the stately Memorial Church, the Main Quad, and the no-doubt brilliant students walking and bicycling from one place to another.

After that, she went to the mall adjacent to the campus, where she wandered through Nordstrom looking at the clothes and accessories.

Toting a shopping bag containing a new pair of shoes and a selection of very expensive makeup, she settled in at a Starbucks to check her e-mail and sip a latte while she waited for Walker's call.

Around late afternoon, she started to worry that he wouldn't call at all. What would she do then? She supposed she'd have to go back to his house and ask the housekeeper to give back the painting. But maybe not right away. What if she left it there for a few days? If Walker didn't call today, it might be because he simply hadn't been home, or hadn't had time to consider Kendrick's work. An extra day or two would increase the chances of Walker really thinking about the painting. But it would also increase the chances of Gen never getting it back. It would suck to go back to Cambria and tell Kendrick that she'd lost his best painting.

It was almost five o'clock, and Gen was pondering her next move—Stay the night in Palo Alto? Go back to the Walker house?—when her cell phone buzzed.

Without introduction, David Walker said, "Can you come back to the house? I want you to tell me about Gordon Kendrick."

Gen spent more than three hours at Walker's house. The housekeeper—whose name was Martina—served dinner, and Gen and Walker discussed Gordon Kendrick over lamb chops, mashed potatoes, and green beans.

She explained the progression of Kendrick's work, and how she'd discovered his paintings online. She'd looked at his overall career, including his early paintings as well as his most recent ones. Gen had thought that Kendrick's paintings were good but not great. More importantly, she'd thought he was moving toward something, some kind of metamorphosis that would ultimately take his work to a higher level. So she'd created the residency and brought him to Cambria to see if a change of scenery could coax greatness out of him.

In her view, it had worked.

She told Walker about Kendrick's initial crisis of confidence, and then his breakthrough.

Walker, an unusually tall man in his early seventies, with a slightly stooped posture and a shock of white hair, listened carefully over dinner without indicating whether he might actually buy the painting. Afterward, he took her on a tour of the house. The inside was as unremarkable as the outside, with outdated furniture and décor that appeared to be from the '70s. But every available surface was covered with modern and contemporary art, ranging from Jackson Pollock to Jeff Koons. Touring Walker's house was like visiting MoMA, but without the uniformed guards around every corner.

Gen was so stunned by Walker's art collection that she almost forgot about why she'd come. Finally, when she was gathering her purse at the end of the evening, Walker shook her hand, then held it tightly in both of his.

"So, how much were you thinking?" he said.

She blinked a few times and realized he was talking about Kendrick's painting.

She named a figure.

He released her hand and went to a side table in the foyer to get his checkbook.

Chapter Twenty-Seven

Gen returned to Cambria the next day in triumph. She was so excited about the sale that she'd considered driving home that night so she could share the good news with Kendrick in person. But then, realizing that she was exhausted, she'd settled for calling him instead. After that she'd called Ryan, because she realized her happiness would not be real unless she shared it with him.

"It was an amazing day, and I needed to tell you about it," she'd told him, clutching her cell phone to her ear in the Sheraton Palo Alto.

"You're amazing," he'd answered in a voice so sexy it made her mentally relive their last intimate encounter.

He said something else, but she was so busy fantasizing she didn't know what it was.

"So now what?" Kendrick asked Gen when she met with him at the guest house the day of her return.

"Now, we wait." She explained to Kendrick that any acquisition to David Walker's collection was big news in the art world, and that Walker's latest purchase would hit social media soon—if it hadn't already. Once that happened, people would start contacting them. If all went well, they could take their pick of New York galleries for Kendrick's show.

Kendrick was so pleased that when Gen wrote him a check for the sale of the painting, he thanked her profusely and didn't even complain about her forty percent.

Gen had been right about word spreading quickly on social media. Within twenty-four hours of the sale, Walker had posted the Kendrick painting on the "New Acquisitions" page of his website. Shortly after that, people began tweeting about Kendrick and his work. And shortly after *that,* Joan Whitley's assistant called Gen, saying Ms. Whitley had reconsidered her earlier refusal, and now wanted to talk about having a show of Kendrick's work.

By then, it was too late. Gen had already made a deal with someone else.

The show was scheduled for the end of September at the Archibald / Bellini Gallery in SoHo. Archibald / Bellini usually was booked a year in advance, but they'd bumped a show titled "Global Warming in Recent Abstractions" to get Kendrick in.

"God, I'm nervous," Gen told Ryan in bed about a week after her return from Palo Alto, when the date for the gallery show had been confirmed. "Jeez. Kendrick's not even nervous, but I can barely function."

"Let's see what we can do to relax you," he said.

"Gen wants me to go to New York with her."

Ryan was lining up a pool shot at Ted's on a Thursday night after Jackson got off work at the restaurant. He and Jackson were playing, and Daniel and Will were standing around heckling them. The bar was mostly empty, as it often was on weeknights, but it still had the aroma of sweat, stale beer, and old carpet.

"For this gallery deal, or is she still talking about moving there?" Will asked.

"As far as I know, her moving there is still on the table. But for now, we're just talking about the gallery deal." He took his shot, and missed getting the six into the corner pocket by a fraction of an inch.

"You going?" Jackson asked.

His shot done, Ryan straightened and backed out of the way so Jackson could take his turn.

"Sure. This is a big thing for her. I want to be supportive."

"Supportive's good," Daniel said.

"Yeah," Ryan agreed.

"But?" Daniel prompted him. Daniel was sitting on a barstool near the wall, a mug of beer in his hand.

"But," Ryan said, "this is it, isn't it? The idea was, she'd hit it big with Kendrick, then she'd have the juice to get back into the New York art scene, and then she could move back there. Well, she's hit it big with Kendrick."

"And you don't want her to move," Will said from the barstool next to Daniel's.

"Well, no."

Jackson lined up his shot and hit the ten into a side pocket.

"Nice shot," Daniel observed.

"So? If she goes, what then?" Jackson asked. "Do you move with her? Or do you do a long-distance thing? Call it off? Or what?"

"Calling it off isn't an option," Ryan said. Just saying the words, just considering the idea of ending things, made him feel a little sick to his stomach.

"So it's serious, then?" Will asked.

"It is for me. I hope it is for her," Ryan said.

Jackson sank the twelve, and Ryan grumbled. They had ten dollars on the game.

"What if she does move? Would you consider going with her?" Daniel said.

"She hasn't asked me to."

"Yeah, yeah," Daniel said impatiently. "If she does."

"It's complicated," Ryan answered. He took a long drink from his beer. "My parents and my uncle are getting old. One brother's in Montana, and the other one has no interest in ranching. Everybody's counting on me to run things out here. If I go … Well. We can hire someone, but it's not the same. The ranch is a family business. We hire someone, that's not family."

Jackson took his next shot and missed. Ryan looked over the table, spotted his next move, and leaned down to line up his shot.

"And the long-distance thing," he continued as he took his turn, "that's complicated, too. Flying back and forth, being apart a lot of the time. I'm in a relationship, I want to *be* with the person. Plus, I'm not a big fan of airplanes."

He hit the cue into the four and sank it into a corner pocket.

"Well, if calling it off isn't an option, what'll you do?" Daniel asked the question that had been keeping Ryan awake nights.

"Shit." Ryan shook his head. "Shit. I guess I'm moving to New York. If she goes. And if she asks me to go with her."

Jackson raised his eyebrows and whistled in admiration. "That's a big fuckin' deal, man."

"Yeah," Ryan agreed.

"You could ask her to stay," Will observed.

"Nah," Ryan said. "Then I'm the asshole who held her back, ruined her career. This matters to her. And if it's important to her, it's important to me."

Jackson chuckled and smacked Ryan on the back. "You're going to make someone a really great wife someday."

"Ah, shut up," Ryan said.

❖

Taking a week off to go to New York wasn't a simple matter. Sure, they had hired hands on the ranch, but nobody who was used to running the place in Ryan's absence. Their best guy, the one who'd been there the longest, was off work with a back injury. That left Joe Barnes, a big hulk of a man who'd come to them about a year and a half ago from a ranch in Nebraska. Barnes was good—he had good instincts and a great work ethic—but he was young, and he'd never been trained to manage the operation. Of course, Ryan's dad would be there, and so would Redmond, in case Barnes got into trouble. Still, Ryan felt shaky about leaving.

Of course, it was entirely possible that part of the shaky feeling had to do with the bigger issue of Gen and New York, rather than this one trip.

Surprisingly, every time he bitched about how he didn't want to abandon the ranch even for a week, Sandra was the one who urged him to go.

"This ranch has been here for a hundred and seventy years, I imagine it'll still be here when you get back in a week," she pronounced, hands on her hips, fuzzy slippers on her feet. "I know you think you're so important we'll all just lay down and die if you take a vacation, but I guess we probably won't."

He scratched at his head and poured his morning coffee. "I don't think I'm that important."

"No? Well, you sure act like it. 'I can't leave! What'll you all do? Oh, what will become of the ranch?' My God. You act like the goddamn sun will stop shining if you get on a plane." She rolled her eyes at him.

"I don't act like that." He stirred sugar into his coffee. "Do I?"

"You've been known to. Good lord, it's like you think we can't function without you here watching over us."

"Well," Ryan said.

She came over to where he sat at the table with his mug. Her voice softened, and she put a hand on his shoulder. "You need to do this, Ryan. Go and support your girl."

He looked up at her, feeling grateful but still a little miserable. "But what if she decides to move?"

Sandra crossed her arms over her chest and glared at him. "There you go, trying to cross bridges you haven't come to yet." She put the hand back on his shoulder. "We'll figure that out when it happens."

"I guess."

"Well, if this one moves across the country, we'll be royally screwed, I guess," Orin said, scratching his belly as he walked into the kitchen to get his coffee.

"Nobody asked you to chime in," Sandra reminded him.

"Well, I guess I get an opinion," Orin said.

"Not on Ryan's love life, you don't," Sandra said. She turned back to Ryan. "Don't you listen to him."

He tried not to. But it was hard.

Chapter Twenty-Eight

The night before Gen and Ryan were set to leave for New York, the girls got together at Rose's house to wish her luck. The cottage, set in a woodsy area east of Highway 1, was tiny, but Gen had always loved it. With its wood paneling, the freestanding cast iron fireplace, and the fact that it was set on a sizeable lot with trees that obscured any view of the neighbors, the place made Gen feel like she was tucked into a secluded mountain hideaway.

Of course, Rose had brought some good wine from her shop, and Jackson had sent a big pan of macaroni and cheese. Because Jackson was Jackson, it couldn't be ordinary mac and cheese, so he'd made it with brie and truffle oil.

The four of them were gathered around Rose's table eating the pasta and drinking a very good Spanish Grenache, talking about Gen's goals for the trip, when Rose brought up the subject of Ryan.

"It's good that he's going with you. It shows he's supportive of your career." She pointed her pasta-laden fork toward Gen. "You don't want some asshole who's going to put himself first, insist that you've got to be the little woman ironing his shirts and … and … I don't know. Baking him cookies. Do not bake him cookies."

"I like cookies," Lacy said.

"It's not about the cookies," Rose insisted.

"No, I get what you're saying. And Ryan's not like that. He didn't hesitate when I asked him if he wanted to come with me."

"Well, he hesitated a little," Kate said.

Gen looked at her. "What do you mean?"

Kate looked uncomfortable. "I shouldn't say anything."

"Of course you should!" Rose insisted.

"Come on, Kate," Gen prompted her. "Spill."

Kate shrugged. "It's just, Ryan talked to Jackson, and Jackson talked to me. Ryan's nervous, is all. He's wondering where this is leading. If you're going to move to New York permanently, and where that'll leave him."

"He didn't tell me any of that," Gen said.

"Of course he didn't," Lacy put in. "Because he's being supportive. It wouldn't be very supportive if he got all angsty to you about what it all means."

"I guess," Gen said.

Rose cocked her head to the side and considered. "It's pretty sweet, if you ask me. I mean, he's worried, and he's maybe wondering if his whole life is going to be uprooted pretty soon, but he's so focused on making you happy that he keeps quiet and pretends he's got no doubts." She nodded thoughtfully. "He might be a keeper."

"Is he?" Lacy asked. "A keeper, I mean. And is he going to get his whole life uprooted pretty soon?"

"You mean, am I moving to New York and will I ask him to go with me?" Gen said.

"That's the question," Kate confirmed.

"I don't know." Gen looked into her wineglass, as though it were a crystal ball.

"You don't know which part?" Rose asked. "Whether you're moving, or whether you're taking him with you?"

"Whether I'm moving. Whatever I do, I kind of can't imagine doing it without Ryan." Just saying the words made her eyes hot, and she blinked a few times, hard.

"Aww," Rose said.

"But his life is here," Gen said. "His family. The ranch. His ... everything."

"Well, if you're not here, then it's not his everything," Lacy said.

"I guess."

"Honey." Kate put a hand on Gen's arm. "You've got to do what's right for you. Ryan will make his own choices. He's in love with you. I'm guessing he'll choose you."

"But I don't even know what I want anymore," Gen said.

"You mean Ryan?" Lacy said.

"No. God. I definitely want Ryan. I ..." She shook her head and looked at the table, trying to think of how to say what she was feeling. "I just thought I had it all figured out, what I wanted from my career. Move to New York, become this hot dealer, this mover and shaker, you know? But now ..."

"Now what?" Lacy prodded gently.

"I'm just confused. That's all," Gen said.

"Well. One step at a time," Kate reassured her. "This trip tomorrow is just one step. You're not moving yet. You're just doing a gallery show."

"Right." Gen took a healthy swallow of the wine. "Right. This is going to be big for Kendrick."

"And big for you," Rose added.

"You can do this," Lacy said. She raised her glass for a toast. "To Gen. Get on that plane and go kick some snooty art-people ass."

Gen drank to that.

Gen found it interesting that, given his financial status, Ryan never even considered flying first class.

"Do you always go coach, like the rest of the huddled masses?" she asked him as they waited at the gate for their plane.

"Sure."

"But why?"

He looked at her as though it were obvious. "You want me to pay an extra two hundred dollars for two more inches of leg room and a glass of wine?"

"I guess not, when you put it that way."

Gen was nervous about the trip, and the airport in San Luis Obispo was so small that she couldn't even enjoy decent shopping while they waited for their flight. When she complained about that to Ryan, he ushered her to a bank of vending machines on one wall of the terminal.

"You want shopping?" he said. "Here we've got a wide selection of soft drinks and snack foods. You name it, and it's yours. Sky's the limit, baby."

She giggled and chose some bottled water and an organic granola bar—selections that he pronounced entirely too healthy for a vacation.

"It's not vacation," she reminded him. "It's a work trip."

"Well, it's vacation for me." Accordingly, he bought a Coke and some Cheetos.

"You know you want some," he said, waving the Cheetos in front of her.

"My body's a temple," she countered.

He lowered his voice and spoke close to her ear. "Well, I know *I* worship it."

She nudged him with her elbow, laughed, and stole one Cheeto from his bag.

❖

"Okay, so listen." It was the day after their arrival in New York, and Gen was scheduled to meet one of the owners of Archibald / Bellini in the bar at the Plaza Hotel. They'd already made their way from the more modest hotel where they were staying, and Gen was giving Ryan a pep talk before they walked in to meet Antonio Bellini. "Just be yourself," she told him. "This is … okay, so, this is a big deal for me. But it's going to be fine. He called me, not the other way around. So I hold all the cards here. It's good. It's going to be good." Halfway through giving Ryan the pep talk, she realized that it was for her and not for him.

Ryan looked amazing in navy slacks, a sky blue dress shirt with the top button undone, and a dark blazer. He was all freshly scrubbed and shaven, and he smelled good, and it wasn't helping her to focus on the task she had ahead of her.

"I can't concentrate when you look at me like that."

"Like what?" he quirked an eyebrow at her.

"Like we've just had amazing sex."

"We did."

"I know. But I can't think about that. Because if I'm thinking about *that*, then I won't be thinking about Gordon Kendrick's show." She took a deep breath and tried to pull herself together.

"Do you want me to go? If you'd rather not have me here, I can see some sights. Visit Times Square or something."

"No! God, no. I need an ally." She squeezed his hand.

"Okay. Well, I'm here. I'm your ally."

"All right."

"You've got this," he said, and kissed her.

His kiss made her knees feel a little bit melty, and that wasn't going to help her nail this meeting.

"No more kissing. If I'm going to focus, there can't be any more kissing," she said.

"Okay. No more kissing." He grinned at her. He'd have to stop doing that, too.

She smoothed her dress—one of the many black dresses she thought of as her gallerywear—and clicked her way into the bar on her spiky high heels with Ryan behind her.

Bellini was sitting at a table by a window under a potted palm tree. She recognized him from a picture she'd found online. She approached him with a confidence she did not feel and extended her hand as Bellini stood to greet her.

"Mr. Bellini, I'm Gen Porter." She shook his hand. "And this is Ryan Delaney."

"A pleasure."

Bellini was a short, mostly bald man in his fifties with thick-framed, round glasses that were so precisely circular that they seemed to be a parody of round glasses—something one of the Muppets would wear in a display of scholarly intellectualism. He was wearing a suit that probably cost two thousand dollars. She recognized two-thousand-dollar suits from when she used to live here, though she hadn't seen one up close in quite some time.

"So, Ryan," Bellini said as they all sat down. "Are you involved in art as well?"

"Cattle," Ryan replied.

Gen braced herself as she imagined where this might go. Bellini might belittle Ryan for his work. Ryan might respond with defensiveness. And then the entire meeting might swirl down the drain like dirty bath water.

Instead, Bellini raised his eyebrows with interest. "Cattle. You're not one of the California Delaneys, are you?"

Ryan grinned. "Well, I imagine there are quite a few Delaney families in California. But that's not what you're asking."

"Ha, ha. No. I'm asking whether you're the Ryan Delaney I read about in *Fortune* magazine."

Gen blinked. Ryan had been in *Fortune* magazine?

"You read that?" Ryan laughed lightly. "They made me and my family seem like these business-savvy moguls. My brother is the one with the business sense. I just know cattle."

"Well, I have to say, it's a thrill to meet you," Bellini said. "Thank you for bringing him along, Genevieve."

Gen's mental GPS navigation system had to reroute to accommodate this sudden change of direction. Bellini not only knew who Ryan was, he was visibly giddy about meeting him. This could be good. It gave Gen a kind of advantage. On the other hand, it wouldn't be good if Bellini was so focused on Ryan that he forgot Gen was there.

"Shall we order?" Bellini asked. A waiter came and took their drink orders—a martini for Bellini, a glass of chardonnay for Gen, and a beer for Ryan.

"I'm thrilled to be showing Gordon Kendrick's work at Archibald / Bellini," Gen said in a bid to get the conversation on track.

"Well, I have to say, I was hoping Mr. Kendrick would be coming as well," Bellini said.

"Ah. Yes. Well, I tried to persuade him to come, but he's recently experienced a remarkable artistic breakthrough, and he didn't want to leave his work." Gen had known the issue would come up, so she had framed it in the best way possible. What Kendrick had actually said was, *You want me to stop painting so I can have wine and cheese and listen to a bunch of blowhards talk about how I 'deconstruct linearity in a post-structuralist world'? The very idea exhausts me. Can't you do it?*

She'd tried to argue with Kendrick, but deep down, she knew he was right, so she hadn't pushed the issue.

"Well." Bellini chuckled. "Far be it from me to separate an artist from his work. Especially when that work is poised to be highly profitable for all of us."

"Let's hope you're right," Gen said.

"Oh, it's not a matter of hoping. Half of the work we're showing has already sold."

The waitress returned with their drinks and placed them carefully on round paper coasters in front of them. Gen was trying to comprehend what he'd just said, and so she ignored her wine.

"It has? But no one has seen the work."

Bellini waved a hand dismissively at her. "I might have passed along some of the digital images you sent me. Just to a few key collectors."

"But we'd agreed not to share the images with anyone until after the show opens." Gen had thought Kendrick's work would have greater impact if it were seen in person. She'd told Bellini that. She didn't want anything to take away from the drama and suspense of unveiling the paintings live, at the gallery.

"Ah, well." He took a drink from his martini. "As I said, sales have been strong. You can't argue with success."

Gen stared at Bellini, who seemed to barely register her presence as he focused on his drink. The guy had flatly ignored the agreement they'd made regarding how to handle the paintings. And now he was unapologetic.

"We had an agreement," she repeated.

"Let's see if you're still cross with me when you see the size of your commission check," he said, winking at her.

"That's not the point," Gen said.

Under the table, Ryan took her hand and squeezed it. She was grateful for that bit of reassurance.

"I thought the point was to sell some paintings," Bellini said. "I've done that, and I will continue to do so." He laughed a breathy laugh, placed his hands on the table, and fidgeted with his diamond pinkie ring. Gen noticed that his watch was Cartier. Did people even wear watches anymore in this age of smartphones? "In fact," he continued, "You'll be stunned at the price I got for *Cambria Pines III*."

She stared at him. "*Cambria Pines III*? That one wasn't for sale."

Bellini made a dismissive sound, something short and breathy. "I know you said that, but ..."

"Kendrick wanted to keep that for his personal collection. He didn't even want to show it, but I assured him that it *wouldn't be sold*."

"Yes, but ..."

"You need to cancel the sale," Gen said.

"I can't." Bellini adjusted his French cuffs. "The original buyer has resold it."

"Wait." Gen pressed her palms onto the table top, her fingers spread. "You're telling me that the painting we agreed would not be sold has already been sold *twice*?"

Bellini shrugged and gave her a tight little grin. "I'm a very good businessman."

"What you are is an assho—"

Ryan squeezed Gen's knee sharply, cutting off the expletive. She took a deep breath and tried to calm down.

Bellini was chuckling—an infuriating laugh that belittled Gen and her petty little concerns about things like integrity. She wanted to punch him in the face, then step on his stupid round glasses.

"Ryan, men like us understand the realities of business, do we not?"

Okay, now the bastard was trying to team up with Ryan, the rich, business-savvy men against the emotional, irrational girl.

"Well, what I understand is that if a man gives his word, he should keep it," Ryan said mildly. "That's how I do business."

"That's how I do it, too," Gen agreed.

"The problem with working with an unknown, small-town gallery owner," Bellini said, carefully straightening his napkin on the table, "is the inevitable naiveté."

The blood pounded in Gen's ears as the phrase *seeing red* took on new meaning for her. "That's just ... I ... Excuse me for a moment, would you?"

She stood, smoothed her dress over her hips, and walked toward the ladies' room with as much calm and dignity as she could muster. Once inside, she let out a roar, kicked the wall until her toes hurt, then slammed a stall door a few times for good measure. A woman in a Chanel suit hurried out of a stall at the far end of the room, gave Gen a frightened look, and then hurried out without even bothering to wash her hands.

Gen pressed a hand to her forehead, looked toward the ceiling, and took a series of deep breaths. She took another moment to find her inner serenity, then returned to the table to face Bellini.

❖

"So, what are you going to do?" Gen and Ryan were walking the five blocks back to their hotel after the meeting with Bellini. The weather was warm, and the sky was a shade of grey that Sherwin-Williams might call "morning fog" or "moonbeam." Fifth Avenue was busy with traffic and pedestrians, with towering buildings to their right and the vast, green expanse of Central Park to their left.

"Well," Gen said, "the first thing I have to do is talk to Gordon. He didn't want to sell the painting. I told him we wouldn't sell it. I promised him."

Ryan shrugged. "I don't see how Bellini could sell it without Gordon's consent. Legally, he'll just have to return the money to the buyer, won't he?"

"Legally, sure."

"But?"

"But, it's complicated. For one thing, Bellini's powerful in the art world. If Gordon pushes the issue and makes him refund the sale, then that's a really big, important bridge to have burned. And the buyers are likely key collectors."

"More important bridges," Ryan said.

"Yes. And art collectors talk to each other. And when they talk, they're not going to frame it as them having bought an artwork that wasn't for sale right out from under the artist. They're going to tell it from their point of view." She shook her head grimly. "By the time the talk circulates, Gordon's going to be seen as a petulant, self-important asshole. Which he certainly can be, on occasion. But still."

They walked through the midafternoon crowds of businesspeople in crisp suits, tourists in jeans and souvenir sweatshirts, and vagrants with their worldly belongings in shopping carts. The city smelled like car exhaust, cigarette smoke, and urine.

"This isn't just about the painting," Gen went on. "It's about Gordon's career."

"So you've got to talk him into letting it go," Ryan said.

"I think I do, yeah. And that really sucks. It's his painting. If he wants to keep it, he should be able to keep it."

"Listen," Ryan said. "Let's get your mind off it. We'll get back to the hotel, change into comfortable clothes, and then we'll do something fun. Act like tourists. You're free the rest of the day, right?"

"Yeah. I just have to make a very uncomfortable phone call to Gordon Kendrick."

"Okay. You'll do that, and afterward, we'll … hell, I don't know. Visit Rockefeller Center."

She grinned at him. "You really want to visit Rockefeller Center?"

"Hell, yeah. This might be work for you, but it's my vacation. I want to see the sights."

"All right." She put her hand in his, and she felt a warm swell of happiness as their fingers intertwined. "Let's see the sights."

After Gen talked to Kendrick—there was some yelling by him, and a good deal of commiserating and placating by her— she and Ryan changed into jeans and comfortable shoes and went back out into the city. They walked through Central Park, visited the Statue of Liberty, and then had dinner at a trendy café overlooking New York Harbor. They would have gone to MoMA, but Gen said she'd thought about art enough for one day.

Of course, having lived in New York, she'd seen all of the sights before. But it was different seeing them with Ryan. His enthusiasm was infectious. As angry as she'd been earlier in the day—as demoralized as she'd felt—she still found herself laughing and smiling as she toured the city with him. They held hands and marveled over the view of the skyline. They ate and drank and talked. They kissed as they looked out from inside the statue's crown.

Later, tired and happy, they made love on the hotel bed until late into the night. Contented, Gen fell asleep in Ryan's arms. She wasn't thinking about Antonio Bellini, or about Gordon Kendrick, at all.

Chapter Twenty-Nine

In the days leading up to the gallery show, Gen had a number of errands to do and details to take care of. She sent Ryan off to do more sightseeing—he wanted to take a guided tour and then ride the Staten Island Ferry—while she visited the framer to ensure Gordon's paintings were being handled properly, met with Bellini again, and talked to an art journalist about a magazine piece he was doing on Kendrick.

When she'd met with Bellini, she'd asked to see the catalog that would accompany the show, but he'd said it wasn't ready. She'd gotten the feeling that he was putting her off, so she'd nagged him about it, calling him repeatedly to ask if it was finished yet, and when she could see it.

She'd known from his tone, and from his repeated excuses, that there was something wrong with the catalog. Even so, when a messenger finally brought a copy to her hotel and she retrieved it from the front desk, she was caught unprepared for what she found.

"It's all about Bellini!" she ranted over the phone to Gordon as she leafed through the catalog. "It's about how he discovered you, and … and how *he* saw something in you, some 'spark of genius,' as he puts it. Apparently, you owe everything to him."

"We've never met," Gordon remarked dryly.

"I know!" Gen exclaimed. "Of course, there's no mention of the Cambria residency. Shit. Shit! And no mention of me. Jesus! To read this, you'd think Bellini was standing there holding your brushes as you worked."

Gordon sighed heavily over the line. "What about the paintings? What does it say about the paintings?"

"Okay, wait. It says … Oh. Oh, no. It says you were inspired by the … wait. The 'clash between man and industry in a post-global-warming age.' What the …"

"Trees," Kendrick said. "I was inspired by trees. And the sky. And cows."

"This is … They've completely misinterpreted your work."

"So it would seem."

"You're calm," Gen said. "Why are you so calm?!"

"Gen." Gordon sounded infinitely patient, something she never would have expected from him when they'd first met. "It's all about the work. None of the rest of this matters. And the work is going better than I ever could have expected."

"Well, that's … Okay. You're right. I know you're right."

"And no matter what the catalog says, it was you. Bellini didn't bring this out of me; you did."

Gen was touched. Her eyes were hot and wet, and she felt a smile come to her lips. "Thank you, Gordon. You know, you've changed since you came to Cambria." She didn't want to tell him he'd been a mess. But she probably didn't have to, because he already knew.

"I feel … It's like I finally know what I'm doing."

She wished she did, too, but more and more these days, she found herself doubting it.

"Well, you're going to be doing it with a lot more money when this is over."

"From your lips to God's ears."

Gen was becoming more and more stressed as the date of the show approached. Bellini was an asshole, the catalog was full of lies, the paintings were being misinterpreted, and she had to grit her teeth to get through any meeting with the Archibald / Bellini people without throwing something.

Ryan, on the other hand, appeared to be having a wonderful time.

Every day, he went out into the city eager to take in the sights, excited about whatever he was planning to do that day. If she had a light schedule with the gallery people, she'd go with him. They would eat at a deli, walk hand in hand through Battery Park, or people-watch on Fifth Avenue. They spent an afternoon at the natural history museum, marveling over the dinosaur skeletons and the IMAX planetarium show.

In the evenings, they made love in the hotel bed, or in the shower, or once—memorably—against the wall. Gen drew the line at doing it on the floor, because one could never know what lurked in the depths of hotel carpets.

"Are you having fun?" she asked him late one night when she was naked and wrapped in his arms.

"Yeah. I really am. But I know you're kind of having a rough time with work." He kissed her forehead tenderly.

"Work? What work?" she said dreamily as she raised her face to his to be kissed.

It was almost over. She and Ryan were set to be in New York for a week, with the gallery opening scheduled for a Friday night at the tail end of the visit. As Friday arrived, Gen was looking forward to wrapping things up and going home to enjoy her victory. By the time the evening ended, she'd have done everything she'd set out to do. She'd found an artist, brought him to Cambria, coaxed him into producing terrific work, and helped him to get his name known among the power people of the art world. She'd brought her own name to the attention of those same power people. And she also, quite likely, would go home with earnings substantial enough to help her relocate to New York.

Right now, though, she wasn't even sure she wanted to come here.

It would be easy to tell herself that Bellini was the exception—that he was just one man who lacked integrity, and that the rest of the New York art world upheld higher standards. But she knew that was bullshit. If she moved here, she'd have to deal with one Bellini after another, one self-absorbed, power-hungry, money-obsessed asshole after another. Bellini wasn't the exception. He was the rule. *She* would be the exception. And upholding her own ideas about ethics and personal character would place her at a distinct disadvantage here.

But that wasn't the worst part.

The worst part was the idea that she might learn to adapt, and that adapting might mean that she would become more like him than she would ever want to admit.

"Do I have to be Bellini?" Gen asked Ryan anxiously as she fussed with her earrings in the hotel mirror.

"I certainly hope not," Ryan said, coming up behind her. He put his hands on her shoulders and bent down to press a kiss against the soft skin of her neck. "That would kind of put a damper on our sex life."

She smacked him playfully with her hand. "I'm serious."

"You're serious about whether you have to become a middle-aged Italian man?"

"I'm serious about … Well, God. About whether I have to act like him in order to compete. You know? He's successful, Ryan. Really successful. If I want to be successful, do I have to turn into a … a …"

"An insufferable, morally challenged narcissist?" Ryan supplied.

"Thank you. Yes."

He gently turned her around to face him. His voice softer, he said, "Gen, that's not going to happen."

"How can you be sure?"

"I can be sure, because I know you."

She looked into his dark, liquid eyes and wanted to believe him. "You think you know me, but …"

"I know you," he said.

And she thought that he did. At least, he knew part of her. He knew her at her best, knew the person she wanted to be. And she realized that the person she wanted to be was very much like him: honest, compassionate, gentle, and strong.

She wanted to be those things not only for herself. She wanted to be those things so she wouldn't disappoint him.

Gen might have had a lot of complaints about Bellini, but she had to give him one thing: Gordon's art looked stunning on the walls of the gallery. The framing was perfect; the lighting was perfect; and the order in which the paintings were presented showed them off to the best possible effect. As she moved through the crowd at the gallery, a glass of white wine in her hand, she reflected that maybe she'd been worried about nothing. Maybe this was going to work out after all.

Katya, Bellini's gallery assistant, stepped up beside Gen, and they both took a moment to look at *Cambria Pines III*, the painting Gordon hadn't wanted to let go. She could see why he'd wanted to keep it. The colors, the brushwork, the sense of movement—this was the painting that most fully captured Gordon's transformation from the artist he'd been to the artist he was now. Though she was still steaming over the fact that it had been sold—twice—she could certainly understand why the buyers had wanted it.

"That one's nice," Katya said, gazing at the painting. She was a five-foot-ten former model with a willowy figure, heavy black eyeliner, and jet black bangs that looked like they'd been cut with the aid of a ruler. Katya was wearing a skin-tight black dress and heels so high and slim that it seemed impossible they could support the weight of a fully grown adult.

"Yes," Gen responded. "It's the artist's favorite."

"You can really see his rage," Katya reflected. "There's a sense of doom. A sort of swirling madness." She moved one dramatically manicured hand in a circular motion in the air in front of the painting, to indicate Gordon's vortex of insanity.

"Rage?" Gen said. "Madness?"

"Oh, yes." Katya nodded sagely. "There's a certain desperation to the work."

"Katya." Gen turned to face the woman, who was so much taller than Gen that she towered over her. "Gordon almost titled this work *Serenity*."

"Ah." Katya nodded. "Irony."

"No. He wasn't being ironic. This painting was inspired by the woods, and the grass, and the … the goddamned serenity of nature!"

"All right." Katya side-eyed Gen and inched a step away from her. "Maybe you're the one with the rage."

Maybe she was. She took a deep breath and reminded herself that it didn't matter how Katya interpreted the paintings. It didn't matter if Gordon was misunderstood, as long as the paintings sold. But she knew that was bullshit. It did matter. Art was communication, first and foremost. She felt a responsibility to ensure that Gordon's message wasn't getting muddled. But it wasn't right to take her frustrations out on Katya.

"I'm sorry," she said. "It's just … this show. It's a lot of pressure."

"Look, I get it." Katya put a graceful, long-fingered hand on Gen's shoulder. "Antonio has been miserable to be around this entire week." Katya rolled her eyes extravagantly. "And speaking of Antonio." Katya shifted her weight to face Gen. "When you get a moment, he'd like me to show you a gallery space a few blocks from here. It's just around the corner on Grand Street."

"A gallery space?"

"You told him you were interested in relocating to Manhattan, right?"

"I … uh … yes."

She nodded. "He has a nice space he's looking to sublet. He thought it might be right for you."

"Oh … That's great." The idea of moving had, of course, been foremost in Gen's mind for a while now. But moving, as a concept, was one thing. Actually looking at gallery space was another.

"Just let me know when you get a break in the action," Katya said. "And I'll run you over there."

"All right."

Katya went to restock the hors d'oeuvre table, leaving Gen standing alone in front of *Cambria Pines III*. Ryan had been across the room chatting with some middle-aged guy with a gold hoop earring and hand-made Italian loafers. Now he'd disengaged from the guy, and he came over to stand beside Gen.

"How's it going?" he asked. He had a wineglass in his hand, and it was still mostly full.

"It's okay." Gen nodded. "Actually, it's crap. But it'll be over soon, so that's good."

"More trouble with Bellini?" Ryan asked in a low voice so he would not be overheard.

"Not really. It's just … It's a lot to absorb." She put a hand on his shoulder. "You must be miserable."

"Me?" He raised his eyebrows at her. "No, no. I'm having a nice time, actually."

"You are?"

"Sure. I'm meeting new people, seeing some very good art. Drinking some pretty good wine." He held up his glass. "And I get to be with you."

"Well … okay. Good. I did notice that a lot of people have been talking to you."

"Yeah." He scratched at the back of his neck. "It seems Bellini let it slip that I'm one of 'the California Delaneys.' I've gotten three pitches for investments that are going to double my money, two pleas from nonprofits that need donations, and two—wait, no, three—women's phone numbers."

She smirked at him. "Let me guess. Katya was one of them."

"Yeah, but I think Bellini put her up to it."

"He probably did."

Just standing there talking to him made her stress melt away, and she found herself with a goofy grin on her face. It was funny how he could do that—how whatever had been wrong stopped being wrong as soon as he entered a room. She'd expected that he wouldn't fit in here—that he would be uncomfortable in the presence of a bunch of pretentious aesthetes who'd spent their entire adulthoods polishing themselves to a high shine. But he'd slipped into the crowd effortlessly, like he belonged there. She was a little ashamed of the assumptions she'd made about him.

"Speaking of Bellini," she began. "He wants to show me a gallery space."

"What, here?"

"Yes. Katya says it's around the corner. He wants to sub-let it."

She saw a moment of hesitation in his face—just a moment—and then he smiled.

"That's great. You should look at it."

"Really?" Part of her was excited at the prospect, and another part of her was disappointed that Ryan wasn't more reluctant about the idea of her moving two thousand miles away.

"Sure. You've been wanting this for a long time. It's an opportunity. You don't want to ignore an opportunity."

"But ..."

"Look." He bent a little to kiss the tip of her nose. "This thing with us isn't going to go away just because you move. I can visit you. You can visit me. When the time is right ... Well. If you decided that you wanted me to move out here to be with you, that wouldn't be out of the question."

"It wouldn't?" She was stunned. She'd always assumed that Ryan was as rooted to the Cambria earth as the pines that lined the shoreline.

"Hell, no. It would take some doing, sure. We'd have to find someone to run the ranch. Maybe talk my brother Liam into moving back from Montana. But we'd work it out. It could be done."

She suddenly felt a little teary-eyed, and she blinked hard. "You'd do that for me?"

"Gen." He put his fingers gently beneath her chin, raising her face toward his. "For you, I'd do that, and a whole hell of a lot more."

"But ..."

"Just look at the gallery space. It wouldn't hurt to look."

"Yeah. Okay."

He was right. It wouldn't hurt to look.

Gen had some more mingling to do before she could leave. She talked to a few collectors, some people from other galleries in Manhattan, a few B-list celebrities, and a number of artists, a couple she'd heard of and more she had not. She distributed her business card where appropriate, and she tried to gently correct misinterpretations of Gordon's artwork when the opportunity presented itself.

Finally, as the crowd began to thin out, she approached Katya.

"I guess this is as good a time as any to see the gallery space," she said.

"Great. Just let me grab the key."

They got their jackets, and Gen told Ryan to sit tight and enjoy the last of the crab puffs, promising she'd be right back. Then Gen and Katya clicked down the sidewalk and around the corner on their spike heels in the cool evening air.

The space was no more than a five-minute walk away. Katya unlocked the door and let Gen inside, and then she flipped on the lights.

The gallery space wasn't large—not really—but it was huge by Manhattan standards. Clean white walls and gleaming honey-colored wood floors immediately made Gen fantasize about the shows she could have here, the artists she would feature, the installations, the world of aesthetic pleasures she could create.

"It's beautiful," she told Katya as she walked the length of the main room. "But I'm sure it's out of my price range."

"Not necessarily." Katya told her the monthly rent.

"Really? That's all?" Gen thought she must have heard wrong.

"I was surprised, too, when Antonio told me. Rents in this part of town usually are much higher." She shrugged. "I suppose he just wants to see you in here. Create an alliance and all that."

It was the "all that" that worried Gen. Bellini was more than a little sleazy in his business practices. If she were his tenant, what unethical things would she be expected to do to keep him happy and keep the rent low?

Still, the place was lovely. She wandered into the back room and then into the small office off the main space.

"How soon would he need to know?"

Katya was inspecting the fingernails of her right hand. "You'd have to talk to Antonio about that. I don't really know the details."

Gen looked around a little more, and then they locked the place up and made their way back to Archibald / Bellini.

The gallery space was like a gift, beautifully wrapped and tempting. But she worried that there might be something nasty hiding inside, something she'd be better off without.

Chapter Thirty

A few minutes after Gen and Katya left Archibald /
Bellini to look at the space around the corner, Ryan
was chatting with an artist in front of a painting titled
Creekside, Delaney Ranch. The artist, a guy who described his
work as "found object" art but who, in Ryan's estimation, really just made things out of trash, was talking about the inanity of
figurative art, an argument that apparently meant art shouldn't
be of anything, or about anything. Ryan nodded his head a lot
and made noises of affirmation, even though the guy's philosophy sounded like a load of crap.

The guy was going into a speech about a particular artist's
"subversive brilliance" when Antonio Bellini came up and put
a hand on Ryan's shoulder.

"How are you enjoying the show, Mr. Delaney?" he asked.

"Call me Ryan."

"Of course. Ryan."

Bellini said some placating words to the artist and then led
Ryan away.

After a little warm-up chitchat about New York,
California, ranching, art, and the common ties of wealthy men,
Bellini arrived at his point. "I'm sure Genevieve has already
spoken to you about what a wise investment a Kendrick would
be. With the attention he's getting—especially with the
acquisition by David Walker—the value of his work is only
going to go up. You should consider it."

Ryan was no stranger to having people try to sell him
"investments." He simply nodded and smiled. "She hasn't
spoken to me about it, actually. We like to keep business out of
our personal relationship." It sounded as though they'd had

some sort of conversation to that effect, but in fact, it was just a matter of courtesy. Gen hadn't tried to sell him a painting because she wasn't a sleazy opportunist.

"Of course, of course," Bellini said, smiling as though he'd expected no other answer. "And yet—it would be a shame for you to miss out on a significant opportunity for profit because of—" He waved a hand vaguely as he searched for a phrase. "—personal considerations."

"Generally speaking, I'm not short of opportunities for profit," Ryan said mildly.

Bellini chuckled. "I'm sure that's true."

He clapped a hand onto Ryan's back as though they were old friends.

"Speaking of profit opportunities, did Genevieve tell you about the gallery space I have available?"

"She did. Katya's showing it to her now." Ryan was certain Bellini already knew that.

"Good, good." Bellini nodded. "I'm sure it's going to meet her needs. And the rent … You know, spaces in this area tend to be very expensive. Of course, not by my standards—or yours, I'm sure. But a woman like Genevieve—"

"It's important to her to do this on her own, without any help from me," Ryan said.

Bellini beamed. "Yes, I got that impression."

Bellini had a point, Ryan was sure of it. Eventually, the man would get to it. Ryan wasn't sure he had enough patience to wait that long.

"You know, I could offer Genevieve the space at a substantial discount," Bellini said finally, after a good deal more posturing.

"Really."

"Oh, yes. But it all depends on sales from the Kendrick show. If it does well, I'd have the ... shall we say ... the leeway to make things work out well for Genevieve."

Here it came. "And how do sales seem to be going?" Ryan said. He was offering a slow pitch over the center of the plate, in the hope that Bellini would hit the damned thing and they could move this along.

"Very well, very well." Bellini nodded. "But ... so far, it's not what you'd call a spectacular success."

"And you need a spectacular success in order to offer Gen the gallery space."

"I'm afraid so."

Ryan wanted to stop dancing around it. He wanted to say: *Let's cut the bullshit. How much are you hoping to extort out of me?* But guys like Bellini didn't work that way. He had to come to it in his own way. Ryan knew guys like this. You couldn't spend your whole life as wealthy as his family was without running into them on an almost daily basis. But it didn't make it any more pleasant. The thing about Gen was that even though she knew this world, this New York art world, she still had a naïve optimism that people would be fair and ethical. Despite vast evidence to the contrary, she still had hope for human nature. It was one of the things he loved about her. One of the many things. It pissed him off that Bellini was trying to use him, but he was used to that. What pissed him off even more was that this asshole was going to kill another little bit of Gen's persistent belief in the basic good of others. For that, Ryan wanted to punch the guy in the goddamned face.

"Well, good luck. There's still time for things to pick up," Ryan said.

"Indeed. I was hoping you could help me with that."

"Were you?"

"Yes. You see, if you were to purchase a painting—one of the larger, more highly prized ones, of course—then that would ensure that I'll be in the financial position to offer Genevieve the gallery space, and at a price I'm sure she'll find workable given her … limited means. And," Bellini spread his hands in a gesture of magnanimity, "it would certainly be a wise investment for you as well. Our Gordon is going to do great things."

Our Gordon. As though Bellini had anything to do with Kendrick's talent. As though Bellini had personally nurtured him. As though they'd even met.

"How much?" Ryan asked.

"Well, it depends on which artwork you …"

"Stop it. How much?" Ryan repeated.

Bellini cleared his throat and told him.

"I see," Ryan said. He nodded. He gritted his teeth and looked at the floor in an effort to hold his temper in check. "If that were to happen, Gen couldn't know about it," Ryan said.

"Of course not," Bellini assured him. "That's the point, isn't it? For her to believe she's pulling herself up by her own bootstraps, as it were? But you and I …" He nodded smugly. "We know the ways of the world."

"This has been an interesting evening," Ryan said after a moment. "It's certainly met my expectations."

He walked away from Bellini and went to the front of the gallery to wait for Gen.

Ryan needed to talk it all over with somebody, but he couldn't talk to Gen. After they arrived back at the hotel, he checked the time. It was still early on the West Coast. While Gen was taking a shower, Ryan called Daniel.

"You know Gen really well," Ryan said when Daniel picked up the phone.

"I guess. I've been showing my work at the Porter Gallery for a while now, so I've spent some time with her."

"You talk about things. You're friendly," Ryan said.

"Sure."

Ryan sighed heavily. "Okay. Then I need some advice." He laid out everything that had happened with Gen, and the Kendrick show, and Bellini.

"I don't enjoy being strong-armed for money. But I also don't want to be too cheap to help her get what she wants, you know?"

"Crap," Daniel said.

"Yeah."

"What did she think about the gallery space?"

"She said it was beautiful. Went on and on about the location, the light, the … I don't know. The 'feel' of it, I think she said. She really liked it." Ryan rotated his neck, trying to stretch out a little of the stress from the day. "Hell. I'm not even sure she wants to move to New York."

"Oh, she wants to." Daniel sounded certain.

"You're sure?"

"Oh, yeah. She's been talking about it as long as I've known her. About how she was going to go back someday, get a gallery of her own, get back what she lost when that shithead MacIntyre screwed her over."

Ryan sighed. "Oh."

"Wouldn't it be more straightforward to help her out with the lease on a gallery yourself, rather than doing all this clandestine bullshit?"

"Well, sure it would. But she'd hand me my ass if I even suggested it," Ryan said.

"Huh. Well," Daniel mused, "you might just want to let it go. I mean, you're probably not too eager to have a long-distance relationship. And what else are you going to do if she leaves, break up? Move to New York?"

"We're not going to break up," he said.

"Okay, then. I'm just saying … it's not really in your best interest to pony up the money."

"I don't care about my best interest. I care about hers," Ryan said.

"Well … I can't tell you what to do, man. But the triumphant return to Manhattan is a key part of what she sees for herself. It hurt her when she got pushed out. It hurt her a lot."

"Okay." Ryan sighed. So much uncertainty was rumbling around inside him. It rankled him to his very core that Bellini might be able to take advantage of him, to extort him. On the other hand, it was just money, and if it could be used to make Gen happy …

The other side of it was that if Gen set up a gallery in a space owned by Bellini, what might he want from her in the future? Ryan was certain it wouldn't end with his purchase of an overpriced Kendrick. Bellini would want more from Ryan—more money, certainly, but probably his influence as well. He'd want to use his "Ryan Delaney of the California Delaneys" connection to whatever advantage he could. And in what ways would he use Gen? But Ryan wasn't naïve about how things worked. He knew having a connection to someone like Bellini could work to Gen's advantage. And she knew it, too. It was possible she could work it to achieve all of her goals. If Ryan didn't stand in her way.

"Look," Ryan told Daniel. "Gen's coming, I've gotta go."

"Good luck, man," Daniel told him. "Whichever way you go, you're going to need it."

The following day, when Ryan took a check in a plain white envelope to Archibald / Bellini, he found Katya alone in the gallery. He placed the envelope on her desk.

"Tell your boss I stopped by, would you?" he said. "And give him this."

Katya rose from her chair, came around to the front of the desk, sat her butt on the sleek, modern desktop, and crossed her impossibly long legs. Her little black dress was very short, and it rose even further with her gesture. Ryan didn't want to look, but he couldn't help it. The legs were right there.

"He'll be back soon," she said. "Why don't you wait for him? I'm sure you and I can entertain each other until his return."

Was she hitting on him? She'd been a little too friendly the night before, sure—she'd been one of the women who'd slipped him her number—but what was this? What kind of *entertainment* was she talking about?

"Thanks, but you don't have to entertain me."

She got up from the desk, walked over to him on sky-high heels, and stepped up so close that her breasts brushed against his chest. She looked up at him through her dark eyelashes, her straight, black bangs brushing the tops of eyebrows that had been groomed to the point that they were barely recognizable as hair.

"It would be my pleasure," she said.

Ryan wondered briefly if Bellini had asked her to screw him in the back room to seal the deal. For a guy like Bellini, it seemed plausible. And then Ryan realized that Gen had once been someone's Katya. She'd worked in jobs like this for guys like Bellini. What had she been asked to do? And for whom?

Suddenly, he could see why she'd had to leave New York in the first place. Because she wouldn't screw wealthy men in back rooms.

A surge of rage shot through him, and the muscles in his jaw bunched up as he fought it back.

"Just give Bellini the envelope."

He took a step back from Katya's breasts and walked out, anger pulsing hard in his chest.

Chapter Thirty-One

"So this is it, then? You're leaving?"

Back in Cambria, Gen was perched on a barstool at De-Vine while Rose stood behind the bar, leaning her forearms on the gleaming wooden top.

"I don't know. I don't know what to do."

"But you like the gallery space."

"Oh God, I love it." She sighed and plopped her head down into her hands. She shook her head, and her curls flopped back and forth. "It's gorgeous. I can see my gallery there, Rose, I really can."

"So what's holding you back? Ryan?"

"It's … a lot of things."

De-Vine had no customers at the moment, as it was barely ten a.m. and the wine tasting traffic didn't usually pick up until after lunchtime. Gen was grateful, because she needed Rose to help her think things through.

"Okay, then," Rose said, nodding her head, which was covered in lilac-colored hair. "Let's do pros and cons."

"All right." Gen lifted her head and straightened on her barstool.

"Pros first," Rose prompted her.

"Okay, pros. One, I've been wanting to go back to New York ever since MacIntyre died. Before that, really. Two, Manhattan is where all the action is, art-wise. I can't really be a player if I'm not there. Three, the gallery space is … oh, jeez. It's just everything I want. Four, New York is … well. It's New York. It's exciting. There's so much to do. It's got that energy."

"Which Cambria doesn't have."

"No."

"Okay, now the cons."

"Cons." Gen started ticking points off on her fingers. "One, Ryan would have to decide whether to come with me or not. If he did, it would really be hard for his family. And for him. Two, you and Kate and Lacy aren't there." Gen started to tear up at the thought of that.

"Oh, honey." Rose reached out and squeezed Gen's hand.

"Three, I love Cambria. God, it's beautiful here. I think I take it for granted sometimes, the natural beauty. I mean, living here every day, I don't know if I always *notice*. But to leave …"

Rose nodded. "I know."

"And four," Gen continued, "I'd kind of forgotten how sleazy people can be when there's big money involved. You know? Bellini's all about the money, he's not about the art. And it's not just him. It's the gallery culture out there. I don't know if I can be that way. Or if I even want to."

"But that leads to another pro," Rose offered.

"It does? How?"

"Because you can go out there and be a force for good." Rose crossed her arms over her chest and raised one pierced eyebrow. "You can be all about the art. Sounds like somebody needs to be."

"Yeah. That's true." Gen nodded. "Yeah."

"So. Who wins? The pros or the cons?"

"I have to decide soon," Gen said, feeling miserable. "The gallery space won't be open forever."

Kendrick was the one who decided it for her.

She went out to visit him at the ranch the day after she returned from New York. She met him at the cottage and told him the good news about his sales—and it was very good news, indeed. After they talked about numbers for a little while, he took her out to the old barn and showed her what he'd been working on. The new canvases were startling in their intensity. Amid abstract bursts of color, images came to her—of birds, of the shoreline, of grassy slopes and clear skies.

"Oh, Gordon," she said with a dreamy sigh. "These are just wonderful."

"So, who have you got lined up for your next residency?" he asked.

"Well … no one. This was kind of a one-time deal."

He looked at her with surprise and dismay. "Genevieve," he said with a scolding tone in his voice, peering at her over his glasses.

She wasn't sure what she'd done to earn his scorn. "What?"

"Why on earth wouldn't you continue the residency?"

"Well, I … The idea was to do this, have some success—which we did—and then relocate to New York." She sounded uncertain and defensive to her own ears.

"That was the idea, was it?" He sounded like a stern professor, about to school his naïve and impossibly immature student. "Genevieve. Come walk with me." Kendrick led her out of the barn and onto a trail that led up into the rolling hills of the ranch.

The morning was cool and crisp, with a light breeze that sent the grass rippling in waves before them. The distant rumble of the waves crashing against the shore mingled with the sounds of birds and the burbling creek off to their left.

"Let me ask you something," Kendrick said. "When you came up with this idea—the idea for the residency—what were you hoping for? What did you imagine might happen?"

"I told you. I thought we'd have some success—"

"But what does that mean? What did you think 'success' would look like? Was it just about money? About selling paintings?"

"No. No, no." Gen thought carefully about her answer. "I had hoped that if I brought you out here, this place—the beauty of it—might inspire you. I could see that you were on the verge of something. I thought if you were here, with the quiet, and the peace … if you could just be with nature for a while, it might, kind of—" She made a shoving motion with her hands. "—push you over the verge."

He paused on the path and turned to look at her. "And how does it feel to know that it did exactly that?"

To hear that, to hear him say it that way, made something within her soar. She blinked away sudden tears. "I … God, Gordon. When you put it that way …"

"Close your eyes," he said.

She did.

"Now, just listen."

She heard the ocean, the breeze rustling in the branches of the trees. Somewhere above, a gull cawed, and something else—some small, winged thing— tittered in the pines. She heard water rush through rocks, and the slow, gentle hum of her own breath.

"Now open your eyes, and *look*."

Carpets of tall, golden grass, shifting in color with the rhythm of the breeze. Sunlight glinting on the ocean. Sleek, feathered bodies gliding overhead. Leaves swaying gently in a private dance. The pattern of the clouds in a cerulean sky.

"This place is magic, Gen," Kendrick said. "That's what you see on my canvases. There's magic here."

She knew he was right, and she knew she had to bring this same magic to other artists. Artists like Kendrick, who needed to be pushed over the verge.

❖

"I know what I'm going to do," Gen told Ryan later that day, when he came to her place after his workday was done.

"About what?"

"About New York. About moving."

He took a deep breath. "I'd better sit down for this." He sat at her kitchen table and focused those dark-chocolate eyes on her. "Okay, I'm ready."

"I'm staying." She felt giddy with happiness, not only with relief because the decision had been made, but also because it was right. This was right. She was home.

"Oh, thank God," he said. She could see the tension drain out of him as he went nearly limp in his chair. "Are you sure, though? I thought you really wanted it."

"I thought I did, too. But going out there, spending time there ... I remembered the downsides. And there are a lot of downsides."

He reached out and grabbed her hand, and tugged her down onto his lap. She wiggled a bit, getting comfortable, as he wrapped his arms around her.

"Are you gonna be happy, running your gallery in Cambria? Is that going to be enough for you?"

"I'm not just going to run the gallery."

He raised his eyebrows. "Oh?"

"No. I'm going to continue the artist's residency. If you're okay with me continuing to lease your guest house and your barn."

"Well, I think we can work something out." He gave her a sexy grin. "What made you decide all this?"

"Gordon."

"Really."

"Yeah. He just … I saw him earlier today. And he …" She found that she couldn't continue, because there were tears in her eyes and her voice was becoming thick.

He rubbed at her back and tucked her head under his chin.

"This just meant a lot to him," she said finally, when she could continue. "It changed him. I want to do that for other artists. I think it's what I'm supposed to do."

"Then that's what you'll do."

Being there with him, thinking about her plans for the future, she could practically hear the puzzle pieces of her life clicking into place. Ryan, her friends, this place. Meaningful work that would bring meaning to others.

"I love you," she said. She'd felt it before now—known it—but this was the first time she'd said it.

He held her tighter, and she could hear his heartbeat against her cheek. "Ah, Gen," he murmured. "I love you too."

Chapter Thirty-Two

She had a lot to do at the gallery after her week-long absence. Alex had done a good job holding down the fort, but there was business only she could handle, and she found that it had piled up while she'd been gone.

She was knee-deep in Excel spreadsheets when Katya called on her cell phone.

"Oh, geez. Katya," Gen said when she answered the phone. "I was meaning to call you."

"Antonio needs an answer about the gallery space," Katya said. "He said, and I quote, 'Do not let her off the phone until she says yes.'"

"Ah. Well, I'm afraid I'm going to have to disappoint him. I'm not taking the space."

"You're not?" She could hear the surprise in Katya's voice.

"No."

"Well. All right. I'll tell him, but he won't be happy."

Gen shifted in her chair and moved the cell phone to her other ear. "I'm not sure why it matters to him. I'm sure he can lease the space to someone else. And at a higher price than he was offering me."

"Of course he can." Katya sounded impatient with her.

"Then why … ?"

"You're terribly naïve," Katya said.

Bellini had said the same thing. Gen was beginning to wonder whether it was true.

"What do you mean, Katya?"

Katya was silent.

"Tell me," Gen insisted.

"Antonio wants you in the gallery space so he can have leverage with the Delaneys. Obviously. You can't possibly think the one purchase was going to be the only one."

Gen started to feel cold. "What purchase?"

"You don't know," Katya said with wonder.

"What purchase, Katya?"

"Your boyfriend made a very large purchase at the show last week. Antonio suggested that it was the only way he'd be in a position to offer you the gallery space at that price. Honestly, Genevieve. Did you think that's what space in SoHo really costs?"

Gen felt sick. She pressed a hand to her belly, as though that might stop the nausea rising there.

"Genevieve?"

"I just … Let me make sure I have all of this straight. Bellini told Ryan that he would give me the gallery space at a rock-bottom price if he made a big purchase. And Ryan did it."

"That about covers it, yes."

"How big a purchase are we talking about?"

With amusement in her voice, Katya said, "I saw the check, Genevieve. There haven't been that many zeroes in one place since the size tags at Fashion Week."

"I … God."

"I'll tell Bellini his cash cow has left the pasture."

"You do that."

Gen ended the call, then placed the phone on the desk in front of her and stared at it.

Alex walked past her and did a double-take.

"Are you okay?"

"Fine." Gen kept staring at the phone.

"Are you sure?"

"Yes." She stood up, stared at the desk a while longer, then snatched the stapler off the desk and hurled it into the wall, where it left a small dent in the drywall.

"Uh oh," Alex said, and quickly found something to do in the back room.

She tracked him down at the ranch. She went to the house first, but of course he wasn't there in the middle of the day. Sandra said he was probably out in the northwest pasture. She put on her athletic shoes and tromped out there, only to find a bunch of lumbering black cows and no Ryan.

She finally found him in the new barn, where he was making cooing sounds to a cow. The cow was shifting uncomfortably from one foot to another, occasionally letting out a mournful moo, as Ryan crouched down and did something to her that undoubtedly would be hard for Gen to get out of her head if she knew what it was.

With a head full of steam, Gen stomped down the rows of clean metal pens, her sneakers crunching on a layer of dirt and hay, until she reached him.

"What the *hell* is this I hear about you writing a giant check to Bellini?" she demanded. She was breathing hard, only partly due to the long walk out here. Her heart was pounding, and her voice sounded slightly hysterical.

"Gen." Ryan stood up, patted the cow, and came out of the pen to stand in the aisle with her.

"You wrote Bellini a big goddamned check, and we both know it wasn't because you wanted a goddamned Gordon Kendrick." She wrapped her arms around herself because that way, it was easier not to throttle him.

"Well." He rubbed at the back of his neck. "Who told you about that?"

"Katya." She spit out the name as though it tasted bad. Which it did.

"Look. Gen." He made a patting gesture in the air in front of him, which she supposed was intended to be calming. It wasn't. "Let's just ... Can we just sit down someplace and talk about this?"

"Talk about what?" she demanded. "About how you thought you could buy off Bellini to get him to offer me cheap gallery space? So you could make poor, inept Gen think she was achieving something on her own? God. It makes me sick to think of you and Bellini scheming behind my back. Do you understand how *humiliating* this is? How demeaning?"

"I didn't mean it like that. I didn't ..."

"Then how *did* you mean it, Ryan? How else could you possibly have intended it?"

He turned and walked a few steps away. He hung his head and put his hands on his hips, then turned back to face her again.

"He—Bellini—said he 'wouldn't be in a position' to offer you the space without a big purchase from me. And I ... You had already gone with Katya to look at it. You were so excited about it. Told me how it was perfect for you. I didn't want to be that guy who was too tight with his checkbook to get you what you wanted."

"What I *wanted* was to prove myself. To make something of myself in that world, *on my own,* without anyone's help. And now ..." She shook her head, her lips pursed tight.

"I thought you didn't want that anymore," he said. "I thought you'd decided it wasn't for you."

"That's not the point."

"Then what is the point? What's the point, Gen?" His voice was raised to a level that was upsetting to the cow, who tossed her head and made a grunting noise.

"The point is that you didn't trust me to stand on my own. You didn't think I could do it without you. And if you're here, standing behind me with your … your Delaney money and your giant almighty checkbook, then I'll never have the chance to try." Tears were spilling down her cheeks, and she swiped at them with her fingertips.

"Ah, Gen …"

"I think I need to go." She turned and walked out of the barn.

"Gen, wait." He started to follow her, and she turned on him, her eyes bright with anger.

"Don't. Just … don't."

She walked out, and he let her go.

Sandra was waiting for Ryan when he got back to the house all dirty and dispirited. He'd barely gotten in the door when she confronted him, her arms crossed over her chest, that Sandra Delaney scowl on her face.

"What had Gen so upset earlier today?" she demanded.

Ryan sighed deeply and rubbed at his eyes. "Not now, Mom."

"Don't you tell me 'not now.' I'm still your mother, and I still expect an answer when I ask you a damned question." Her graying ponytail bobbed with vehemence.

"Mom … Please." He couldn't look at her, and he felt like shit. It wasn't enough, apparently, to have one woman he loved yell at him. Now another one appeared ready to tear his head off and throw it at him.

"Ry." Her voice was softer now, and the softness ate at him even more than the anger had. "What happened? Come on. Sit down and tell me."

They went into the kitchen, and he sat at the kitchen table, staring miserably at the tabletop. He told her what he'd done, and what Gen had said. His voice sounded pathetic, and he knew it, but he couldn't seem to change it. When he was done, Sandra sat across from him and shook her head.

"God, men can be idiots sometimes," she said. Despite the harshness of her words, her voice was gentle. "You misread that situation, boy."

"Yeah. I'm starting to get that."

"A girl like Genevieve doesn't give two shits from a rat's ass about your money. She wants your *emotional* support, not your financial support. I'd have thought you'd have figured that out about her by now."

"Well, I guess I should have, but I didn't. I can't undo what's done. So how do I fix this?"

She leaned back in her chair and gave him a hard look. "If I were you, I'd give her a little time. Then I'd go find her and grovel."

He nodded slowly. "Yeah."

"But I wouldn't be surprised if it doesn't work."

The idea that it might not, the thought that he might not be able to set this right, made his chest hurt. "Why not?"

"You didn't just lie to her. You didn't just scheme behind her back. You hurt her feelings. And a woman's feelings can be slow to heal."

"Ah … shit."

"Wait. And then grovel." Sandra went to the refrigerator, got out a bottle of beer, and set it in front of Ryan. "I figure you need this right about now." She patted his shoulder—a quick and businesslike *pat-pat*—let out a grunt, and walked out of the room, leaving him alone with his beer and his regret.

Chapter Thirty-Three

Gen was crying, and Rose was holding a carton of Ben & Jerry's Chunky Monkey and a spoon.

"Here." She held the ice cream and the spoon out to Gen. "It's not happiness, but it's pretty damned close."

Gen grabbed at the carton as though it were a life raft and she were at sea in the middle of a hurricane.

"Why?" she moaned. "Why would he *do* something like that?" She tore the top off the ice cream carton and began shoveling with the spoon.

They, along with Kate and Lacy, were gathered at Kate's house on an emergency mission to nurse Gen through the crisis. It was dark out, and Jackson was at the restaurant working the dinner service. Gen's eyes were red, her skin was blotchy, and a flurry of crumpled Kleenex surrounded her like little shipwreck victims.

"Oh, honey." Kate put her hand on Gen's forearm. "Men like to fix things. He saw a problem—you wanted the gallery space—and he tried to fix it."

"But I didn't even *want* the gallery space! I'd decided that I wasn't even going! He was fixing a problem that didn't exist!" She waved the spoon and the ice cream carton around for emphasis.

"But he didn't know that," Lacy said.

"He would have if he'd *talked* to me! And why are you all on his side?!"

"We're on your side," Rose said. "It's just …"

"It's just what?" Gen demanded. She spooned more ice cream into her mouth.

"Well … it's just that he thought he was helping. He was trying to help."

"But he was 'helping' by being patronizing and demeaning," Lacy said.

"Exactly!" Gen pointed the spoon at her. "That's … That's exactly right." She looked down at the ice cream. "Why am I eating this? I don't eat junk food."

"You do today," Rose said.

Gen put the ice cream and the spoon down on the coffee table in front of her and slumped back onto Kate's sofa. She put her hands over her face and scrubbed at it.

"He doesn't even get it. I was yelling at him, and he was just … He asked me what my *point* was."

"Oh, God," Lacy said. "I hate that. That's the worst."

"Right?" Gen said. "If he doesn't even understand why I'm upset, then how … how …"

"Make him understand." Kate rubbed her arm some more. "Explain it to him."

"No." Gen pushed herself up off the sofa and started to pace. "No. I'm not going to explain it. I shouldn't have to explain it. The bottom line is, he thought I wouldn't be able to do the things I wanted to do without his help. He thought I was incapable on my own. Isn't that cute, Gen trying to be this New York art big shot. Isn't it adorable? I'd better rush in with my giant phallic checkbook and save the goddamned day." She picked up a throw pillow from one of Kate's chairs and hurled it to the ground.

"When you put it like that, it really does sound bad," Rose conceded.

"It sounds bad because it *is*." Gen came to rest in front of her friends. "If that's what he thinks of me, if that's how little he respects me, then how can we have a relationship? What future could we possibly have?"

"I still think he deserves a chance to learn from his idiot mistake," Lacy said. "I've known him a long time. He's a good guy."

"God. I thought … I thought …"

"You thought he was the one," Kate said.

"I really did. Is that stupid? Was I stupid?"

"No, honey. Just in love," Lacy said.

"Well, it's the same goddamned thing."

"It probably is," Rose agreed. "If you're not going to finish that ice cream, you mind if I do?"

Ryan tried to call Gen, but she didn't pick up, and then his calls went to voicemail. He tried to text her, but she didn't answer. He went over to her place, but she wouldn't answer the door. If she'd acknowledged him in any way—if she'd yelled through the door for him to go away, even—then he'd have been able to make his case and maybe get her to talk to him. But as it was, he was left standing there feeling like a jerk.

His mother had told him to give her time, but he'd been too impatient, and he'd started in right away with the calls and the banging on her door. Maybe his mother was right.

Dispirited, he went home and sulked.

He felt misunderstood—surely if she thought about it she could see his good intentions—but he also felt like a goddamned imbecile. He should have known that conspiring with Bellini behind her back, no matter what his intentions, would backfire on him if she ever found out. And that was the problem with lies and secrets. People always found out. His dad had taught him to live his life in such a way that he wouldn't need to hide anything, because his actions would be above reproach. When had he forgotten that?

Restless, he went out to the old barn to check on a heifer that had been showing some early signs of BVD. He'd checked on her earlier, and he didn't really need to go out there again for a while, but he needed to do something to get his mind off Gen.

He checked on the calf, then tried Gen again on his cell phone. She didn't answer. He put his phone back in his pocket, paced a little bit, and then retrieved the phone again.

"You told me to write the check, and now Gen won't speak to me," Ryan said when Daniel answered the phone.

"I didn't tell you to write the check. I told you that she really wanted to go to New York."

"How is that different?" Ryan demanded. He came to rest in front of an empty stall and leaned against the railing.

"It's different because when *I* call her, she picks up," Daniel said.

It wasn't a bad point.

Gen had no choice but to get on with things. She was miserable and lonely, and she couldn't sleep without missing the feeling of Ryan's body next to hers. But that didn't mean she could just sit on her ass and cry. She had a gallery to run. And she had an artist-in-residence program to organize.

Gordon was set to go home in a week or two, and it was time to figure out who would take his place. She hadn't even set up a formal application process, but all of the publicity Gordon had received—and the attention she'd received as an extension of that—meant that artists were contacting her on a daily basis wanting information on the residency. She hadn't originally intended for it to be an ongoing program, so she had some catching up to do. And obviously, the artist she chose would not be staying at the ranch. It would be too awkward if she and Ryan weren't together anymore. She needed to find a new place.

"You could just forgive Ryan," Alex suggested when Gen assigned him to start looking for rental properties that would work.

She could. God knew she thought about it every day. Forgiving him would be easy. What wouldn't be easy would be living with the fact that he didn't think enough of her to believe that she could achieve her goals without his help. What wouldn't be easy—or even possible—would be trying to be her own person while living under the shadow of his wealth.

So she contacted artists, looked at the rental places Alex picked out, and worked on an application process for the residency. The McCabes had only agreed to sponsor the program for one five-month period, and when she approached them about continuing it indefinitely, they'd balked. So she drafted a letter to David Walker, reminding him of Kendrick's astounding progress during the residency and asking him to sponsor the program so that other emerging artists might have the same opportunity.

The work helped her.

Keeping busy helped her.

If she hadn't been busy, she'd have spent all of her time thinking of Ryan and how she felt when he looked at her with those limitless eyes. If she hadn't been constantly in motion, she'd have spent a lot of time crying and feeling sorry for herself. As it was, she felt a dull ache in her middle every day, as though she were suffering from some sort of virus. She felt as though her world had been skewed off center, so that everything looked wrong and seemed off-balance. Thank God for her friends and her job. If she hadn't had them, she'd have risked vanishing into her grief.

❖

Ryan couldn't eat.

He was getting through his day-to-day life okay, except that the very sight of food made him feel sick, so that he picked at his meals and then shoved back from the table with some excuse about being tired or having work to do.

It wasn't good, a man with a job as physical as his going hungry, but there was nothing for it. Eating was what you did when you had hope and optimism. Eating was what you did when you wanted to be well and thrive, and he just honestly didn't give a shit about that anymore. He wanted to, but he couldn't seem to do it.

It hurt that she wouldn't even talk to him.

The fact that she couldn't even try to see his side of things made him wonder if he'd misjudged her. But it didn't matter if he had. No matter what she did, no matter what she was, he loved her with a desperate certainty that couldn't be undone. His feelings for her were unmanageable, uncontainable, vast like that endless Cambria sky that held the stars, the moon, and all of the unthinkable galaxies beyond.

His side didn't matter.

Nothing mattered but Gen.

He was sure that he'd survive this, that he'd learn to get along and just live his life. But caring about what was left of that life? Well, that was another thing entirely.

Chapter Thirty-Four

The day Breanna came to see her, Gen was working on a list of finalists for the next spot in her residency. She'd asked Alex to set up phone interviews with some of the most promising candidates, and she was sorting through their information when she heard the front door of the gallery open.

She looked up and there was Breanna, standing in the doorway looking uncertain and tentative.

"Breanna," Gen said. She felt a hard knot of pain in her chest. "Come on in. Is everything okay?"

"No." Breanna came into the gallery clutching her purse in front of her. "No, it's not okay. Can we go somewhere and talk?"

Gen sat across from Breanna at a café table at Jitters, Gen with a mug of coffee in front of her, Breanna with her hands wrapped around a cup of tea. Alex was manning the gallery. It was midmorning, and the coffee place had a smattering of customers working on laptops or chatting over lattes and scones.

"So, what is this about?" Gen said once they were settled. She'd always liked Breanna, and part of her sorrow over losing Ryan had to do with the loss of his family as well.

"It's about you. And Ryan. He's miserable, you know. He's … I've never seen him like this. He works, and he comes home, and he does all of the usual things, but … he's not there. Not really."

The thought of him unhappy made the backs of her eyes feel hot with unshed tears.

"Oh."

"You didn't even hear him out. You didn't even let him try to explain."

"There was nothing to say." Gen blinked hard to clear her vision.

"Yes, there was. But he won't say it. He's too proud. So I have to say it for him."

"Breanna …"

"Just listen to me. If you won't listen to him, listen to me." Something in her voice made Gen stop protesting.

"All right."

Breanna took a sip of her tea and then set the cup carefully back on the table. "A few years ago, before you moved to Cambria, Ryan was involved with a woman."

Gen felt a knot in her chest at the thought of him with someone else. It didn't matter that it had happened before he met her.

"He was … They were very serious," Breanna went on. "He was thinking marriage, kids, the whole bit."

"What happened?" Gen wasn't sure she wanted to know.

"She tried to take advantage of him. Her parents' business was failing—because of their own incompetence—and she wanted him to bail them out. He said no, and it ended them."

Gen was appalled. "She broke up with him over money?"

"If you'd asked her about it, she would have said no. They didn't break up right away. But …" She shrugged. "That was the beginning of the end for them. She started picking fights over little things, finding fault with him over this or that. We all knew it was about the money."

"God," Gen said.

Breanna leaned closer to Gen. "You have to understand how complicated it is for him. The money—it makes everything harder. More confusing. There's always the question of whether a woman really wants him for him. And if she needs money for something … for anything, really … it becomes this minefield he has to navigate. If he gives it to her, he wonders if she's using him. On the other hand, if he doesn't …"

"Then he worries that they'll leave," Gen finished for her.

"Right. And that doesn't even touch on the issue of the family."

"The family?"

"Well, it's not Ryan's money, individually. It belongs to the family. He takes that responsibility seriously. He doesn't want our parents to think he's being frivolous or foolish. That's so important to him. He really worries about how they see him."

Gen pulled a paper napkin out of the metal dispenser on the table and started twisting it in her fingers. "So when this thing with Bellini came up …"

"He was damned if he did, and damned if he didn't."

A fat tear spilled down Gen's cheek and plopped onto the table. "Yeah. I can see that."

"And, Gen." Breanna looked at her intently. "When he didn't know what to do, he erred on the side of making you happy. For all the good it did him."

Gen let out a shaky sigh. "And I wouldn't even talk to him."

"Well, you might want to reconsider that," Breanna said. "That thing with his ex-girlfriend was bad. But this? This is worse."

Gen tossed the mangled napkin aside. "But … he gave Bellini that money because he thought I couldn't handle things on my own. He didn't respect me."

Breanna shook her head, frustrated. "God, Genevieve. He's a man. Do you really think he thought it through that far? He saw something you wanted, and he thought he could get it for you. He was …" She waved her hands around in front of her, groping for a metaphor. "You were a hungry cave woman and he speared a mastodon for you. It's that simple!"

Gen laughed through a throat thick with emotion. "And I wouldn't even eat the damned thing."

Breanna nodded. "Pretty much."

"Okay." Gen wiped at her eyes. "Okay. Thank you for telling me."

"You're welcome. Now, what are you going to do about it?"

"I'm not sure."

Breanna shook her head in a gesture of pity and scorn. "If you let him go over this, it's going to be a big mistake. He loves you. I mean, he *really* loves you. And he's a good man, Genevieve."

She got up from the table, gathered up her purse, and walked out of the café.

When Breanna was gone, Lacy came over to the table, cautiously, and sat down across from Gen.

"That looked intense," she said. "Are you okay?"

"I might be an idiot," Gen said.

"At least you won't be lonely," Lacy said, reaching for Gen's hand and squeezing it in hers. "It's a big club."

She didn't know what to do, and she couldn't quite get it straight in her head.

Ryan loved her. He did what he did because he wanted to help her. What he'd done had been patronizing and demeaning, no question. But there was every chance Breanna was right—

he hadn't thought of it that way. He hadn't thought at all. He'd simply seen a chance to get her what he thought she wanted, and he took it.

The background of the thing—that he'd lost a relationship in the past because of a reluctance to come through with money—did change things. He hadn't wanted to lose Gen the way he'd lost the woman who came before her.

But then he'd lost Gen anyway.

Then there was the question of exactly how important Gen's pride was to her. Did she care about her ego more than she cared about Ryan? Right about now it didn't seem that way. She felt broken without him, wounded, as though a part of her body were missing. And the thought of him suffering, too—it made her feel a range of emotions from sorrow to guilt. He hurt because she was too stubborn to even talk to him.

"I don't know if I can do this," Gen told Kate one morning before work, as they were standing on Kate's deck, drinking coffee and looking at the roiling ocean.

"Do what?"

"Stay mad at Ryan."

"Oh, Gen," Kate said. "Then don't. Just don't."

"Is it that simple?" Gen turned to Kate, the silvery horizon at her back.

"It can be," Kate said. "He didn't mean to hurt you, you know."

"I do know that."

"But?"

Gen sighed. "I don't even know anymore. I don't even know why I'm holding onto this."

"Then don't," Kate said again.

"Yeah."

"I think he's it for you," Kate said gently. "I really do. Do you want to let him go because of this? Because of money?"

Gen shrugged. "It sounds stupid when you put it that way."

"Well. That's something to think about."

Gen had to help Kendrick move out of the guest cottage. His residency was finished, and he was scheduled to fly back to Chicago the following day. She'd promised that she would help him by picking up the paintings that he'd be taking with him so she could have them crated and shipped to his home address.

She was nervous about going to the ranch, because she worried that she might run into Ryan—and she also worried that she might not. She thought she was ready to talk to him, but she didn't know how it would go. There was a good chance that he was so hurt by now by the way she'd shut him out that he would close the door in her face if she went up to the main house.

Still, she thought she had to try.

As she drove her car up the road that led to the guest house, she felt a little sick and quivery, as though some dark creature were gnawing at her insides. She just wanted to feel okay again; she wanted to feel whole. And she didn't think she could do that without Ryan.

At the guest house, she found Kendrick amid the disarray of packing. He was dressed in jeans and a T-shirt, and he looked rested and happy.

"How's it coming along?" she asked.

"Good, good. Though I really hate to go." He faced her and stuffed his hands into his jeans pockets.

Gen grinned at him. "I remember when you couldn't wait to get out of here."

"Yeah, well." Kendrick looked at his feet and smiled, embarrassed. "I can't thank you enough. For everything."

"Oh, Gordon." Impulsively, she rushed forward and hugged him. At first he didn't hug her back—she imagined that he was taken aback by her sudden gesture—but then he put his arms around her and squeezed.

"Yes, well," he said after they'd separated. He was blushing slightly. "I have the canvases for shipping."

"Good."

He showed her the paintings stacked against one wall of the little house, and she browsed through them. She gazed in awe at the stunning images, bursts of vibrant color that hinted of the wind, the water, birdsong, the rush of the creek over rocks.

And then she saw it.

"Gordon. What's this?" She pulled away the top canvases so he could see the one underneath.

"Ah. *Cambria Pines III.*"

"This is the one you didn't want to sell. But Bellini sold it anyway. How did you get it?"

Kendrick looked at her, puzzled. "I thought you knew."

"Knew what?"

"It arrived here about a week after the show in New York. The note enclosed with it said it was from you. I just assumed you'd worked things out with Bellini."

"What? I ..."

And then she knew where the painting had come from.

"I ... Gordon, I have to go. I'll be back for the paintings. Later. I have to ..."

She hit the door at a near run.

She had to find Ryan.

Chapter Thirty-Five

He wasn't at the house. Of course he wasn't—it was the middle of a workday. Still, she almost wept with frustration. Breanna had answered the door, and she stood in the doorway looking at Gen.

"I need to see Ryan," Gen said, breathless.

"Well, it's about time."

Breanna wasn't sure where he was, so she called him on his cell phone. He didn't answer.

"Cell service is sketchy out here," Breanna said, though Gen already knew from her own experience that it was true.

"Please," Gen said. "Do you have any idea where he might be? I really … I just need to see him."

Breanna put one fist on her hip and regarded Gen. "Well, he said something about a fence in the southwest pasture."

"Great. Good. How do I get there?" Gen was already stepping down off the porch on the way to her car.

"Can't get there by car. You've gotta ride."

"Oh, God," Gen said.

Smirking, Breanna led Gen to the stables. They saddled up two horses—the chestnut named Bailey that Gen had ridden before, and a gorgeous black mare Breanna called Molly. Breanna gave Gen some gentle instruction as she used the mounting block to climb atop Bailey's back.

"You ready?" Breanna asked as Gen settled into the saddle, feeling a little scared, intimidated by the size of the animal.

"I guess." At least her discomfort with the idea of riding was crowding out her fear about seeing Ryan again. That was something.

They headed out on a trail that led into the hills past the old barn. They moved at a walk, which Gen assumed was for her benefit.

"Could we hurry?" Gen called ahead to Breanna.

"Fine by me. But are you up for it?"

"I ... Yes. Let's just go."

"All right." Breanna nudged her horse into a trot, and Bailey followed suit. At first the jostling was alarming, and Gen worried that she'd be thrown off and under the massive animal's hooves. But Breanna called instructions to her, and soon Gen was following the horse's rhythm and feeling pretty sure that she could do this.

Gen knew the ranch was big, but it seemed like they'd been riding forever before they finally arrived at the southwest pasture. Breanna brought Molly to a stop, and Bailey came up alongside her.

"Doesn't look like he's here," Breanna said, unnecessarily. Gen could see that for herself. The countryside was dotted with the big, black bodies of cows grazing or just standing around—but no Ryan.

Gen let out a little frustrated moan.

"You want to go back, or you want to try the new barn?" Breanna said.

"Breanna!" Gen shouted at her.

"Okay. New barn it is."

They turned around and went back onto the path.

By the time they got to the new barn, Gen's ass was sore and she was nearly weeping with the need to see Ryan. The horses trotted up to the barn, and Ryan appeared in the doorway. A couple of ranch hands were unloading hay bales from a truck. They looked at her and then at Ryan with curiosity.

She scrambled to get down from Bailey's back, which seemed impossibly high off the ground. Her foot got stuck in the stirrup and she stumbled backward. Ryan was there to catch her.

The feel of his body against hers as he righted her made tears spring to her eyes. She wanted to melt into him and then stay there, warm and safe, forever.

"Gen," he said, stepping away from her after she'd gained her balance.

"Oh, God. Ryan, I need to talk to you. I need …"

"I think you two can take it from here," Breanna said. "You'll get her and Bailey back to the house?" she asked Ryan.

He nodded, and Breanna led Molly at a trot down the path that led back the way they'd come. As she went, she looked over her shoulder and shot them a satisfied smirk.

"What's going on?" Ryan said when she was gone. "Did something happen?"

"You bought Kendrick's painting," Gen said.

"Ah, Gen." He rubbed at the back of his neck. "Look. I'm sorry. I know I shouldn't …"

"No." She interrupted him. "You bought the one he wanted to keep for himself, and returned it to him."

"Well." He stood there with his hands on his hips, looking uncomfortable. The ranch hands had stopped unloading the hay and were watching them openly.

"Don't you two have something to do?" Ryan asked them. They ducked their heads and disappeared into the barn.

"Ryan. Giving that painting to Gordon was the most thoughtful, generous ... just about the *kindest* thing I've ever seen."

"I didn't ... It wasn't ... It just seemed like the right thing to do."

Being told he was kind and generous made him look like he was standing on a rusty nail. His discomfort with the praise, with the attention from his selfless act, made her melt. She simply could not imagine waiting another moment before being in his arms.

"I ... Ryan ... I should have *talked* to you. We should have ..."

"Come here."

She ran to him and he enfolded her against his warm, hard body. She didn't belong in New York. She belonged here. Right here.

"I never said I'm sorry," he murmured into her hair. "I never should have given that check to Bellini behind your back. Gen. I'm sorry."

"I'm sorry, too." She pressed her cheek to his chest, feeling the rhythm of his breath, feeling his heartbeat. She pulled back a little and looked up at him. "I shouldn't have shut you out. But, Ryan, I have to be able to do things on my own. My career ... If I'm going to be successful, I have to do that alone. I can't always be wondering if you somehow made it happen for me."

"I know. I should have understood that about you. My mother did. She called me an idiot."

Gen's mouth quirked into a half smile. "Well, maybe you were. Just a little bit. But you were a very sweet idiot."

"Well, that's something."

She looked into his face and saw something change there. Relief had turned into desire, and his mouth claimed hers in a kiss.

It started out soft, tentative, questioning whether this was okay, if they were okay. Then, having gotten his answer, he deepened the kiss until the heat of it spread through her, lighting her aflame.

She held him to her tightly, wanting him more than she wanted to take her next breath.

He pulled back from her a little and looked around him.

"We've never done it in the new barn," he said.

"There are a couple of guys in there."

"I'm their boss. I'll tell them to get lost."

"There are cows," Gen said. "What about the cows?"

"They're going to be scandalized," Ryan said, grinning.

"I guess they'll get over it," she said.

He picked her up into his arms, and she let out a delighted shriek as he carried her into the barn.

Gen was in the gallery a couple of days later, feeling deliciously satisfied after spending the night with Ryan at her place, when her cell phone rang.

"Gen Porter."

"This is Hillary Ramsey, David Walker's assistant. Is this a good time?"

Gen sat up straighter in her chair. "Of course."

"Mr. Walker received your proposal regarding his sponsorship of your artist's residency program, and he asked me to set up a meeting with you to discuss it."

"He did?" Gen realized she probably sounded shocked and stupid, but she needed a moment to absorb the information.

"Is next Tuesday satisfactory? Mr. Walker would like to come to Cambria and see the property where the artists reside."

"I ... That's ... Yes. Next Tuesday is great."

They set up the meeting. Gen couldn't wait to tell Ryan.

❖

"I guess that means you'll want to keep renting the guest cottage," Ryan said, grinning, when she told him that evening at her place.

"Well, yes. If you didn't have other plans for it."

"I think we can work something out." He pressed a quick kiss to her lips. "No break on the rent, though. Since you want to do things on your own."

"Of course." She grinned and wiggled a little in his arms.

Ryan shook his head, a look of dismay on his features. "You know, you'll probably have to come out to the ranch a lot, if you're going to keep the residency program going."

"I suppose."

"It'd be a lot easier on you if you lived out there. Less wear and tear on your car."

She felt a jolt of electricity through her veins, and her heart sped up.

"Ryan ... That's ..." Then her excitement was tempered by the reality of the situation. "It'd be awkward, me living with you in your parents' house."

"Not if we were married."

She pushed back from him, her mouth open in shock.

"Married?"

"Of course, we'll want to build our own house eventually. We'd still be on the land with my folks, but we'd have some privacy."

"Oh, my God, Ryan."

"I don't need an answer right now. Just think about it. And in the meantime, let's, you know, practice a little. Doing stuff that married people do."

He flopped down onto her bed, pulling her along with him, and she fell on top of him with a squeal.

"We might need a lot of practice," she said.

"Well, we'd better get on it, then."

So they did.

Acknowledgments

I'd like to thank my husband, John, and my daughters for their constant support. When I was busy writing, when I was worried about the details of publishing, when I talked on and on about plots and characters, they were endlessly patient. I love you guys.

I'd also like to thank the people of Cambria, who welcomed the first book in this series, *Moonstone Beach,* so warmly. I feel like an honorary Cambrian now, and I can't think of a nicer thing to be.

Made in the USA
Las Vegas, NV
29 April 2023

71303910R00194

,eed's Readers' Group

,'s website at www.lindaseed.com and sign up for
newsletter to get the latest information about new
events, giveaways, and more. When you join, you'll
"Jacks Are Wild," a Main Street Merchants short story,
,o cost. The story, featuring Kate and Jackson from
oonstone Beach, is only available to newsletter subscribers.

Stay in touch with Linda at the following places:

E-mail: linda@lindaseed.com
Facebook: www.facebook.com/LindaSeedAuthor/
Twitter: www.twitter.com/LindaSeedAuthor
Pinterest: www.pinterest.com/lindahseed/